The
Trouble
with
Weddings

The Trouble with Weddings

SHARON
OWENS

POOLBEG

Published 2007
by Poolbeg Press Ltd
123 Grange Hill, Baldoyle
Dublin 13, Ireland
E-mail: poolbeg@poolbeg.com
www.poolbeg.com

© Sharon Owens 2007

Copyright for typesetting, layout, design
© Poolbeg Press Ltd

The moral right of the author has been asserted.

13 5 7 9 10 8 6 4 2

A catalogue record for this book is available from the British Library.

ISBN 978-1-84223-298-9

Typeset by Patricia Hope in Caslon 10.75/15.5

Printed by
Litografia Rosés, S.A., Spain

www.poolbeg.com

Note on the author

Sharon Owens was born in Omagh in 1968. She moved to Belfast in 1988, to study illustration at the Art College. She married husband Dermot in 1992 and they have one daughter, Alice.

Her bestselling novels *The Tea House on Mulberry Street*, *The Ballroom on Magnolia Street* and *The Tavern on Maple Street* are also published by Poolbeg Press.

Acknowledgements

With many thanks and best wishes to everyone at Poolbeg and Penguin, especially Paula Campbell, Gaye Shortland and Clare Ledingham. A huge thank-you to all the terrific people in the media who have supported me along the way, and to my wonderful agents, Ros Edwards and Helenka Fuglewicz. And to all the readers who've sent such lovely letters and cards, a major thank-you. Once again, this book would not have been written without the love and support of my husband Dermot and daughter Alice. I love you both.

For Dermot

1

Dream Weddings

November 2006

H I, THERE.

Oh, wait a minute.

Just had another text in from Julie.

Fifth one today from Julie, that is.

She needn't worry – I can manage on my own for a few days.

Yes, I did warn the violinists they'll have to wear full-length brown fur coats to the Patterson wedding. And yes, I have hired brown fur coats for all seven of them, in the correct sizes, yes, to be delivered from London in good time for the occasion. And yes, I have checked the coats will be security-tagged and fully insured for their little trip to Carrickfergus.

And, *send*.

God love those poor guys, they don't know what they've let themselves in for. They'll be sweltered playing Tchaikovsky up to their eyeballs in mink but Narnia is *huge* at the moment, theme-wise. Huge as anything, I just can't tell you. At least they won't have to turn up in beaver costumes or appear as wicked elves with long pointy boots on their feet. Both of those ideas were mooted by the bride's mother but Julie put her foot down. She likes a laugh, does Julie, but we always have the reputation of Dream Weddings to think of. The bride is dressing as the Snow Queen in palest blue fur. With a two-foot-tall delicate silver crown attached to the top of her head with extra-strong elastic. And the groom is going to surprise her with a sleigh on wheels when they come out of the church after the ceremony. Obviously if it actually snows real snow on the day, we're laughing. And it might just do that 'cos the wedding's on Christmas Eve. But if Mother Nature lets us down, we're going to fill the carpark with three tons of rice-paper flakes. No expense is being spared – the bride's family owns an international haulage company. Well, I have to admit Miss Patterson does look exquisite in that blue fur and, you know what they say, you can't take it with you. (And the Pattersons do give a lot of money to charity so that's okay.) We're even going to make it 'snow' inside the ballroom at the end of the night. Nothing in this business surprises me any more. Wait a minute, now Julie's texting me about the rice paper. Yes, I have obtained permission from the hotelier to shake bags of paper flakes from the rafters in the ballroom. We've lined up three game teenagers who're going to be dressed as snow-clouds.

And, *send.*

Julie's in New York this week, would you believe? I say

this week but really it's only for four days and then she's flying on to Los Angeles with Henri. Henri's a financial whizz and big-time deal-fixer and also Julie's new boyfriend. He's cultured and polite and extremely good-looking. Eyes so dark you'd think they were made of black glass. And muscles! Well, forget about it. Even his muscles have muscles. When I first met Henri I thought he was gay, his clothes were that perfect. But Julie assured me he definitely didn't play for the other side.

"He's only French," she said.

I'm sure he has a flaw of some kind but we're still waiting to see what it is. Henri's in New York to set up some meetings with an elite group of arthouse film directors and an even more elite group of serious actors (darling), and Julie's there to attend one of the biggest bridal fairs in the developed world.

Oh! There's the phone again.

"Hello. Dream Weddings, can I help you? Our brochure? Of course, if you just give me your address? I'll pop one in the post. Yes, we are very busy at the moment. Fully booked for the next two years, to tell you the truth. Yes, really we are! Yes, you can book now for November 2008 if you forward our little holding fee – it's all there in the brochure. Okay? Lovely. Thank you so much. Cheerio."

I told Julie, don't come back to Belfast with a load of frilly white dresses and traditional veils and posies because we are *so* getting into the fantasy wedding market these days, it's not funny. Ever since that rock-star wedding we did a few months ago, Dream Weddings has been absolutely inundated with calls. I mean hundreds and hundreds of phone calls and e-mail enquiries from prospective brides and grooms. And even married couples wanting to renew their vows and have another party because they feel they missed the boat, style-wise, first time round. Honestly! The women all wanting Gothic gowns and fairytale capes, and kitsch pink limousines and pink champagne, and Victorian black bouquets and I don't know what else. And the guys are binning the top hat and tails and going for snazzy tailoring. And super-short ceremonies are the order of the day now, with no embarrassing speeches or the endless reading out of dreary telegrams at the reception afterwards. Most of the men we've met would rather die than attempt public speaking so we have a professional speechmaker on our books and he's getting gigs right, left and centre. I'm telling you, it's definitely the end of the white wedding as we know it. Goodbye to the blushing bride and all that.

Today's woman knows what she's getting on the honeymoon. And a good thing too. As Julie always says to me (and only to me, mind you), what's the big deal about white weddings anyway? I mean, no woman would dream of buying a car without taking it for a test-drive first. Julie's words, not mine. So why on earth would she throw in her lot with *any* guy before she's made certain-sure he can treat her tenderly when the lights go out?

And Julie should know. When it comes to men and weddings, Julie Sultana wrote the book. And that's why Julie will never get married herself. Ever. I mean, she says she won't but I hope she will, one day. But for now,

Julie says she's still looking for Mr Right and she's having a lot of fun doing it and you can't blame her for that.

Oh, my name is Margaret Grimsdale.

Mags, for short.

I'm Julie's PA at Dream Weddings.

2

Bill & Mags Forever

THEY SAY YOU NEVER FORGET YOUR FIRST LOVE. I certainly won't. I'm still married to mine. God knows what I ever did to deserve such a scrumptious husband but there you go. Life isn't fair, I suppose. Though growing up in a rain-drenched Belfast in the 1970's must have counted for something. We're from wildly different backgrounds but we compromise on the big issues and we discuss things calmly and we muddle through.

My husband Bill was a Punk, you see, when I first met him in 1984 in the Limelight Club. Leaping across the dance floor with some lengths of industrial chain (from the hardware store) round his neck. And I was a Goth in plum lippy and a vintage bridesmaid's dress I'd bought in Oxfam and dyed black in a basin in the yard.

Bill's favourite band back then was The Blades (a Dublin-based outfit) and they're still in his personal top five. According to my other half, The Blades' debut (and as it turned out, their only) album, *The Last Man In Europe*, was the best piece of recorded music ever produced in the western world. Cover's nice, too. Black and white moody shot of the band with some derelict gasworks in the background. Very urban decay. Bill had the original album cover framed and it's been hanging in our bedroom forever. Funny to think that cover is actually older than our children.

Bill was a little bit more sensitive than your average Punk and I was a lot more outspoken than your average Goth and so we managed to bridge the cultural divide. It's not always been easy. Bill has a huge collection of nearly 10,000 vinyl records, twelve bass guitars and four massive amps. And I'm a tidy-freak. But with some built-in shelving in the sitting room and the guitars wall-mounted on the stairs, we've managed to steer a relatively peaceful path through two decades of marriage. It's very hard to dust behind the strings on a guitar and I can't abide dust so Bill switched the light-bulbs in the hall to a dimmer grade some years ago, and I have to say I don't notice the dust half as much as I used to.

He insisted the house be painted brilliant white, inside and out, however. All clean lines and modern furniture. The man has a wallpaper phobia. Bill says wallpaper reminds him of people dying of tuberculosis in the 1940's. Expiring in the bed with starched handkerchiefs over their mouths, hushed voices on the landing and all that caper. Doesn't matter if it's that new shiny 'statement wallcovering' that's featured in fancy magazines nowadays, he can't stand it. Ditto, knick-knack cabinets and swirly carpets. I agreed with Bill's decision as long as I could have some colour in the bedrooms. Well, in Alicia-Rose's. She's our only daughter. Our three boys haven't ever been bothered about the décor. So our children grew up in an all-white house except for Alicia-Rose's room which was pink, pink, pink. Compromise, you see: that's the secret of a happy marriage. It also helps if your husband has a cute bubble-butt and lovely smooth feet and is very good at giving erotic massages.

I always knew Bill was in bad form when he got a faraway look in his eyes and started wondering aloud why The Blades didn't make it when The Clash did, and wasn't it a shame they never got the recognition? And Bill knew I had rampant PMT when I took to the bath with a copy of some interiors magazine and a nice glass of Merlot to cheer myself up. Then he checked the chart we keep on the inside of the wardrobe door with my PMT days blocked out in blue marker, stayed out of my way for a day or two and remembered to rinse his cereal bowl and put it in the dishwasher and not leave it to dry up on the arm of the sofa. Otherwise he'd get the 'I have to do everything in this bloody house' lecture from me. What I'm trying to say is that we were very much in love. I never thought anything could or would come between us. When you've loved someone for twenty years you know what they're going to think and say about ten seconds before they do.

It was so romantic, that balmy summer in 1984 when our two worlds first collided. Bill had a short white Mohawk and knee-high blue leather boots with steel plates on the shins. And I was going through my 'Granny dress and plaits' phase. But everyone said we looked right together and we were so in love we just knew we could make it work. Think Billy Idol as a sensitive young man teamed with Wednesday Addams as a bolshy teenager and you'll get the general idea. It was all harmless fun, you know: dressing up in the 1980's. There was nothing else to do and no money to do it with. At least we were using our imaginations and not just going slowly mental in front of a computer like kids nowadays.

The night Bill and I met was simply magical. I was eighteen years old and Bill had just turned twenty. Within five minutes of clocking one another we were oblivious to our surroundings, utterly lost in a passionate kiss. I thought I'd died and gone to heaven. But when Bill walked me home from the Limelight Club we were hassled by a gang of drunken thugs. The usual bad language and colourful threats, will they never get bored of it? I was terrified. Mobile phones hadn't been invented then (or at least the ordinary person in the street didn't have one, only the rich-o yuppies in London) and there wasn't a policeman in sight. Bill ignored them for a while but they became increasingly aggressive. He whispered to me to project an image of utter calmness and he asked me if I had anything in my handbag he might use as a weapon. I happened to have a steel comb with a sharp end (they were still legal then) as well as a large can of extra-strength hairspray to keep my blunt fringe straight, and between us we managed to frighten them off.

I say that like it was an equal thing but what

happened was, Bill suddenly stopped walking, stood in front of me, waved the comb at the thugs and invited them to have a go.

"You're a dead man, freak!" they shouted.

"Fair enough," Bill replied levelly, "but one of you losers is going down with me. Now who's it gonna be?"

While I wielded the hairspray menacingly in the background, hoping I could at least give the rotten creeps some stinging eyes or something. For about two minutes there was an ape-like stand-off with lots of crouching and side-stepping going on. It would have been quite interesting if it weren't for the fact we were about to be murdered. Bill didn't move an inch. I don't think he even blinked. I thought the big, fat thug in the beer-stained tracksuit would have been the first to launch himself on Bill but then again the smallest one with the darting eyes did look the maddest of the bunch.

"I haven't got all night," Bill said at one point.

Amazingly, they backed down and we escaped without broken bones. Bill stood his ground until they were out of sight.

"Thank God I didn't have to use this thing," Bill said as he handed the comb back to me. "Bunch of sad cases, really."

"Would you really have stabbed one of them, Bill?" I said to him quietly as we resumed walking.

"Don't know," he replied after a short pause. "I could have out-run them on my own, no problem. But I forgot to ask if you were a good runner. Are you?"

"No, sorry. Actually, I'm rubbish."

"Well then. Come on, let's get you home."

I was weak-kneed with relief. And lust.

There were five of those hooligans so obviously they'd picked on us because they thought they'd have the advantage, but Bill has a theory that most violent men have personality disorders too. And that's why they were so angry when they saw us strolling along the moonlit street. Simply because we were happy and they were not. I think Bill had a valid point that night anyway because when I read this article in a magazine recently I discovered a few interesting facts. Apparently, a rough childhood can lead to the brain being hardwired into negative patterns. So our thuggy friends probably couldn't 'do' normal life because they didn't have a normal childhood and 'normality' is a way of life that must be learned *before the age of six*. Imagine that. After the age of six it's too late to change anyone's personality in any major way. Even therapy can only make them aware of why they are the way they are. But it's too late to actually change them.

But anyway, Bill knew how to look after himself on the streets of Belfast after dark and I suppose that's how we managed to have such a great social life when we first got together. We were married just a year after that eventful night and we've been together ever since. We have four children (aged eighteen, nineteen, twenty and twenty-one) and a mortgage nearly cleared. We're law-abiding taxpayers, never been on the dole. It's all very suburban.

Bill's father is English, hence the curious surname. Grimsdale. It's always reminded me of cobbled streets and clay chimney pots. And Norman Wisdom calling out to Mr Grimsdale in those old black-and-white comedies. Do you remember them? When Norman was a milkman? Sometimes, I do that when I've spilt a cup of tea over the bed or something. I'll yell, "Mr Grimsdale! Mr Grimsdale!" in my best Norman Wisdom accent and Bill will come running with a tea towel.

We've only ever had one major disagreement and that was over my boss Julie's recent fling with a barman from County Galway. Now, Julie Sultana is a terrific girl and for the fourteen years that we worked together in Dream Weddings she was always the living embodiment of style, poise and confidence. I'd be tying my long black hair up with a scrunchie and complaining about the summer heat and she'd be spritzing herself with designer water and wearing sunglasses by Chanel. But when she went off the rails last summer, she really pulled out all the stops. I mean, she did some things I would never have thought of in my wildest dreams. And I've got quite an imagination if I do say so myself. Yes, Julie opened my eyes on several subjects, I can tell you. And that was all the more surprising because I never had her down as the rebellious type. Who'd have thought the sort of person who drives an immaculate white Mercedes convertible with scented tissues in the glove compartment would ever have got up to the sort of shenanigans that Julie did last summer?

3

The Café Vaudeville

So, I knew Julie had something big to tell me when she suddenly snapped her laptop shut one day last July and said brightly, "Mags Grimsdale, put down that tiara and get your coat on, will you? I'm taking you out for coffee – to the Café Vaudeville, no less."

"Really?" I said. "Even though we're snowed under with Janine Smith's wedding? I mean, these whacking great corsages will take hours to finish."

"Yes, yes. I'll work late to get them made up. Come on."

I should mention at this point that Julie's wedding-planner business is run from a decommissioned lighthouse on the outskirts of Belfast. Julie owns the entire building but we've only decorated the top three floors and we use them as an office, a kitchenette and a storeroom, respectively. Interesting story, how Julie came to be the owner of such an unusual building – we'll get to

15

that in good time. You might think it was a bit crazy to run the business from a lighthouse when it had nothing whatsoever to do with the sea but honestly the free publicity was tremendous. The novelty value was priceless, it really was. The women of Belfast were queuing up to huff and puff their way round the endless spiral of stone steps before finally collapsing into our tiny, circular office with spectacular sea views. And they were usually so blown away by the whole experience, they didn't think to query the bill which was an added bonus. That's Julie for you, the consummate businesswoman. And that was before we *really* went meteoric with these fantasy weddings that are suddenly all the rage.

We're a good team, Julie and me. We're very good wedding planners (if I do say so myself).

But anyway.

So, yes, I leapt from my seat like a Jack-in-the-box. You see, I just adore the Café Vaudeville. All ruby-red walls stencilled with fanciful gold loops and swirls, Moroccan lampshades in yellow and blue ceramic studded with glittery jewels, massive red-glass chandeliers and all sorts of lovely dark corners and shadowy nooks to sit in. There's a wicker sofa with curtains draped over it like a little tent. So Bohemian, you simply can't imagine. Who'd have thought our creaking old city would ever in a million years have something so beautiful just tucked away on Arthur Street like it was nothing special? It's a bar and restaurant by day and apparently it's *the* place to be seen posing in after dark. But Bill and I rarely went out at night then, what with the kids needing their supper, and lifts here and there, and various school uniforms and outfits to be pressed and so on. But I always did love going out for coffee and Julie knew I was hopelessly enchanted with the red chandeliers.

So even though it wasn't her favourite place to eat (she enjoys the New York modernity of Deane's Deli with its trendy dark-grey walls and giant bowls of fresh olives on the counter) she'd still chosen to take me there and that's how I knew there was something on her mind.

"Oh, what a lovely-dovely treat," I murmured as I switched on the answerphone and closed the windows in the lighthouse. Obviously burglars couldn't have got in at that terrific height but sometimes the seagulls are brazen in their attempts to nick what's left of our sandwiches. Quite frightening, seagulls are, when they're standing on your keyboard.

So, as I said, I knew she had some special news to impart to me but you can't ask with Julie. No, you can't go jumping the gun and demanding to know what's going on or trying to guess what it is or making silly jokes or anything. You just have to bite your tongue and wait and Julie will tell you in her own good time. So I fetched my glad rags. A floor-length black wool coat with giant jet buttons on it and my old-fashioned black-velvet handbag.

I'm an ex-Goth. Did I mention that? Well, I say ex. I'm more of a forty-year-old institutionalised 'post-Goth' who's allergic to anything floral or flouncy, and I don't know what else to wear now I've turned forty. Blimey, it sounds so strange to even *think* I'm forty years of age. I mean, I'm still eighteen in my mind. I gave up the studded belts and the black nail polish when I had my first child, naturally. I'm not an attention-seeker. But I didn't go mad and buy myself a billowy pink frock with enormous white collars on it either. Like those dresses Princess Diana wore when she was expecting William and Harry. I mean, you can't suddenly swap comfortable biker boots for those fiddly little sandals that let in the rain and give you chilblains and bunions. And the fashion scene is so expensive. A completely new wardrobe twice a year? On my budget? Don't make me laugh!

Yes, so that was the day Julie and I went to the Café Vaudeville together for the last time before it all kicked off. Julie drove us into town in her white convertible, chatting all the way about inconsequential things, giving nothing away about the bombshell she was about to drop on me from a great height. (I've never learned to drive; I'm useless with gadgets in general.) In fairness to Julie, she hadn't a clue that day just how it would all end for her, either. Sometimes it's the decision you make on the spur of the moment that determines the rest of your life. Oh, well.

We found a parking space near the Art Deco BBC building on Bedford Street, popped some coins in the meter, a short walk and suddenly we were in through the main doors. Bit of a queue at the entrance but Julie knew the head waitress and we got sneakily siphoned off the line and ushered through to a side room, all the while pretending to be there on business. I waved a couple of A4 envelopes in the air as if we were delivering a business quote of some kind. Works every time. Naughty us! We ended up seated on a low leather banquette in the coffee bar (good) next to a gaggle of chain-smoking women in skin-tight double-denim (not so good). Is there anything worse on the larger figure? And they were smoking like trains, filling the air around Julie and me with a thick blue cloud of acrid smoke. But even that couldn't take the edge off my buzz. I just love opulent interiors, they make my heart beat faster. In my next life, I swear I'm going to come back as a mirror in the Palace of Versailles.

"Café mocha and a chocolate square for you, Mags?" Julie asked and I nodded happily. Women are supposed to have curves, aren't they? So why on earth do so many girls like Emma have eating disorders these days? Emma was my eldest son Alexander's girlfriend at the time. What a drama that was!

I'm tall for a woman, five foot eleven inches and let's just describe my figure as voluptuous. Hour-glass figure with 'strong' ankles, that's me. I'm a life-long devotee of the wide-leg trouser. I mean, why bother with healthy eating when there's usually nothing in the grocery cupboard but a stale loaf of wholegrain bread, a small can of tuna in brine and a messy bottle of out-of-date salad cream? That huge choccy square in the Café Vaudeville must have weighed two pounds, but really, I'm not in bad shape considering I'm a mother of four. I had mine young, you see. So my tummy zapped back in again like an elastic band. My hips are thirty-nine inches but my waist is still only twenty-eight! Some women I know hate me for it but there's no point reminding them I spent my twenties and thirties at the kitchen sink while they were sunning themselves round the holiday spots of Europe.

Now they're all plunging into motherhood for the first time and my eldest two are already at university. Well, Alicia-Rose is at university. Alexander dropped out when Emma was first diagnosed with anorexia.

So Julie ordered a pot of tea for herself (and a plain scone) and for a while we just sat there soaking up the ambience, saying nothing, deliberately looking straight ahead. Then Julie stood up and said she was going to powder her nose and off she went striding through the afternoon crowd, attracting admiring glances from the men and envious shrugs from the women. I suppose she wanted to gather her thoughts before she made her big announcement.

Julie is gorgeous-looking, did I mention that? She looks much younger than her forty-one years. She's never had to go without her sleep, I suppose. Though they do say women without children can age faster than mothers but that theory certainly doesn't apply to Julie. You'd easily take her for thirty. She's tall as well, just one inch shorter than me but she's fine-boned and elegant to go with it. Graceful and willowy with a platinum-white bob, palest blue eyes, delicate tiny ankles, a light honey-gold tan and clothes to die for. Mostly white linen tops and skirts, lots of ruffles round the hem and outsize mohair flowers on the waistband. Dry clean only. Nothing cheap and trendy from your UK chain stores for our Julie, oh no. She shops only in exclusive boutiques staffed by women of a certain age who've had plastic surgery and whose fingernails are so long they must have to employ some lackey to get the lid off their toothpaste at night.

Even the loos are nice in the Café Vaudeville, by the way. All matt-black walls with giant lily motifs hand-painted on, and marble sinks. Clean as a new pin, they are. I was tinkering with the idea of a black bathroom in my own house, actually. Black walls would have contrasted beautifully with the white suite and I could have had a Roman blind made up in that lovely pattern that's mainly white with ancient Greek dignitaries' heads printed on it in grey. I remember thinking to myself, I'll have to see if Bill is agreeable to a stone urn and black walls in the lavatory one of these days. And if not, then we'll just have a black chandelier. Meanwhile, I got stuck into the chocolate square because I knew that if Julie's news was negative in any way I wouldn't be able to eat in front of her afterwards. I'm a very practical sort of girl. With four children and a full-time job, I have to be.

Those chocolate concoctions are heaven on a plate, aren't they? So rich and sticky. Full of grated coconut, flaked almonds and syrupy cherries that burst in your mouth. I almost forgot about Julie as I enjoyed the delicious taste of it. It reminded me of Christmas. I do love Christmas even though I'm not very religious. Well, it's a Pagan festival first and foremost, isn't it, I suppose? All bright lights, evergreen branches and feasting in the depths of Midwinter? Before some *men* had the bright idea to torment us all with the fairytale of a virgin birth. Little did those wise-guys know, most women wouldn't mind a virgin birth if it meant they never had to experience another dimply sweaty beer belly and BO 'pits looming over them in the bed, ever again.

21

Think about it.

"I'm leaving Gary tomorrow," Julie said simply when she returned from the ladies' room in the Café Vaudeville. Sitting demurely down again on the banquette and smiling at me. And then she went on supping her tea and cutting her plain scone up into neat little cubes.

"Come again," I squeaked.

And I literally did squeak because she laughed and called me a mouse. A squeaky little mouse. She can turn quite defensive when she's cornered, can Julie. You'll see that as the story progresses.

"Margaret Mouse, you do surprise me," she said, almost sniggering. "I thought you Goths were unshockable. Don't you chain each other up for sex in the cellar and drink blood for breakfast?"

"You're thinking of high-ranking civil servants," I told her wearily. "And Bill was a Punk, not a Goth. And what you're describing is *Fetish*. Apart from the bit about drinking blood, which is plainly ridiculous by anyone's standards."

Honestly, so many people these days get Goth confused with Fetish. They are completely opposing concepts, don't you know? Those flimsy sex-shop undies don't float my boat. Never have. For Goths (the real purists I'm talking about now) eroticism means fully dressed or completely bare, and nothing in between.

"Come on, Mags," she said, "you can tell me. Doesn't Bill ever dress up for you? Like on your birthday or special occasions? I bet he looks dead sexy in tight leather trousers and a studded dog collar."

"Oh, Julie. You know I prefer lace-trimmed cotton pillowcases and handwritten love letters. Please tell me you're joking about leaving Gary."

"I'm not joking. Gary wants to get married and start a family and I don't. That's it in a nutshell. So there's no point in going on with the relationship. There's just no point."

"Now, wait a minute, Julie. Slow down and think about this logically. Can't you tell Gary how you feel about having children? I'm sure he would understand. He loves you to bits."

"There's no time for soul-searching, Mags. We're both over forty. It's now or never for Gary. I haven't told him I'm not ready for marriage and I don't think I *can* tell him face to face. He won't be amused, you know? Recently he's been nagging me to set a date for our wedding and asking why I can't decide on a venue for the reception. He won't be expecting anything as drastic as this and he won't take the news lying down."

"You're right, there," I said. "He won't let you go if I'm any judge."

"You see what I mean?" she replied, her blue eyes wide in exasperation. "You know yourself what would happen if I tried to leave Gary in a mature and sensible fashion. He'd wreck the house. His house, remember. Not mine. And the renovations cost an absolute fortune. I can't stand confrontation, Mags. You know I can't abide shouting and pleading and tears dripping off people's chins. And slamming doors give me palpitations. It's all so untidy, so unnecessary. Look, the decision is already

23

made. What I want you to do is tell Gary for me. Please. Will you? You're so good at this emotional stuff. I'm begging you, Mags."

I was stunned.

"The thing is, Julie, I'd rather not get involved in your relationship with Gary," I said when I'd recovered from the shock. "In any relationship really. It's usually the messenger that gets shot, in my experience."

"Oh, Mags!"

"No, really," I insisted. "Although I do appreciate the compliment about me being emotional and so on, thank you very much. But you know this information ought to come from you directly. Are you sure you won't change your mind about talking to him?"

"No, I simply can't face the man, absolutely not. So either you do it or I leave him a note on the kitchen table."

"But that won't be the end of it, Julie. Won't Gary come to the lighthouse, looking for an explanation?"

"I don't think he will, actually. He's a very proud man. A few days to brood and he'll bounce back. It's better if I just vanish. Out of sight, out of mind."

Oh, as if, I thought to myself. You don't know Gary, of course, but he's deep. He's not a bounce-back sort of man. So for his sake I ploughed on, though I had a feeling it wouldn't do any good whatsoever.

"What about your things?"

"What things?"

"What things, she says! Your six-figure wardrobe, lady! Your clothes and all your other possessions in Gary's

24

house? I mean, you'll have to go back to fetch them, won't you? You'll see him then. You'll have to talk to him *then*?"

Gary lives in a rustic farmhouse on the outskirts of town but of course on the inside it's packed with luxury fittings, a dream bachelor pad.

"I'm going away tomorrow morning for two weeks so he won't be able to find me," Julie said. "I'll tell you the location but no-one else is to know. I don't care what happens, you mustn't reveal to Gary where I am. I've thought about this from every angle and it's definitely what I want to do. As for my clothes, most of them have been spirited out of the wardrobe already, allegedly taken to the dry-cleaner's. What's left, he'll probably throw in the bin. Along with my fancy blender, my chrome shoe-racks, my nice shower gels and so on. I wouldn't blame him."

"Oh, Julie. Are you sure about this?"

"I am, yes. Thank my lucky stars I still have my apartment. I was tempted to sell it last year and buy a holiday home in Italy but then there was that scaremongering about the cheap flights coming to an end. So I changed my mind. And to be honest with you, somehow I just knew I'd be needing it again."

Julie kept her pristine all-mod-cons apartment in a converted flour mill in Saintfield when she moved in with Gary three years before but he didn't know that. She doesn't have a lot of faith in love everlasting, I'm sorry to say. Yes, I realise that does sound strange coming from a wedding planner but there's a lot of money to be made in this game and Julie is nothing if not financially astute. And as I said before, we *are* very good at what we do.

"So, I'm leaving Gary tomorrow," she said again, just like that.

I was deeply unsettled. I don't like change, not even in the lives of other people. Then Julie poured another cup of tea and drank it slowly, gazing up at the red-glass chandeliers and with only the hint of a tear in her eye. What a trooper Julie is, I thought. At the time I supposed she had her reasons but I couldn't figure out why she would want to break up with her lovely boyfriend. I was sure he would have liked the chance to discuss things and maybe they could have reached some sort of compromise. Gary Devine was the best-looking man I had ever seen in real life. Conventionally handsome, if you know what I mean? The living image of Andy Garcia. Big honest eyes, thighs rounded and hard like telegraph poles, thick head of glossy black hair. (And it's not even dyed, like mine is.) Great lover, too, according to Julie. She never went into details. She just laughed once and said Gary definitely knew what he was doing in the bedroom. Nicely spoken, he was. Never used to swear in the company of ladies.

What does Gary do for a living, I hear you ask?

Says a lot about a man, doesn't it?

Well, Gary's a riding-instructor with his own stables in Crawfordsburn. Julie met him in 2003 when she was learning to ride a horse. She was seeing this older man called Bert at the time and she was tinkering with the idea of getting married. Only tinkering, now, she hadn't set a date or anything. She was talking about a Robin

26

Hood theme, hence the horse-riding lessons. Bert was a paper products (loo-roll) millionaire and a very keen rider himself. Julie didn't love Bert but he was filthy rich, as it were.

"People will always need toilet tissue." That was Bert's motto.

We had quite a few laughs over it. Until Julie fell off the horse into a deep puddle of sticky black mud and Bert laughed his head off. Big mistake. Nobody laughs at Julie twice. She swiftly dumped Bert for Gary Devine, just as soon as she'd washed off the mud in the stables' showers. Julie moved in with Gary that evening, actually.

"I'm going to stay in a new spa in Galway." That was Julie's follow-up nugget of news. She took a thick gold-edged business card out of her handbag and laid it gingerly on my knee. "That's the name of the place, there. They've got shocking-pink armchairs in the foyer."

So they had. There was a picture of the foyer on the business card. Shocking-pink armchairs, all present and correct. Lots of glass walls and exotic flowers in tall vases. An indoor stream and some gorgeous hunks in white towelling robes standing casually by the stairs. Having a cosy little chat, by all accounts. It all looked so natural and spontaneous. Not! Bully for you in your white robes, I thought resentfully.

Normally I'd be extremely impressed with shocking-pink armchairs in the foyer and gold-edged business cards but that day I could feel the sands of time shifting beneath my feet and I knew that both our lives were on the cusp of major change. Don't ask me how I knew. I mean, Julie was only breaking up with her boyfriend. It happens all the time. People get together and they split up again. But this was different. Call it a woman's intuition. I just knew the transition period would be long and difficult for everyone concerned.

"I see," I replied in a whisper.

"Super place, so I hear," Julie added. "I expect I'll spend more time lying by the pool than being slathered in smelly potions and all that caper but I'm so looking forward to the peace and quiet. Windows right down to the ground, they have. See? It's like being outside except, of course, it's warm."

We both peered at the card again. It did seem a 5-star sort of operation which was only what I expected of Julie Sultana. She wasn't likely to lie low in a rural guest-house with Camberwick bedspreads and crumbs in the jam. Julie is nothing if not stylish.

And then, break-up announced, she got on with the rest of the business instructions.

"Now, Mags, will you be able to cope with Dream Weddings on your own while I'm away? Only, my mobile will be switched off in case Gary rings me. Which he's bound to do. Let's see, there's that peasant shindig coming up tomorrow afternoon for a start. I should never have taken them on as clients. What possessed me? Janine Smith and the rest of her motley crew! Never less than six of them clumping into the lighthouse for appointments, sometimes with small kids in tow. Mags, no more Under-12's in the lighthouse! We don't want one of them falling down the bloody stairs. Right?"

"Yes, Julie."

I thought, see! She *does* care about children.

"We don't want to be hit with a crippling lawsuit," Julie added. "Just when we're starting to do so well."

Oh, I thought. Good point, all the same. We didn't want any little ones breaking their necks. Those steps are only four inches wide on the inside tread. And the banister is a rope which isn't as easy as you'd think to hold on to, the way it loops up and down to the fixings.

"No more children in the lighthouse, agreed," I parroted.

"And the dress will take a team of engineers to put on, silly mare. She'll be killed trying to walk down the aisle, honestly she will. She'll probably faint with heat exhaustion. Make sure you're close by with the Rescue Remedy, Mags. Why *do* women get so carried away on their wedding day? It's only a piece of paper when all's said and done."

Well, that last comment was very telling, I thought to myself. But I said nothing.

"It's okay, Julie," I muttered. "I'll manage."

I was terrified, to tell you the truth. I always wanted Julie and me to go together if we had to meet clients in their own homes and attend weddings and so on. But I could see she was having some sort of crisis. Shame about Gary, though. I'd always thought Gary was very nice. I hoped she'd miss him so much she'd come home after ten minutes of 'forest sounds and hot stones', make it up with him and still be available to help me squash the bride (the aforementioned Janine Smith) into her pumpkin coach. And we still weren't convinced the extra-volume pink tulle (fifty layers of it) Janine had ordered wasn't highly flammable. And the bride and groom were both heavy smokers.

"I'll check my mobile once a day for messages," Julie added. "Around lunch-time, probably. Emergencies only, mind. Don't contact me unless Janine Smith actually gets hurt falling out of the pumpkin coach. You know what, don't tell me anything about that vile wedding. I'm so ashamed of the entire farce. And don't agree to put a shot of her on our website, either. Little wannabe. Let her give *Closer* magazine a ring instead. We're not an elitist set-up, Mags, but even I draw the line at plastic tiaras and nylon nipple-skimmers."

Nipple-skimmer is what we in the business call a low-cut bridal gown. Just a private trade joke. I nodded mutely. You can't argue with Julie. That's another thing you've got to understand if you want to be Julie's friend. You can't ask searching questions and you can't argue with her if you don't agree with what she says. She's very stubborn, is Julie. Anyone else would assume Julie was a bit of a spoilt madam, not letting people have their say, but not me. I knew her too well, you see. And I knew all about Charlotte and Sidney. And they're the reason I let Julie get away with blue murder sometimes.

4

Charlotte & Sidney

CHARLOTTE AND SIDNEY WERE JULIE'S PARENTS BUT she didn't love them very much when she was growing up. In fact she hated her father, in particular, so much that she also hated anyone who was even *called* Sidney. She once put the squeeze on this man called Sidney McCreevy. He was asking for it, mind you. Wouldn't settle the bill for his daughter's wedding and it was well into six figures, what with the way plans had expanded during the run-up. And Julie can't be doing with late payers. We could have gone to court but that would've dragged on for years so Julie decided to take matters into her own hands. She threatened to tell Mrs McCreevy that her husband was up to no good with his secretary. Julie knows all the gossip in this town. Julie and her five best friends, The Lisburn Road Coven: they know *everything*. That's how Julie came to be the owner of the lighthouse on Lagan Road. Sidney McCreevy gave it to her in lieu of a cheque. And he's still seeing his secretary to this day.

Marriage is a curious thing, isn't it?

How many couples do you know? Forty or fifty, probably. And how many of them can you honestly say are blissfully happy? Come on, now. How many couples do you know, for a fact, go rolling about on their Habitat rugs every weekend? Not many, I'll wager. Well, me and my Bill are actually a bit like that except with rugs from Ormeau Carpets instead of Habitat. But most marriages are a little mundane like a Cheddar-cheese sandwich curling up at the edges. That's Julie's opinion and maybe she's right? I'm not being smug, you understand? I'm only going by what I've been told on the maternity wards. Some women will really dish the dirt on their husbands when they've recently had their undercarriage stitched up like an army blanket while hubby sits watching 'a qualifier' on some pub telly. But to continue with Julie's theory, most wives don't really fancy their husbands and, like cheap bread, the poor guy looks grey in a certain light but he's better than nothing. And the wives ask themselves, well, who gets to eat gourmet food every night? So they make do with their man (the equivalent of a Cheddar doorstep) and they tell themselves it could be worse and at least he doesn't batter them round the scullery when he gets drunk and if he wasn't there, who would cut the grass and put the shelves up? Right?

Okay.

But Charlotte and Sidney, Julie's parents? Oh dear. Brace yourself for this. It's not pleasant. They were completely mad. Both of them. Absolutely *mental*, doolally, bonkers, up the left, round the twist, gaga, potty, basket cases. We're not supposed to use those derogatory words any more, are we? It's not politically correct to say someone's a Grade One Nut Job. We're supposed to say that people are dealing as best they can with some serious issues and they're having a spot of therapy at the moment or they've had a hard life and that's why they're a little 'eccentric'. Fair enough. But Charlotte and Sidney were in a league of their own when it came to marital disharmony. They were a poster campaign for quickie divorces. They drove each other insane in that big house on the edge of the city, surrounded by sycamore trees. And poor Julie was a thoroughly miserable witness to their outrageous carry-on. It was a nuclear war in that house from what I gather. Each of them with their finger poised above the red button, waiting for the mushroom cloud of Armageddon to erupt.

Married her for a bet, that's what Sidney said to Charlotte when they returned from their honeymoon in Bundoran in 1964. She still had the silver horseshoe wedding charm dangling off her wrist.

"Guess what? I married you for a bet, Charlotte my darling," Sidney said when he'd carried his new bride over the threshold of his rented rooms in the Holy Lands district of South Belfast.

"I beg your pardon?" Charlotte said, tapping her ears with a pink vinyl clutch bag. "Can you say that again, Sidney? I don't think I heard you right, my sweetness."

"Yes indeed, I married you for a wager! Now, Mrs

Sultana, where's my dinner? The kitchen is through there. I'm extremely partial to a little bundle of shredded Savoy cabbage lightly fried in bacon grease. Only, don't use too much, my love, as I prefer my rashers crispy. Thank you very much."

Charlotte, rather predictably, keeled over like a ton of bricks onto the worn linoleum and would you believe he left her lying there in a heap and went for a nice long soak in the bath. He was an evil man, that Sidney Sultana.

He seemed to draw strength from the misery of others, Julie's father. Never missed a wake, for instance. Always first at the front door to shake hands with the grief-stricken family, swiftly followed by a good long gawp at the deceased. Or as Catholics persist in calling them, 'the remains'. Nice. Sidney actually kept a count of the wakes he had attended on the back of an envelope, tucked into his car's sun visor for handiness. I'm not making this up. Now, I've always found prolific wake-attenders to be very strange characters. I'm not talking about close friends and relatives, you understand? I'm talking about those people who pop into every wake in town when they were only ever a casual acquaintance. Morbid voyeurs asking questions about the circumstances of the death.

"Did he suffer at the finish? Were there any last words?"

Or,

"Was she conscious at all, the poor woman? Did she know the end was nigh?"

Gives me the heebie-jeebies, people like that. I might dress like a vampire's grandmother sometimes but

I'm no coffin-chaser, believe you me. I've always found death to be a very upsetting subject. I love beautiful things: jet beads, ornate gates and bedsteads, lace curtains, beaded handbags, long-stemmed wine glasses. Men with good bone structure. Ostrich feathers, Roman noses and red roses. But death and all associated subjects? I don't want to know, missus. Just wanted to clear that up.

So, yes, day one of married life for the Sultanas. Charlotte drops like a sack of spuds into the corner and he nips off for a sandalwood bubble-bath. The wretched woman should have crawled out of that tenement house on her hands and knees when she came to, and she might have done just that except Julie was already on the way. A brave little speck of hope in a marriage that was doomed from the very beginning. Charlotte was feeling unwell during her last few days at the seaside, you see. A fluttery feeling in her tummy, she told Julie years later. And she just knew she was pregnant. So being a good wife, she pretended she hadn't heard what Sidney had said, pretended she hadn't fainted onto a pile of old newspapers and punctured bicycle tyres. And off she went to the corner shop to purchase some new potatoes, a fresh Savoy cabbage and a pound of lean bacon.

Tragic.

Some background for you?

Okay.

Sidney Sultana was a betting man. He loved a gamble. He loved a good bet. He owned a chain of betting-shops across Belfast and a shiny big BMW saloon car which he kept in 'mint' condition at all times because he never knew when he might be able to offer a lift to a pretty young girl. Oh yes, he was always on the sniff, the dirty dog. Before his marriage to Charlotte and during it. Up to all sorts of tax dodges, he was. Kept a mountain of cash around the office, the bank never saw the half of it. Sidney had lived in rented rooms all his adult life even though he could easily have afforded a decent house. I've never been able to work out why he did that. Well, that's neither here nor there, is it? Maybe he worried that some of the customers he'd bankrupted would burn him out? Maybe he simply didn't fancy the upkeep?

Whatever.

Basically what happened was, his old poker associates bet him ten thousand quid that he couldn't wed a lady from the upper classes and of course Sidney went all-out to win that ten grand. Even though he was rotten with money already and didn't need it. He pursued Charlotte relentlessly and when he got her to fall in love with him, well, her disappointed family had no choice but to swallow their distaste and arrange the nuptials as best they could. The reception was like a Laurel and Hardy film, so I believe, with Charlotte's posh relatives hiding behind potted palms in the hotel, to avoid having to converse with the riotous Sultana tribe.

Charlotte's father reluctantly signed over a plot of land as a wedding present and Sidney finally became a homeowner. He built a vulgar great house on the land with three garages and a swimming pool even though neither he nor his heartbroken bride could swim a stroke. As a little twist though, he built the house facing away from the view just so his wife couldn't enjoy the scenery unless she was standing at the sink in the scullery. The despicable excuse for a man. He taunted Charlotte with that bet through every day of her nightmare pregnancy. He flaunted his mistresses before her, buying them gifts of perfume and satin underwear and leaving them lying round the house for a day or two with gift tags attached. (The gifts, not the mistresses.) He embarrassed his wife in front of their dinner guests. Time and time again he made a show of her, criticising her prim and proper clothes and her dowdy taste in footwear and her lumpy mashed potatoes.

He didn't have it all his own way, though. They never had another child because after the baby was born Charlotte refused to share a bed with Sidney ever again. She was a doormat, certainly, but she wasn't a masochist. She thought he might be planning to wear her out with back-to-back pregnancies so she moved into one of the other bedrooms (taking Baby Julie with her) and she had a lock put on the door. Of course, any fool knows the average lifespan of mothers in this country used to be something laughable like forty-five in the years before contraception became widely available. Thousands of women ended up in early graves. Anaemic and under-nourished, forced to scrub and cook all hours, they simply collapsed with exhaustion beside the mangle. A bloody disgrace it was. Hard to believe it's still going on in developing countries, isn't it? This quiet annihilation of women.

Anyway, Julie heard them rowing about sex, in the garden one night when she was about seven. Sidney shouting that Charlotte wasn't giving him what he was entitled to by law and in 'the eyes of the Catholic Church'. And her vowing to 'hack it off' with a knife if he ever came near her. It was a complete mystery to Julie why they carried on like this for ten years. And Sidney didn't relent in his atrocious behaviour for one single minute. Personally, I think it was a class-thing and Sidney hated Charlotte because she was educated and refined but that doesn't explain why he married her to begin with. I mean, if he'd wanted a common wife with a rampant libido and a swarthy tongue in her head, why the hell didn't he propose to someone like that instead and save us all a lot of bother?

Such trouble to go to for a wager!

Sidney shouted at Charlotte and he threw things at the wall above her head and he even took an axe to the kitchen in the new house one night when he'd had too much to drink. It was almost as if he was trying to drive his own wife to suicide. That's what Julie thinks, looking back. Sidney knew full well that Charlotte was a sensitive sort who wasn't used to such deadly melodrama but he didn't care. In fact, he delighted in seeing her weep with despair. Stuck-up cow, he used to call her. She would cry for hours on end and beg him to explain why he'd married her if he hated her so much and he would always yell back, "How many times, you stupid woman? I married you for a bet!"

"But why?" she would moan. "Why, Sidney?"

"Because I felt like it. That's why!"

And off she would go, bawling again. Lying on the

38

carpet like a sick cat, sobbing her lungs into spasms, while Sidney calmly read the newspaper and Julie cowered in her own bedroom eating custard creams. A monster in beige polyester slacks, that was Sidney Sultana, Esquire. And Charlotte was a gutless drip of a woman who didn't have the brains to get the hell out of her sham marriage before her only child was emotionally damaged for life. Like I said, a couple of out-and-out nut jobs.

They do say fact is stranger than fiction.

You must be in despair for Charlotte by now and I wouldn't blame you one bit. A lot of these battered wives are asking for it, you might even dare to suggest. Whimpering like a dog in the corner, letting him get away with it over and over. Clearly she was stressed to the point of madness. But what Sidney hadn't reckoned on, and this was the bit you couldn't make up (you'll enjoy this), was that Charlotte was a devout Catholic who simply couldn't *countenance* divorce let alone the mortal sin of suicide. And that if she were to step discreetly in front of a train or go to her own family solicitor to see about procuring a divorce, then she'd go straight down to the fiery furnace. And she'd never see Saint Peter and the Pearly Gates. So Charlotte wouldn't leave Sidney despite his best attempts to make her life a living hell. Besides, she had nowhere else to go, I daresay, and no career with which to support her child. She didn't want to admit to her family that she had made a dreadful mistake and she didn't want to become one of those stoic Lone Parents waiting in line in the Post Office for a government handout. But the main reason was definitely religious. So she stayed put in the big house and did her best to keep out of the firing line.

By 1970, however, Charlotte felt worn out. Julie remembers the very day her mother finally abandoned all efforts at keeping up appearances. She said it was like a light going out in Charlotte's eyes. The wretched woman stopped crying and she stopped speaking to her husband altogether. She didn't cook for him any more, didn't clean the house, didn't answer the phone, nothing. She reckoned the sin of sloth would be worth only fifty years in Purgatory and she was willing to suffer that much to spite Sidney Sultana, she told Julie. Dust piled up in the corners, newspapers toppled off the armchairs and the milk turned mouldy on the doorstep.

Sidney tried to weather the storm. He wore his clothes for weeks without washing them, then he buried them in the garden and bought more. He ate burgers and chips from the local fryer and he heated up Fray Bentos pies in the oven. He drank Lucozade and brown lemonade if there were no teabags left in the kitchen. He was livid with rage but he didn't know what to do with this silent wife who would not look him in the eye. He invited people home to dinner (squads of them) in an attempt to embarrass Charlotte back into domestic servitude but she stayed in her room and wouldn't even come downstairs to say hello. She gave him nothing but the silent treatment. And he couldn't hit her, you see, even though he threatened to because then she'd have had the bruises as evidence of cruelty and she could have got him arrested and banned from the premises altogether.

And Charlotte couldn't *kill* Sidney. Obviously she couldn't kill him though she often told Julie she wanted to, because that would have been a mortal sin of the very worst kind. No, Charlotte was lining her heavenly nest with the feathers of pain and suffering. And cold-blooded murder would have put the mockers on all of that, big style. And Sidney wouldn't hire a housekeeper to cook and clean for the three of them because then Charlotte would have got away with lying about, officially doing nothing all day long, and he wasn't having *that*. It was therefore a classic case of stalemate.

Well, then the balance of power suddenly shifted irreversibly. It was hard to tell what exactly happened and of course Julie was only a child and can't be expected to remember the details with any perspective. But she told me that one day in 1972 when her mother was getting ready to go the shops, she hesitated on the doormat for a few moments and then she put down her shopping basket on the hall carpet and went straight back to bed.

"I'm tired," Charlotte said quietly. "So very tired."

Julie was left sitting on the bottom stair, wondering when her mummy was going to get up again after this strange afternoon nap. And as the evening wore on, Charlotte did indeed trail out of bed to prepare a shepherd's pie out of some leftovers for herself and Julie. But she vowed never to leave the house again until the day either herself or Sidney died. She stayed in her room for the best part of three years, ordering groceries and household supplies over the telephone and leaving the money for them in a neat row of small brown envelopes on a marble half-moon table in the front porch.

When Sidney eventually realised (and it took him several months to work it out, he was that selfish and stupid) he had taunted and tortured his own wife into a state of chronic and profound depression where she was emotionally dead inside, he was afraid. Very afraid indeed. But he couldn't go calling in the doctors, do you see? Do you understand the pickle he was in? Never mind the dust now, to hell with the dust and the mouldy milk. Charlotte had become Belfast's answer to Mrs Rochester. The shameful mad wife to be hidden from society at all costs. A shadowy figure pacing the house at night so that Sidney was afraid to go to sleep in case she opened him up with a carving-knife. He'd pushed her too far and he had run out of ideas.

Even then, in my humble opinion, it was not too late to salvage the Sultana family – on an individual basis, obviously. Sidney could have told all to his GP, got Charlotte some professional help and fled to England or somewhere far away from the whole sorry saga. Julie could have been fostered out to some sensible middle-class family and the three of them could have begun to live again. Even a half-life would have been better than the conveyor belt of misery they were all seemingly strapped to. But no. Sidney Sultana had dug a hole for himself and he was determined to go on digging. He couldn't get the psychiatrists and the Social Services in on the act because then he would have to tell the world what a wicked man he'd been. They'd probably arrest him and try him for cruelty. He couldn't let Charlotte go and he wouldn't let Julie go. He was trapped in his big back-to-front house with a zombie wife and a silent child and there was nothing he could do about it. Sidney Sultana, hoist by his own petard. It was the most delicious revenge, though Julie paid dearly for her parents' stubbornness with the loss of a happy childhood. We mustn't forget that.

To summarise, Sidney had collected his ten thousand pounds, married a toff and got a plum plot of land beside the sea handed to him. He'd fathered a pretty daughter who would care for him in his dotage, and he'd gained a ticket for life into Belfast's polite society. Such as it was. (Or still is.) Sorted.

What he got instead was a wife who jumped at the slightest noise, who hoarded tins of corned beef and novelty teapots in her bedroom. A resentful daughter who hated him so much she bit his hand in front of the bishop one Cemetery Sunday when he tried to pat her head in church, and the knowledge that all his mates in the poker club pitied him and looked down upon him. Even his painted-up floozies deserted Sidney in the end when they thought Charlotte might be committed to an asylum, and the scandal would explode around all of them like a volcano. Sidney Sultana had always been a loose cannon but when he became a social leper as well (and even the small-time gamblers would not drink with him lest they say the wrong thing and offend him) it drove him over the edge altogether. He became almost as much of a recluse as Charlotte. He sat downstairs in the lounge for weeks at a time, watching horse-racing on the television and phoning out for Chinese takeaways while Charlotte stayed in her room sipping endless cups of tea and nibbling on cooked ham slices. Julie pottered about on her own, forging her parents' signatures on school notes and doing her best to look clean and presentable. She never spoke to her father except to wish him well on his birthday, when she would present him with a home-made card featuring a car she'd drawn using felt-tip pens. Sidney couldn't prove it but he always did think that Julie's glitter-car was shaped rather like a coffin. She could see the suspicion in his eyes, she told me.

"Will you look after me when I am old?" he'd ask Julie from time to time, apparently yearning for a wicker chair and senility. And Julie always told him she would like to take care of him, certainly, but Charlotte would probably need her more. He couldn't fault that reply, could he? It was only the truth.

And so, Sidney's ruined life stretched ahead of him like an endless ribbon of pain and sorrow until one stormy night in 1975 when he decided he could take no more of it. He was fifty and losing his hair, it has to be said. And he was developing that peculiar figure some men get, when their stomach bloats out like a Space Hopper and their hips disappear altogether. He had to buy braces to hold his beige polyester slacks up, it was that bad. The floozies laughed at him when his once-pert posterior began to sag and then caved in completely. Charlotte literally wouldn't look at him even when he threw the hall-table out onto the driveway one day, scattering brown envelopes right and left. And his own daughter was giving him drawings of coffins for his birthday. The relentless diet of Chinese takeaways had caused a bleeding stomach ulcer that refused to heal and he had no friends left in the whole wide world. Sidney Sultana realised far, far too late that being an evil bully and a cruel beast has its downside.

Loneliness and despair.

What happened next?

Well, you might ask.

He died, of course. What do most bullies do when they have run out of victims with which to amuse themselves? He expired in a puff of black smoke and a ball of red and orange flames on the very stroke of midnight. Like the devil he was. Julie, the poor waif, was only ten years of age when Sidney Sultana topped himself. Drove his big fancy saloon car straight into a landmark oak tree on the road back from Portstewart. He'd been seen earlier that day walking along the beach by several day-trippers. Just walking casually on the beach, they said, eating an ice-cream cone with two big Flakes sticking out of it. A chocolate V-sign, if you will? They remembered him because he'd been wearing a showy overcoat and talking to himself about novelty teapots.

It was gruesome, so they told Charlotte afterwards. The crash scene was 'well and truly fierce'. Firemen did what they could to cut Sidney out of the wreckage but he was a dead duck and no mistake. Car was in bits. Pity about that beautiful car when you come to think of it. Leaping off a cliff would have been more environment-ally friendly. And besides, he might have hit another vehicle on his nocturnal suicide-mission. But that's just me being practical again. Maybe he didn't have the guts for a cliff-top leap? I'd say hitting that old oak tree head-on was a quicker way to bow out.

The police came to the door of the Sultana residence in the middle of the night and Julie answered it in her bright red nightgown with ladybird buttons down the front. (Charlotte had stopped answering the door years before.) A strangely calm Julie summoned Charlotte to the hall, and then the tragic child proceeded to make tea and hand out chocolate biscuits individually wrapped in bright green foil, to the small party that sat beneath a hideous painting of some famous racehorse, executed (so to speak) in oils with a palette knife. The police told Charlotte the sad news with suitable gravitas and she promptly hung her head and cried her eyes out. With sheer relief rather than genuine grief, it has to be said, though the coppers weren't to know that.

"You're quite sure it was him?" she kept asking them. "You're quite sure there's been no mistake? A short, stocky man with a heavy sheepskin coat and two gold sovereign rings on his left hand? And he's officially dead? He's not only been brought to the morgue and left there till morning? A doctor has definitely signed the death notice? Do you have any actual proof of the death, about your persons?"

You couldn't make it up.

Julie said she would never forget the change in her mother's face that night. The ten years of lunacy and misery just seemed to fall away and Charlotte's narrow green eyes became bright and animated. Yes, it was definitely Sidney Sultana, Rest In Peace. Dead at last. Dead as a Dodo. Thanks be to God. Charlotte danced on the kitchen table when the policemen had taken their leave. Kicking up her heels and fluttering her fingers like a cheesy cabaret star.

"Dat-a-dat-a-dah!"

Picture the scene.

"Don't you worry about me hating your father," Charlotte said to Julie in a breathless rasp. The sudden bout of exercise had fairly taken it out of her, I expect. "I won't go to hell now," she said, stamping her feet on the wooden tabletop. "I can always tell it in Confession and get absolution. I couldn't go to Confession before, do you see? Because I wasn't really sorry for hating that horrible man. And God won't forgive you if you're not truly sorry, and God knows every thought in your head so there's no use pretending. But now I *can* be sorry and mean it because my husband's stone dead and he won't be coming back. *Hip, hip, hooray!* Oh, the shopping I'll do now! I'll shop till I drop. Till the two legs buckle beneath me in Anderson McAuley's. I might even open my *own* shop! I'll get away from this hateful house and all the years I've wasted in it."

"Yes, Mummy," said Julie.

Doolally, all the way.

Poor Julie, can you even begin to imagine what that night must have been like for her? And the child still at Primary school? So you've got to make allowances for the woman, haven't you?

Anyway.

47

You'd think Sidney Sultana would have done the decent thing at the end and made it look like an accident. Wouldn't you say that was the least he could have done after what he had put them through? So that Charlotte and Julie would be well provided for by the life insurance? But no, the vile and twisted little snake had left a goodbye note pinned to the wall of the office in one of his betting-shops. And he'd left most of his money to charity for reasons which escaped everyone who knew him. So Charlotte got nothing in the heel of the hunt but a lot of averted eyes at the funeral service.

Charlotte didn't care about the neighbours, though. Couldn't have cared less about any of them at that point in her life. Her depression was instantly cured and she had quite a portfolio of property to sell, what with the house and the betting shops so she was going to be fine financially. Despite the house being built the wrong way round and the betting shops being located in slightly dodgy areas. Her heart was yelping like a randy rooster under those black widow's weeds and she couldn't get the mourners shifted out of the mansion fast enough when Sidney was finally planted. She practically ripped the paper plates out of their hands and shoved them through the double doors of the mansion, their mouths still full of egg mayonnaise.

Later that day Charlotte took a taxi (with Julie in tow) back out to the grave and, with the aid of a litre of petrol, set fire to the bouquets the undertakers had left on Sidney's plot for the sake of respectability. (She hadn't ordered any.) In their place, she dropped a cardboard box containing his Hank Williams records, his bronze bust of Johnny Cash, his brown-glass ashtray that was shaped like a vintage car and his awful oil painting of the racehorse.

"Goodbye, Sidney," Charlotte said softly to the burnt-out fake grass covering the grave and then she spat on it for good measure. "And good riddance to bad rubbish." It was the only time Julie had ever seen her mother spit. Charlotte always used to say that the government should reintroduce the death penalty for spitters as a clever way to rid society of all idiots and perverts (who were spitters to a man), so it was quite a shock for Julie to see her dear mater pucker up with such unfettered gusto.

Yes, marriage is a curious thing.

Which is why I didn't quiz Julie in the Café Vaudeville that day when she told me she was leaving Gary. You can't really blame Julie for not wanting to marry Gary, can you? Even though he was gorgeous in every way and even though he treated her like a princess. As they say nowadays, Julie has some 'serious issues' where marriage is concerned. I mean, I've seen Julie blanch visibly at the mere mention of Savoy cabbage. And she won't travel in a dark blue BMW, no matter who's driving it. And we don't use brown envelopes at Dream Weddings. At the time in question we had pale blue and pale pink ones printed up specially with our logo on the top-left corner.

Every cloud, mind you.

Julie's a magnificent wedding-planner, the best in the business. Why? Because she thinks weddings are a complete and utter waste of time. She thinks any woman who wants to get married is soft in the head.

"Half of all marriages end in divorce," she says, "and most of the marriages that do survive are like those dried-up Cheddar-cheese sandwiches. Dreary but better than an empty plate. Well, I won't be stuck with a dried-up sarnie, Mags, no way. I want a lifetime pass to the gourmet buffet table."

May I remind you those are Julie's words, not mine.

I reckon guys like Sidney are few and far between, and that most men are only doing their best. But that's why Julie never gets flustered if the cars are late, never gets in a twist about the flowers or the catering arrangements. Because at the end of the day, she just doesn't honestly *care* about weddings. She does a good job for her clients, I'm not saying she's an absolute maverick. She does care about the reputation of Dream Weddings and she works long hours and most of the time the brides are delighted with our services. But she retains enough cynicism to stop herself from getting completely obsessed with the subject. And I don't think anyone in her shoes would be any different.

Shame about Gary, though. I wasn't looking forward to that little chat, I can tell you.

5

The House on Eglantine Avenue

I HAD A GREAT LIFE AS A TEENAGER. OH BOY, DID I ENJOY myself or what? In the space of about six months when I was eighteen I discovered liquid eyeliner, the coolest group on the planet (Bauhaus), the unbeatable combination of Pernod and blackcurrant and the sensuous caresses of my husband-to-be, Bill Grimsdale. Every night of the week or so it seemed, I was down at the Limelight Club pushing and shoving my way through a sea of rock fans, cigarette smoke and raging hormones. I got kicked in the face once by a crazy mosher high on adrenaline and possibly drugs and I didn't even care. The music was so loud it interfered with my heartbeat and sometimes I forgot to breathe if there was a really good song on. I loved The Pixies, The Banshees, The Fall. Basically anything that was loud, outrageous and exploding with emotion and angst.

That's the thing about Goths, for those of you who

don't know any personally. We're lovely people: pacifist, artistic and generally vegetarian. We're no threat to the fabric of society whatsoever. Take Punks, for instance. The music is great. 'Making Plans For Nigel' by XTC is particularly excellent but the fans are unpredictable, I find. Could be pussycats like my Bill, could be insane like the mosher who nearly blinded me. It's impossible to tell on first appearances. Take my advice and be polite to Punks because your condescending expression could just be the final straw for one of them. Nu-Metal fans and the School-Rock brigade, now they really are a bunch of immature idiots with far too many tattoos and body-piercings. Not likely to attack you but they probably will take a leak in your topiary tubs. And of course your vacant-stare, always-in-a-gang, baseball-hat-loving 'Chavs' are the ones most likely to stab you for a tenner and spend it on lottery tickets. Never turn your back on a bunch of Chavs, they're the most dangerous of the lot. I'd rather get stuck in a lift with a group of Hell's Angels. But Goths are harmless enough.

Small point, Goths are not to be confused with people who are simply wearing black clothes. If you have a tan of any kind you don't qualify as a Goth. If people never laugh at your shoes you don't qualify as a Goth. If you don't find the moss-covered ruins of ancient castles emotionally uplifting, forget it. And of course, true Goths are never violent in any way.

What else can I tell you?

I failed my 'A' levels but I didn't care. They were useless subjects anyway. I can't even remember what they were called now. Social something-or-other and Media-whatnot. Not worth the paper I bought to write my essays on. I was considering trying to get onto some practical course at the Tech, like hairdressing, but I hadn't yet managed to pass any exams. But Bill said not to worry about formal qualifications. He explained that he was a fully-trained plumber and making relatively good money. He'd already worked out that deferred gratification was just that: deferred. So he'd got himself trained and he'd passed his driving test and he was out on the road earning a living when most lads his age were still learning how to open a tin of spaghetti hoops on campus and sticking up posters of Betty Blue.

From day one we were inseparable. I fancied Bill so much it was embarrassing. He'd only have to touch me and I'd vibrate with pleasure. And he seemed to feel the same way though I was quite skinny then and wore far too much eyeliner. I was always getting red eyes from my mascara bleeding into them in the heat of the club. On the plus side, I did get accepted onto a hairdressing course and life went on as normal. We spent all our spare time together and friends joked that we'd be getting married soon and could they come to the wedding? It was hard to find a private place to 'court' so we became expert at having a quick fumble standing against a wall and with all our clothes on. And then I forgot to take my pill and the jokes became a reality.

I wasn't embarrassed to be pregnant so young. My mother was very disappointed in me and strangely, that was the main reason I felt I was doing the right thing. She was vaguely unhappy most of the time (until she left my father) so any advice she gave me was bound to be seriously flawed, in my estimation. I told (well, I boasted really) to everyone that I was 'up the spout' and I had my long hair cut into a nice crisp bob to prove how grown-up I was.

We got married in a civil ceremony in the City Hall when I was eight months pregnant with our first child. I was nineteen and Bill was twenty-one. (It wasn't planned, naturally, but I think we were such a perfect match hormonally it was inevitable we'd have four children within four years.) Two of the cleaning ladies at City Hall stood in for us as witnesses, still wearing their lilac tabards with name-badges attached. Valerie and Lil were their names. They kissed us on both cheeks afterwards and threw some confetti they'd found left behind on a windowsill. Lovely women, I wish we'd kept in touch. We went across the road to the Wimpy for a beanburger and a Coke when we'd signed the register, proudly wearing our matching wedding rings, pleased as punch with our outrageousness. Bill said to the girl behind the counter, "I'll have a beanburger as it comes, please, and *my wife* will have extra pickles." We didn't invite our families and friends to attend the ceremony because it was our special occasion and we wanted to keep it all to ourselves. We wanted to keep our wedding day pure and not get it bogged down in arguments over seating plans, and prawn cocktails versus vegetable soup. And anyway, neither one of us was particularly religious, and Bill was reared a Protestant and I was reared a Catholic and it would have been awkward.

My parents are a bit odd, that way, slightly prejudiced. They can't help it; it's the way they were brought up. One of my Dad's ancestors, a mild-mannered farmer from county Tyrone, was mistaken for an IRA man and murdered in 1919 by the Black and Tans. With his own pitchfork, to add insult to injury. So Dad blamed everything that ever went wrong in this country on 'the British presence'. He was a good man, my father, but he never could get past the political situation which I think was a great pity. He once threw a perfectly good punnet of strawberries in the bin because there was a tiny Union flag on the label. Lovely big strawberries, they were. And we didn't have a lot of money in those days.

He shipped our family over the border to Donegal for a fortnight every year to escape the 12th of July Orange Order parades. The lot of us weighed down with flasks of tea and picnic blankets. You do know, of course, about the countless road blocks and general anarchy that occasionally kicks off in this place, during the marches commemorating the triumph of Protestant William of Orange (newly crowned William III of England) over the Catholic rebellion of 1690? I think my father was almost hoping there'd be a civil war back home in the North just so he could justify investing in that old caravan in Mullaghmore. Glued to the radio, he was, from seven in the morning till midnight. Even took it down to the beach and tucked it in behind the blue nylon windbreaker. Come the news pips, he'd raise his hand for silence and any child who spoke during the bulletin would get a light slap on the back of the head. The barest sniff of a riot and he'd be on his feet, shouting, "Hush now, weans, it's startin'. It's startin'! Our Lord in his infinite mercy bless those left behind!" We used to go to the amusements and hide, even if we had no money left for the carousel, my two sisters and me. He was that embarrassing. Dad hated Ian Paisley (the leader of the Democratic Unionist Party) with a passion. I think he hated 'Big Ian' a lot more than he ever loved us.

Such a pity.

Protestants don't bother me, I have to say. Or Protestantism as a concept, pure and simple. So they have extremely plain churches and they can get divorced and still hold their heads up in public. What's wrong with that? They're not quite so indoctrinated as Catholics are on religious matters, but a lot more likely to join the army and get themselves killed. Swings and roundabouts. Mind you, I've always found Protestants to have exceptionally clean homes. You could eat your dinner off the floor, usually. My dad always said that was the guilt manifesting itself for what they did to Ireland for 800 years. Our own house was fairly rough and ready. We'd a sack of coal in the corner of the sitting-room and Mum never decanted milk or lemonade into jugs.

Everyone understood about the wedding, I must say. In fact, they were quite relieved. Probably the thought of a heavily pregnant bride wearing black lace and biker boots wasn't exactly their idea of a big day out. We couldn't afford a luxury honeymoon and anyway the whole honeymoon-thing was a bit of a turn-off for both of us. We were used to kissing and cuddling in the dark urban streets of Belfast. Fully dressed and only half-sober. Until I got in the family way, of course. Then I gave up the Pernod and so did Bill, out of solidarity. White sandy beaches were not appealing to us back then, perched as we were on the verge of parenthood. We rented a doll-sized terrace on the Ormeau Road and bought a baby's crib and a kettle.

And then a lovely thing happened.

Our relatives (Bill's mostly but some of mine too) got together, held a whip-round for us (the little cross-community angels) and collected several thousand pounds. We were itching to nest-build so we used the money as the deposit on a wreck of a house on Eglantine Avenue. A big Victorian house with two bay windows, three reception rooms and one bathroom but space for three more. Six bedrooms! It had been let to students and was in a terrible state. The doors had been kicked in, the carpets were soaked with beer and wine, the kitchen sink had been split in half with a brick and the 1950's loo was a health hazard. But Bill had been told by a builder-friend of his that peace was surely coming to Belfast after twenty long years of conflict and that property prices would really take off in the nineties. This builder was buying every house he could, fixing them up quickly and letting them out again. Less than ten thousand, some of the inner-city terraces were selling for in 1985. He said he'd be a millionaire when the troops pulled out and he was right. A millionaire, several times over.

I wish my father had bought a small property in Belfast all those years ago instead of that ancient caravan

SHARON OWENS

beside the sea. He was still glued to the radio, still expecting a civil war, the day peace was declared in April 1998. He said it was only a false sense of security and banned my mother from going into the town centre for six months in case she got caught up in any trouble. Mum got so bored under house-arrest she gave up her interest in local politics on New Year's Eve 1999 and left my father for another man. The rep from British Telecom, actually. Dad gave the guy short shrift on the doorstep but Mum noticed a twinkle in his eye and slipped him her mobile phone number. They hooked up a few days later and within weeks she'd gone to England to be with him. She went on to have a fantastic facelift in Harley Street with her redundancy pay from the hosiery factory where she'd been working since the linen mill closed down. She lives in Devon now and runs a sweet little B&B with her BT lover. Roses round the door, basket full of wooden badminton racquets in the hall; the works. Good for her. It might not last forever, she says, but in the meantime she's having a whale of a time. Dad said, what else could you expect from the British? They'd taken his country and now they'd carried off his 'beloved wife' into the bargain.

Anyway, Bill worked a miracle on the house on Eglantine. He really did. Ripped out the kitchen the day after we moved in and we had to live on sandwiches for a few weeks while he replaced it with freestanding pieces from various salvage-yards. We had a Belfast sink years before they became popular again, a pine dresser with shiny red plates in neat rows and a big wicker basket full of red apples on the kitchen table. It's all country-chic nowadays in the magazines but Bill had the vision, twenty years ago, to transform that house – and he was so sexy-looking when he was covered in rubble and dust! Combined with an exquisitely shaped bare back and Billy Idol looks, well, let's just say we had no problems conceiving a sister for Alexander after he was born in 1985. Alicia-Rose, we called her – she was born in 1986. And then two more boys after that, Andrew and Christopher, 1987 and 1988. Alexander, Alicia-Rose, Andrew and Christopher. Our children! We were a proper family with a laundry basket on every landing and neat rows of shoe-shelves that Bill made for the cupboard under the stairs in the hall. A bottle-green carpet in the playroom for the boys (in what had been the drawing room) with beanbags and a big television. A white four-poster for Alicia-Rose with yellow fairy-lights on the ceiling. It was all so utterly perfect. And when the youngest, Christopher, started school in 1992, I looked about for a little part-time job and that's how I met Julie.

At the time I did wonder why a glamorous woman like Julie would want to hire someone like me to share a very small office with her. (We started off in a Portakabin on the Boucher Road.) But now I know it was because she glanced into my shopping basket during the interview and saw a packet of custard creams nestling beside my hat and gloves. The only thing she'd felt any affection for in her life to date.

6

The Smith Wedding

So NEXT DAY, GOOD AS HER WORD, JULIE SIMPLY DROPPED off the radar. I woke up in Bill's arms, missing her already. Our bedroom is gorgeous, I just have to tell you about it before I go any further. The walls and the ceiling are painted a very soothing shade of ivory. (Bill relented on the colour front eventually.) There's a clear-glass chandelier from Homebase though it really does look antique and we have a magnificent nickel-coloured Victorian-style bed complete with curly headboard and footboard, handy to hang vintage handbags on. Fat white pillows and duvet, and a fluffy red wool throw and cushions for warmth. The curtains are red too and there's a big silver-edged mirror opposite the window. Two white bedside tables with stacks of CDs on them in wicker baskets and no less than four alarm-clocks in case we sleep in. A huge white-painted wardrobe with white hatboxes on the top, full of my junk-jewellery and the children's keepsakes: their first shoes, first winter mittens, first cuddly toys, school reports and photos.

None of the kids are Goths, by the way. That would have been pushing it. We never dressed them in black, not even for family funerals. All four are completely conservative dressers by nature. Alicia-Rose is a vision in poker-straight blond hair and diamante-studded jeans – she's at Art College. She's very fond of white – sometimes we tease her she looks like a commercial for Philadelphia cheese. The boys wear baggy jeans and casual tops mostly. We enrolled them all at non-denominational private schools and we're tremendously proud of them. Alexander is studying architecture at Queen's. Well, he *was* studying architecture before his girlfriend Emma depressed him with her eating disorder and he dropped out, citing stress. The two youngest boys play rugby for their school in national competitions. I love my children so much it makes my heart ache sometimes. For years I had been dreading the day they all moved out and scattered across the country or maybe even the globe, God forbid.

So, with Julie vanishing off to the top-notch spa in Galway (the one with the shocking-pink armchairs) I had to attend the wedding of Janine Smith on my own. And then I was going to have to call Gary and tell him Julie and himself were no longer an item. I wished I could just ask someone else to live the next twenty-four hours for me, and go back to sleep. But obviously that wasn't going to happen so I sat up and reached for my robe.

"Oh, Bill, I'm not looking forward to this particular wedding," I said grumpily. "I'd better book a taxi now to take me to the bride's house and I hope she's not had second thoughts about the pink tulle. They look like the sort of family who might turn nasty if anything goes wrong. I so wish Julie was going to be there."

"Where is Julie?" Bill mumbled from deep under the duvet. "You didn't say she was going away."

"She's visiting her mother," I replied, quick as a flash. "Just took a notion."

Julie's mother, Charlotte, lives in Dublin nowadays in a one-bed penthouse apartment in Malahide village. She runs a tiny fashion boutique there, about eight foot across at its widest point. But she's used to confined spaces, I daresay, after that three-year sit-in, in her bedroom in the back-to-front mansion all those years ago. The boutique's painted lime-green inside and furnished with turquoise cabinets, and oval mirrors with pink and red glitter frames. She stocks French jeans and handbags mostly, as well as cute peep-toe shoes from Italy. Everything Charlotte sells comes gift-wrapped in the softest tissue paper and accompanied by a free key-ring in the shape of a glass strawberry. That's the name of her boutique: The Glass Strawberry. Charlotte's hair is about one inch long and dyed pillar-box red. She has loads of celebrity friends and you'd never guess she was the type of woman who once spat on her husband's grave and danced a jig on the table when she first heard he was dead. Just goes to show how the human psyche can recover from difficult circumstances. She's never remarried, though. She says one life sentence is enough for any woman and two would be foolhardy. She has a miniature dog of some kind for company. His name is Jasper.

"Look, I'll move my plumbing jobs to tomorrow and I'll drive you to the bride's house," Bill said sleepily. "Will that do?"

"Would you really?" I gasped, absolutely delighted. "That would be fantastic, Bill! The rest of the week, there's only phone calls and paperwork to get through. It'll be a cinch."

Famous last words.

"Sure, no problem. I'll wait outside in the car all morning. And you can take a couple of spare frocks from the lighthouse stockroom with you in case the bride has changed her mind about the pink whatsit."

"Bill Grimsdale, I love you," I said, almost in tears.

"Love you too," he said and went back to sleep for half an hour.

I raced happily down to the kitchen, put the kettle on and made a big pot of tea. I could hear the kids stirring in their rooms, feet padding into various bathrooms. I used to love mornings in that big house when the sun was filtering through the lace curtains in the breakfast room. Listening to the clatter and crash of cereal bowls and juice glasses. The best thing about teenagers is, they can dress themselves and brush their own teeth. Well, usually they can. Unless they're already twenty minutes late for school and then it takes them half an hour to tie their shoelaces and comb their hair. And if you shout at them to hurry up, they forget their science projects and games kits and have to come back again to fetch them.

So there we were, an hour and a half later. The children off to school. Bill and myself all tidy and presentable, cruising back from the lighthouse with the boot of the car full of demure white silk and some tasteful accessories when my mobile phone rang. It was Gary.

"Hi, Gary," I said at once, way too brightly. Bill gave me a look.

"Have you seen Julie yet, today?" Gary asked, a note of worry in his voice. "Only she looked a bit down-in-the-dumps this morning at breakfast and I wondered if there was anything going on? She said goodbye instead of see-ya. Julie never says goodbye."

"Um, Gary, listen," I blurted out, "can I call you back later this evening? I'm a bit busy at the moment. En route to a big wedding as we speak."

"Sure," he said in a puzzled voice, "though I'll have seen Julie myself by then, won't I? Cheerio." He switched off.

"What was that about?" Bill asked, taking a left turn.

"Nothing, nothing at all," I said, pretending to check my make-up in the passenger's mirror to avoid having to look at my husband. "Gary's just getting impatient for Julie to set a date for their wedding, that's all. He's trying to work out why she's taking so long to choose a venue but I'm not getting involved."

"But you said you'd call him later."

"Oh, I know I did but I'll forget to!"

"Good girl! Though I have to say, I'm looking forward to Julie's wedding," said Bill, smiling. "Lordy, Lordy, there'll be some style on that momentous occasion. No doubt you'll be roped in to play Matron of Honour? I've never seen you in peach satin before!"

"And you never will, my darling! I wouldn't wear peach satin for all the money in the world."

"I would!" Bill laughed. "I'd wear a peach satin G-string to the Vatican. On second thoughts –"

"Don't even go there," I scolded him, in fits of laughter, and the tricky subject of Julie's wedding was mercifully dropped.

I couldn't tell Gary, you see. Or Bill. I couldn't tell anyone. I was buying myself some time that day, even a few hours might have made all the difference. I remember telling myself not to worry, that Julie would take the head-staggers in Galway and come rushing back to tell me she was only suffering from monumental PMT or she'd just freaked out because she was forty-one. And Gary would never have to know that she'd been considering leaving him. And Bill would never have to know Julie's personal business. I felt very protective towards Julie. After all, she did have to witness her mother setting fire to her father's final resting place (that fake grass apparently smelt horrendous when it went up) so she was obviously worried sick about becoming a wife herself.

I'd been planning to tell Gary that Julie was just off on a little mystery holiday for a day or two (I couldn't say she was visiting Charlotte in Malahide because he might have called her there) and she'd be home soon and everything would be back to normal.

"Do you think I look nice?" I said to Bill then, because I knew that he knew there was something fishy going on.

They're quite easily distracted, men.

"Lovely, as ever," Bill replied automatically. "I like that big green flower in your hair."

I was trying to look classy that day. I had on a black trouser suit with a green-glass choker and several velvet moss-green bracelets. My hair was pinned up in a loose topknot with the big silk rose tucked in at the side. And I was wearing green faux-suede shoes and clutching a matching handbag. My eye make-up was very restrained also, and my lippy was bronze not red.

I had all the accoutrements I might need for the day and I was fairly confident I could manage, now that Bill was going to be sitting outside in the car. Providing much-needed moral support.

We arrived at the house. I took a few deep breaths and went in. It was much smaller and shabbier than I'd expected, considering what had been spent on the wedding. But you find that sometimes. Those living on a tight budget like to show off at weddings while the wealthiest clients opt for a plain white shift-dress, and one tiny orchid and a few blades of ornamental grass in their bouquet. They have nothing to prove, I daresay. I was so unbelievably grateful that Bill was outside in the Chrysler because as soon as the front door closed behind me, I knew there was going to be a problem. The atmosphere was very strained. Mrs Smith was shaking some yellow tablets into her hand out of a little brown bottle and Mr Smith was pouring himself an extra-large vodka.

"Okay, tell me what's wrong," I said, taking another deep breath.

They both pointed to the ceiling and shook their heads wordlessly. They'd clearly driven themselves hoarse begging Janine to be sensible. The bride-to-be was locked in the bathroom, sobbing loudly and occasionally throwing jumbo bottles of shampoo and bubble bath against the door.

"I'm not coming out!" she shouted suddenly. "I'm not coming out and none of you can make me!"

"Janine? Are you all right?" I said cheerily, advancing up the stairs. "You can tell me, sweetheart. Tell your Aunty Mags!"

"She won't listen to reason," said her mother crossly, coming up behind me and then the poor lady coughed noisily before swallowing her yellow tablets.

"What is it?" I asked quickly. "Is it the dress? Has it been damaged during delivery? Maybe we can rearrange the layers?"

"Oh, the bloody dress is fine," said her mother. "But one of her so-called mates told our Janine last night that the gown of her dreams is a glorified toilet-roll cover and the entire street is killing themselves laughing over it. She's been crying ever since. All night she's been crying. I could string that vicious cow up by the ears, I really could. She's only jealous. Our Janine adored that blasted dress and now she won't wear it and it's too late to get another one. I swear, when it comes to marriage the women in this family are cursed."

By this stage, Mr Smith had wandered out to the hall where he propped himself up against the front door and watched us with eyes that seemed unable to focus properly. Mrs Smith gave her husband a hard stare and he swallowed the vodka in one go and burped loudly.

"And it's not because she's changed her mind about getting married?" I whispered extra-softly. "She hasn't had a falling-out with her young man?"

"Oh no, she still wants *him* but not the pink dress. She must think we're made of money," said Mrs Smith. And then she leaned in towards the bathroom door and shouted, "We're not made of money!"

"Go away! I hate all of you!" roared Janine and she dissolved into a fresh bout of sobbing.

At this rate she'd be dehydrated, I thought to myself. Another typical day in the life of Dream Weddings. I realised Janine Smith had just discovered she wasn't a diva after all, but a normal shy girl who just wanted to get through biggest day of her life without anything going wrong. Plans you dream up in the privacy of your own bedroom can be a whole different ball game in real life.

Ask Julie Sultana.

"As it happens, I have some spare stock in the car," I said to the bride's mother. Loud enough so that Janine could overhear. "Of course, the pink tulle was fabulous on Janine. She looked amazing in it but if Janine really doesn't want the pink any more, I have other dresses with me. More conservative styles, if that's what she wants today."

The sobbing on the other side of the bathroom door stopped abruptly. Janine opened the door an inch and wiped her eyes dry on the back of a multi-coloured bath towel spelling out Majorca in giant gold letters. I felt so sorry for her, I forgot how nervous I was myself.

"What sort of dresses have you got?" Janine wanted to know. Her hair was stiff with lacquer, puffed-up to the size of a small armchair and her make-up was a dreadful shade of dark-orange. Only she'd forgotten to do her ears and they were still white.

"Janine, sweetheart," I began. (Julie always calls the brides 'sweethearts' and they seem thrilled by it.) "Why don't you pop into the shower and wash off that foundation and hair mousse and we'll start again? Okay?"

"Ah now! Am I that awful?" she wanted to know.

"Nothing wrong with you, *sweetheart*, but we'll need to start again, won't we? And style your hair to match the new dress? And I don't want to mark any of the gowns with foundation, okay? They're very *expensive*."

Hoping that would entice her to co-operate.

"I'm not paying for a new frock," said Janine's father at once, seemingly back in the loop. "I can't pay for as much as a new safety pin. I'll be in hock to the credit union for three years, as it is."

"You won't have to pay," I told him gently. "It'll be a gift from Dream Weddings." Julie had whacked on her usual fat profit margin so I thought I could get away with donating a dress. The really nice ones don't cost that much, off the peg.

"There's no time to change anything," Janine whimpered and her eyes filled up again. "The pumpkin coach is coming in an hour. And I don't want that now either," she added hopelessly. "I don't know what I was thinking of. It's all such a tacky mess."

"Bloody hell!" cried Mrs Smith, wringing her hands

and flinging the bottle of tablets at the wall. "Our life savings wasted! Are you trying to put the lot of us in the funny farm, my girl? You've been nothing but trouble since the day you were born!"

"I never asked to be born," said Janine at once, her face flushing alarmingly.

"Charming," Mrs Smith sighed, looking pointedly at her watch and then at me. "Makes you so proud, doesn't it?" she added bitterly. "To see the way your kids turn out."

Janine's angelic blue eyes suddenly became glowing spirals of rage. "You fuckin' shut your mouth or I'll shut it for you!" she roared into her poor sedated mother's shocked fizzog and I knew then, whatever life might throw at Janine Smith in the future, she'd be more than able to cope.

"Now, now, ladies! There's no need for a family ding-dong! There's loads of time to fix this," I assured Janine and her mother, both. "Look, Janine. You do as I say and have a nice relaxing shower. I'll cancel the pumpkin coach and you can travel to the church in one of the other cars."

"I don't want the outsize corsages," Janine said defiantly. "They'll be a laughing stock and all."

"Okay," I said. Almost fainting with relief because I'd forgotten all about the corsages and they were still in the lighthouse, in a box under Julie's desk.

"Christ!" said Mrs Smith.

"I have some spare buttonholes in the car," I told them brightly. "Cute little white ones, you'll love them."

"Will there be a refund on the coach?" Mr Smith asked and I had to shake my head.

"Sorry, I'm afraid it's too late for that," I told him gently.

71

He sighed heavily, staggered back to the sitting room and sank into one of the armchairs, clutching the bottle of vodka to his chest.

"I'm tired," wailed Janine. "I'm too tired to get married now. Mum, tell all the guests to go home!"

"Come on, Janine, sweetheart, we can do this. Your mother will fetch you some tea and toast and I'll get my stuff from the boot. You'll look amazing. And after the ceremony you can have a quick nap in the car on the way to the hotel, in your new husband's arms. It's a half-hour drive. Yes? Right. You're a size 8, aren't you?"

"Yes, Mrs Grimsdale."

"Call me Mags, please. Quick, quick, into the shower with you! Sweetheart!"

"Okay, Mags." And the door closed again.

"God bless you," said Janine's mother and she shuffled downstairs to get the tea ready, glad that someone else was taking charge of her indecisive daughter.

When Janine re-emerged from the bathroom twenty minutes later she looked like a different person. Tiny and pale with a long wave of chestnut-brown hair, she was prettier than I'd ever seen her. I quickly blow-dried her hair into a single loose ringlet and pinned a spray of white silk roses behind her right ear. Then, I covered her tear-stained face with the palest foundation I could find in the Dream Weddings make-up case, added some soft pink blusher and natural brown mascara. No jewellery was necessary except for a pair of tiny silver studs in her ears. And then I tried a fitted white-silk bodice with a delicate white tulle skirt on her. She looked radiant. Finally, her too-long nails were clipped and shaped and I gave her one of my own rings, a pink-glass flower from Angel At My Table.

"There you are! You've still got your bit of pink for good luck," I said. "Now, what do you think of your new image?" I led her out to the hall mirror. "Grace Kelly didn't look this good on her own wedding day."

"Grace who?" Janine said, admiring herself.

"Never mind, sweetheart. She was a film star. You look absolutely beautiful."

Janine was so pleased she threatened to start crying again and ruin her make-up so I convinced her to calm down and have some of the tea and toast.

"You'll need to keep your strength up for the photographs," I told her, pinning an apron over her frock and she nodded and sighed, and calm was restored. Ten minutes later the cars pulled up at the kerb and she was ready to face the public. I pulled Janine's massive bridal bouquet into about six pieces and handed one of them to her. She really did look beautiful. When she went out of the front door she saw a large crowd had gathered on the pavement. There was a moment or two of stunned silence and then a round of tumultuous applause.

Hooray!

Janine waved graciously to the onlookers and folded herself into the limousine like a true princess. I like to think I started a personal journey for Janine that day. I've no doubt she'll end up winning style awards. When the wedding party had exited the estate with much shouting and cheering and beeping of horns, I hurried back to Bill and we set off for the church too. Just in case we were needed but I'd a feeling we wouldn't be.

"I don't know what I'd have done without you," I said to Bill, shaking with relief that I hadn't let Janine (or Dream Weddings) down.

"What do you mean?" he said, laughing. "I've only been sitting here the whole time, reading road maps. Should have brought a good novel with me and some tea and sandwiches."

"You were there for me, darling. That's all I needed to know," I told him warmly. "How can I ever repay you?"

"You can buy me a black Volvo S80," Bill said, and we both burst into fits of laughter.

The rest of the day went like a dream. Janine didn't get roaring drunk now she was transformed into a delicate beauty, and her new husband didn't get sloshed either for fear she might abandon him in the dining room for a more sophisticated man. They apparently sat holding hands demurely until ten o'clock when they said goodnight to the guests and stole up to the bridal suite.

But I was back home by that time and sitting on the bed in my lovely bedroom, trying to work out what I could say to Gary Devine.

7

Jay O'Hanlon

DAY TWO OF JULIE'S HOLIDAY. I'D MANAGED TO convince Gary that Julie had driven all the way down to West Cork to look at a new range of bridal shoes, and she'd decided to stay the night and come back the following day. I was hoping he'd not attempt to follow her there as it was too long a round-trip to leave the stables unattended without organising holiday cover. And he agreed with me that West Cork was a bit far for a surprise visit. So far, so good. But of course the man wasn't an idiot.

"Why hasn't she called me herself then?" Gary asked, rather reasonably. "Her phone has been switched off for two days now."

"Must be a network problem," I told him. "Or maybe there's no signal where she is? I mean, she called me from a pay phone. Honestly, I wouldn't worry about it if I were you."

75

"Well, I am worried, Mags. Look, if she gets in touch again, will you please ask her to phone me? I'm worried sick, here. Usually if Julie's going to a trade thing, I go as well and make a city-break of it."

"Okay, Gary. I'll let you know the minute I have any definite information."

Which was almost the truth, I remember thinking. And Julie will surely come home soon.

How wrong I was.

At eleven o'clock on the morning after Janine Smith's triumphant makeover, and just as I was relaxing on the balcony of the lighthouse with a tall mug of instant coffee, who should call me but Julie. To say – wait for it – she'd spent the night in a hayloft with someone by the name of Jay. Some local man by the name of Jay O'Hanlon who was a dead ringer for Sean Bean when he played Sharpe in that hit telly series. You know the one set in the time of the Napoleonic campaign? Sean Bean with a military jacket, lots of gold buttons and a constantly grazed cheekbone?

I thought I was hallucinating. I actually held my mobile at arm's length and stared at it, thinking that Julie was playing some extended practical joke on me. The sudden break-up with Gary, Janine Smith's histrionics and now this hayloft nonsense? I really thought I'd be featured on some comedy show where they make fools of the unsuspecting public.

"Julie," I said slowly, "fair enough, you've had your fun. Now, can you come up the stairs and into this office and get some work done? I've just made coffee, the water's still hot."

"Mags, I'm not joking. Jay and I lay in each other's arms talking and kissing until the sun came up. Me, Mags, of all people, lying on a stack of hay half the night!"

"Let me get this straight, Julie. Did you just tell me you've cheated on your long-term boyfriend, the wonderful man that is Gary Devine? The man you are going to marry when this moment of madness has passed?"

"No," she said right away, "I didn't cheat on anyone. Gary and me have split up. How did he take it, by the way? Was he inconsolable?"

"*By the way*, she says casually! You're a dark horse, Julie Sultana. Pull yourself together for five minutes, woman, will you? Julie, listen to me. I didn't tell Gary anything," I said desperately. "He thinks you're in West Cork, looking at shoes."

"But why, Mags? Why does he think I'm there?"

"Because if he tries to trace you using mobile phone records, he'll find out you're in the South of Ireland anyway."

"But why didn't you tell him we're finished? It doesn't matter to Gary who I spend the night with any more. I want him to be free to marry a younger woman and have the family he craves so badly."

I sighed heavily.

"Honestly, Mags! I thought I explained all of this to you already?"

I sincerely hoped Julie wasn't going to drift into a ten-year fog like her mother had done. Poor Charlotte was never the same after she measured her length in that rented hallway in the Holy Lands district. I mean, red hair at her age? Well, okay, maybe it's not so crazy in light of what I did myself a few days later. But Julie's love life seemed to be teetering on a knife-edge and suddenly I was queasy with fear for her. I edged my way in off the balcony and knelt on the kitchen floor. My head was spinning. I felt as if I had vertigo though usually I'm used to the sound of seagulls calling and the wind whistling up and down the stone staircase of the lighthouse.

"Okay, Julie, so you want a trial separation? I can understand that. You want to take stock, yes? No-one would blame you after what you witnessed as a child. But I can't tell Gary you're leaving him because you don't want kids. I can't talk about the subject of having children with Gary, Julie. It isn't fair on him. And I don't want to see the two of you break up anyway. How can I convince you both that children aren't worth splitting up for when I have four of my own? I'll go to see Gary with you and I'll be just outside the door but the actual words will have to come from you. Julie, please be reasonable. You'll have to come back to Belfast and see him yourself."

"I'll not come back," she said crossly and I could almost see her pouting. "I'm on holiday. I really need this holiday, Mags."

"Call him then."

"No. There's no point. He'll only race down here and cause a scene."

"Please, Julie! This isn't like you. You're strong. You know you are. Write him a letter then, if you must? Just don't ask me to drop him for you, please. You haven't told Gary about your weird childhood, have you?"

"No, and you mustn't tell him either. Just give him the message and let's have an end to it."

"Look, Julie, this little escapade has gone far enough," I said, biting my nails with the stress of walking on such micro-fine eggshells. "You can't put me under this kind of pressure even if we are best friends. I know you love Gary and this is just a case of cold feet. I blame your parents, personally. This is simply a childhood trauma that's come back to haunt you. You know Gary would never be like your father – he's a good man and you will *so* regret ditching him like this. I want no part of it. Now, come straight home. Okay?"

"Mags," she said gently, "I know you think I'm losing my mind but I'm not. Last night, I felt like a teenager again but it was like being a teenager with brains, if you know what I mean? We talked and talked and we could have slept together at one point when this amazing kind of energy happened between us but we didn't go down that road. Not yet anyway. Jay's only twenty-eight. He's gorgeous, Mags!"

"You haven't slept with him? Thank God for small mercies! At least no real harm has been done, then? You haven't officially cheated on Gary? What age did you say that fella was, by the way?"

"Oh Mags," she said sadly, "infidelity isn't just about sex. We connected, do you understand? We felt easy together, at peace under the stars. Look at the way I'm talking, Mags. I never used to talk like this. I'm opening up in ways I never imagined. Last night, I didn't worry about my age, about my wedding to Gary, about the fact I can't have children. I block things out, you see? I always have. So do you, Mags. I thought you would understand."

Let's take a moment.

You know, it's amazing how things can change in one generation, isn't it? My parents went to school in bare feet in the summer and were working full-time by the age of twelve, my father as a shop delivery boy with a big black bicycle, and my mother as a cleaner in the linen mill. By contrast, I was still buying pop posters when I was eighteen and taping the charts for hours every Sunday night, painstakingly writing down all the titles on cassette cards. I lived in a sort of bubble for most of my childhood, that's the truth of it. I didn't like to hear or see anything that might upset me so I blanked it out and created a little world of my own in my bedroom. I had all my posters in there, my books and cassettes, a beanbag and cushions, a blue plastic crate of make-up and cheap jewellery, incense sticks and a bedside lamp that looked like an oil lamp but wasn't really an oil lamp. Bill still teases me about my 'bubble-mentality' and asks me how my 'bubble-integrity' is at stressful times in my life. He understands, though, why I put so much effort into creating our perfect home. It's because I want to create a perfect world but deep down I know I can't.

Julie couldn't have children.

I couldn't believe it.

"What was that you said? What was that you said, Julie? You *can't* have children?"

I never knew Julie was infertile. She never brought the subject up and I'd always assumed she wasn't the maternal type.

"Years ago, on holiday. I caught an infection off this idiot. A cheesy nightclub-crooner with platform shoes. It didn't matter to me, Mags, when I found out. I didn't want children anyway but I should have told Gary before he wasted three years of his life on me."

"Julie, is this what it's all about?" I tried to be extra-gentle. "Is the break-up with Gary because you *can't* have a child together? I'm sure Gary will understand – you know how calm and sensible he is? At least give him the chance to talk about this. I can't believe you won't even see him after what a decent bloke he's always been. You can't be in love with this Jay guy after only knowing him for five minutes. This isn't a Hollywood movie, Julie."

"Who said anything about love?" Julie said then, sounding utterly bewildered. "I don't love Jay. I just love who I become when I'm with him. I'm different, a better person. It's easy for you, Mags, sitting there in your little palace on Eglantine Avenue with your chattering brood round you. And Bill making all the decisions. Your whole life is one big certainty. I'm living from day to day, Mags. Here and now is all I have."

Well, I didn't like that comment about Bill making all the decisions but I let it slide. Single women without kids can be quite naïve sometimes, I find. It's not their fault. They have no idea how much hard work and serious responsibility motherhood and being married actually is. All they see are the glossy adverts on telly for Mother's

Day gifts. They know nothing of the agony you go through when your child makes their own way to and from school for the first time. God, I was in bits for weeks with all four of mine. Imagining them smiling and laughing as they stepped out in front of a juggernaut. Still, you can't rattle on about these things or you get labelled neurotic. And you can't walk the kids to and from school yourself after they turn eleven or the poor mites will be crucified by their peers. In fact, eleven is pushing it. My kids made me wait round the corner from the school gates and pretend I was sitting at the bus stop. If there were any other children about, they wouldn't even walk beside me or speak to me. What's *easy* about that?

"But you have Gary," I reminded her.

"Not when he finds out my tubes are blocked. Look, I'm on my own in this world. Well, there's my mother but she's too busy with her precious boutique to talk to me like a normal mother would. Poor cow."

"You have me," I said. "You can talk to me."

"Oh, I've tried talking to you, Mags and you won't listen. You're a hopeless romantic. Look, I've got to go," she sighed then. "Tell Gary today, please? Will you? Bye for now."

"Julie, wait! Are you testing Gary? Do you want him to come to Galway and find you? Like Richard Gere and Debra Winger in that film and she was wearing his hat at the end? Should I tell him where you are but let him think he dragged it out of me? Julie?" I almost shouted into the phone but she had already hung up.

I was left with the uneasy feeling that Julie was perhaps feeling very vulnerable at the moment and maybe she needed to be rescued from this Jay, whoever he was. Some dope-smoking Casanova who'd take advantage of her? A smooth-talker with wandering hands? A daydreaming poet who'd make her fall in love with him and then move on to his next muse? I almost fainted with worry.

So although I felt guilty to the core, talking about Julie behind her back, I decided I'd call Bill and ask his advice. Naturally, I knew exactly what he'd say but I wanted to hear him say it anyway. I said Julie wanted me to finish with Gary for her and that she was in hiding in Galway until the deed was done. Bill told me it wasn't my problem, just like I *knew* he would. He said I owed Julie my loyalty and respect for being a good employer but that I wasn't her doctor, her shrink, her mother or her agony aunt. Well, that's men for you, the bottom line is they're very logical. Of course I wasn't Julie's personal psychiatrist but I still wanted to help her. Bill said I should give Gary the name of the spa and let him sort it out himself. That's what he'd prefer, Bill said, if he was in Gary's shoes.

But I couldn't do that because I hadn't told my husband about Jay O'Hanlon and the hayloft and Julie deciding to 'open up' after forty-one years of being a super-tough survivor.

It wasn't even lunch-time and I was in turmoil. I went to the office to try and organise my thoughts. Incredibly, I just sat there thinking that all-white really is very cold to live with and that the office could have done with two coats of Soft Truffle (by Dulux) and some pretty desk-lamps. And maybe a soft rug to take the bareness off the floorboards.

And then Gary phoned to say he was coming to the lighthouse to take me out for lunch. Digging for more Julie-info, obviously. I told him I was far too busy for lunch and he said he'd swing out by the lighthouse anyway and maybe we could go for a short stroll along the shore. My skin was prickling with panic. He hung up before I could think of an excuse why we couldn't meet. Like I had scurvy or something terribly contagious?

And then my mother called me from Devon to inform me that my – wait for it – 'silly old sod of a father' had passed away.

"What? *Who's passed away? My da?* Mum, have you been drinking?" I croaked, switching from mouse-mode to toad-mode. "Get out of that, will you? Dad's only sixty-eight."

"Drinking, is it? I never touch the stuff, Margaret. You know I don't. Honestly, what a thing to say to me. Now, your father's gone to a better place and so on and so forth, so let's get down to the nitty-gritty. The thing is, my dear, you'll have to arrange the funeral, all right?" she said brusquely. "I simply can't get away in the peak season and anyway, we *are* properly divorced so I'm not the next-of-kin any more. You are. You're the eldest child, Margaret."

"Me? Arrange a funeral? But you know I'm not religious! I can't go asking his priest to say the Mass. I don't even know who his priest is. I don't know what to do! You know Bill and I aren't religious, Mum."

"That's your problem, Margaret. I've always told you to keep in with the clergy and now you know why. Because sooner or later you'll need a priest and then where will you be with your trendy ideas? I'm sorry but I've already given the hospital your name. As of now, I am not to be contacted any more *re* my ex-husband."

'Re' meaning, with reference to. It's the only modern lingo my mother knows and she uses it at every opportunity.

"Well, that's very handy for you," I snapped, a huge lump of sadness forming in my throat. That day, I almost wished divorce wasn't available in the British Isles because clearly one of the spin-offs of divorce is that we children have to bury our fathers these days, instead of the estranged wife having to do it. "I can't believe this is happening," I gasped, experiencing my first hot flush since meeting Bill in the Limelight Club. "What the heck *happened* to him? Can you tell me that before I order the coffin? Or are you too busy with your toast racks and your butter curls?"

"Don't be cheeky, Margaret. It's not my fault the man died. You know he had no time for me or anyone else outside of Stormont."

That's the name of our local parliament building, by the way. Though it hasn't seen much action these last few years.

"So?"

"So why do you think I should be upset? Any woman

who could cook and clean would have done him for a wife. As long as she kept her mouth shut and didn't interrupt him when he was watching the news."

She had a point there.

"Go on, then," I grumbled. "Tell me the rest of it."

"*Apparently*, one of the neighbours found him sitting at the kitchen table with his head on a sliced loaf. They broke in when they noticed the milk hadn't been collected from the doorstep for three days."

For one awful moment, I thought my father had been murdered and horribly mutilated by some psychopath. Care in the community isn't what it was, you know. But no. No such drama. He'd only fallen asleep listening to the radio as usual and died peacefully of heart failure. Maybe the exhaustion of waiting for a civil war had finally sapped his life force? I should have visited him more often but it used to put me off when he started up about how society had forgotten the 1981 hunger-strikers, before I'd even got my coat off. And he always told me I was pale as death even though he knew that was how I *wanted* to look. I mean, how could he forget I was a Goth when he never forgot the anniversary of Bobby Sands' death? But anyway he was gone. And the worst thing was, he'd been sitting there with his right ear firmly pressed to an Ormo thick-sliced loaf for a day or two before he'd been found. I couldn't even cry, I was that stunned.

"Oh Mum, this is terrible. I feel so absolutely *terrible* about this. Are you devastated?"

"No, dear. I only married him in the first place because he had a decent car."

"Well, that's nice to know, that I'm only alive today because you liked the look of my father's wheels!"

"He was so handsome when we first began walking out together, Margaret. And he could have gone a lot further in that job of his, if he'd done some exams and kept at it. I really thought I'd caught myself a prince. All the girls round our way had their eye on him, you know. But then he went all funny into politics and he made nothing of his life. Now, don't worry," she said kindly, easing up on me a little bit. "It won't be in the papers. They've already assured me it won't. This sort of thing happens all the time to poor folk who live by themselves. I suppose he should have had an arrangement with a neighbour where they'd call each other every morning at a certain time? That's very popular nowadays, you know? With so many people living on their own in our society. But of course your father was too pig-headed to entertain anything normal like that. He's at peace now, how ironic. He can go to heaven and meet the 1916 Easter Rising gang and tell them where they went wrong. Greatest armchair-general this country has ever known, your father. And God knows we had plenty to choose from."

That's my mother for you, a very dry sense of humour.

"Do my sisters know yet?"

"No, Margaret. I thought you'd prefer to break the news to them. You were always so close, the three of you. As thick as thieves always."

"Oh, thanks, Mum!" I was so looking forward to *that*. No doubt she was thinking of the cost of calling Australia.

She's very careful with money, is my mother unless you're talking about face-lifts and then it's no expense spared.

"That's okay, love."

"What will I do, though, after I've phoned them?" I asked her. "I've never arranged a funeral before. Let alone a funeral for a devout Catholic and hardline Republican-sympathiser."

"Don't be like that, Margaret. It doesn't suit you, dear. Look up *Undertakers* in the Yellow Pages, for heaven's sake. What do you think you're supposed to do? They'll fetch your father from the mortuary and tidy him up, I expect. I wouldn't bother with a big do. It'll be nearly as expensive as a wedding but it's up to yourself. If you're willing to pay for it, you go ahead."

"When are you coming over?" I said, making a mental note to pop a basket of fresh towels in the guest-room. It'll be lovely to spend a few days with Mum, I thought. Even if the circumstances were so awful. "Will Tone be coming with you?" Tone is her boyfriend's name. Well, he's really called Tony and he's fifty-nine but she calls him Tone. She's sixty-four.

"Oh no, Margaret. I can't make it to Ireland at the minute. I'm up to my eyes here with cooked breakfasts and afternoon teas. And Tone wouldn't feel comfortable, dear, going to a funeral with so many Nationalists kicking about. Keep this to yourself now but he once had a relative in the UDR."

The Ulster Defence Regiment.

"But you've got to come *to the funeral*," I pleaded.

88

"Mum, I need you here. You're not seriously going to miss it, are you? You must be there for my sake and for Ann and Elizabeth, too. Remember them?"

My sisters. *Her daughters.*

"Oh Margaret, please control yourself! You always were the Drama Queen in the family. Why on earth would I want to parade myself about Belfast and have the entire city talking about me! The merry divorcée? And poor Tone dragged along into the bargain? Are you mad? It would only be harder for the family, not knowing whether to sympathise with me or blame me for your father's death. Or give poor Tone a hard time about his relative being in the UDR. My money's on the blame-game. Your father never ate properly after I left him. It was only the milk deliveries that kept him alive all this time. Why single men can't be bothered to cook is beyond me. There's nothing to it, just peeling the odd carrot and chucking in a stock cube. Laziness, is all it is. Oh! Got to go. Someone's at the front door. It might be a guest. Bye, love."

Someone at the door, my bum in chives! I knew she was fibbing to get me off the line. There was a hint of a Devon accent this time, too, I noticed. Well, I suppose she was only trying to blend in. When you're from Northern Ireland you get weary of clocking the concentration on people's faces as they try to work out which side of the fence (or Peace Line) you're from. It's easier to do an accent and deny any connection. I've done it myself at Heathrow. I'm very good at the Bolton accent, if I do say so myself, after watching Peter Kay videos non-stop for several years. I could be Peter's understudy. If I had the nerve to go onstage, that is. Blimey Charlie!

"Bye, Mum."

But she was already off the line.

My father was dead.

The news finally began to filter through.

Bubble-integrity dropped alarmingly as the realisation reached my overloaded brain. Before I'd even put the phone down, I was howling like a toddler who's dropped his ice cream in the sand and knows there's no chance of persuading his parents to buy him another one.

"Dad, oh Daddy," I wailed, sounding as high-pitched as the seagulls. "What a waste of a life! What a terrible waste! You could have taken up fishing or built a model railway in the back garden. What do other men do in their spare time besides watching qualifiers? Oh God!" I reached for a handful of Julie's trademark scented tissues and settled in for a good old mope but immediately there was another phone call.

Without hesitation, I picked up. I was hoping it might have been one of my sisters and that maybe they'd have heard about the tragedy already. We could have had a lovely long chat about what might have been, and those endless summers we spent hanging round the carousel looking for dropped coins in the parched grass.

But it was Alexander (my eldest child) and he was in pieces. Sobbing and crying and shuddering with exhaustion.

"Mum, I don't know what to do!" he wept. "Everything's gone wrong."

"Jesus Christ! Alexander, tell me, son. Tell me

immediately," I commanded him, unable to wait for a single second in case the house was on fire and he needed to be reminded to phone the fire brigade.

"Oh, Mum!"

"Is anybody hurt? Is one of the family hurt?"

"I don't know what to do."

"Alexander Grimsdale!" I screamed. "Tell me *right now*."

"It's Emma," he cried, blowing his nose a bit too close to the receiver. "She's broken up with me, Mum."

I deflated with relief, like a hot-air balloon that's just been shot down.

"Oh, Alexander! For fuck's sake! You nearly gave me heart failure," I said. The mere mention of heart failure reminded me of my father and I resumed crying too. "Is that all? You'll make it up with her again, son. Don't you always? You've split up six times this month alone."

Emma's a beautiful girl but she was very moody with it, around the time she was anorexic. I knew she had an eating disorder the day I met her three years ago because she was very thin and claimed to have an awful lot of food allergies. I mean, I felt sorry for Emma but you can't help wishing your son had fallen for one of those no-nonsense girls on the hockey team instead. You know the ones with legs like tree-trunks and healthy pink complexions? Personally, I have to say that Emma manipulated my Alexander a little bit. He was utterly obsessed with her fragility and her other-worldness. And she wore the most expensive shoes. At the time, I didn't trust anyone who wore designer shoes, I must admit. I think it showed a narcissistic streak if a person considered their own flippers too good for humble chainstore clobber. But maybe I was just being an inverted snob. (In light of what happened later.)

"You don't understand, Mum. Emma's *pregnant* but she won't talk to me about it and she says she doesn't know if she's going to keep the baby. Mum, you've got to see her and talk to her for me? Please, Mum? You've got to make her love me again. I want the baby, Mum, and I want Emma to marry me!"

And he blew his nose again, louder this time.

Well now.

What do you make of that, I thought to myself.

A moody, anorexic and beautiful young woman who's pregnant with my obsessive son's baby. What's a girl to do? I could feel my brain cells dragging out the shutters and nailing them up. Too much to deal with, too early in the day. It was time to be Supermum. That's what we get paid the big bucks for! (I wish.)

"Where are you, Alexander? Are you at college? Go sit with some friends, yes? I'll be right there, my darling."

But he was at home in his bedroom, it transpired. Reading Emma's letter and considering an overdose. He was listening to Bill's copy of Radiohead's first album. I could hear it in the background. Another few minutes of that and he'd be ready to leap off the attic windowsill onto the wrought-iron railings below. Teenage boys are like that, you know. On a hair-trigger, emotionally. They're not faking it to get out of washing the car. They really don't understand that teen angst is a passing phase and if they can just hang on in there till they're twenty-one or twenty-two, they'll become somewhat desensitised to pain and suffering like the rest of us oldies. Enough to keep going when it all seems rather bleak and pointless, at any rate.

"Alexander," I said. "Listen to me, son. Switch off that music at once. *At once*, do you hear me? And go downstairs and set the kitchen table for lunch, for you and me. Yes, just do as I say. I'll bring home fish and chips and we'll talk about this properly. It's not the end of the world. No, it is *not* the end of the world. Emma's frightened but she'll come round. You've got to be strong, Alexander. She's going to need a lot of support, whatever happens. Now, can you manage without me for half an hour until I get there? Or will I call your dad? Only he's on an important job today."

And he was, too. Fitting a rain-shower for a celebrity client. Tina Campbell, lovely girl who reads the news here. Nice choppy blond crop, arty jewellery, pink jacket, genuine smile. You'd like her.

I was going to ask Alexander to take in the washing for me as there was loads of it and it might have occupied his attention for a while but then I stopped myself. I didn't want to go placing him in close proximity to a few metres of strong, plastic cord. That *bloody* Emma, I thought to myself and I almost laughed with hysteria. I'd always thought she was too skinny to conceive.

Alexander said he'd try to hold himself together for thirty minutes though he couldn't make any promises. I hung up and called a taxi straight away. I think I screamed at them to come "immediately if not sooner" but I can't be sure. They know me well enough by now anyway – they would have understood it was just another domestic emergency in the Grimsdale household. Weeping uncontrollably, I peeled back my ears for the taxi's beep. Hating myself every second for not being able to drive. For goodness' sake, children of seventeen can drive but anyway there was nothing for it but to clatter down the stairs with my legs feeling like melting jelly and lock up the lighthouse. It was only as the taxi was speeding off down the road that I remembered Gary was coming out to see me. But Gary had been demoted several steps down the ladder of domestic emergencies and it was all I could do to keep calm in the back seat of one of First Class's finest motors. I'll calm Alexander down first, I decided. The children are my top priority, always have been. Then we'd contact Emma and assure her we'd do anything she wanted. We'd mind the baby for her somehow while she went to classes at university, we'd do the babysitting in the evenings. Anything she needed, whatsoever. Even if she didn't want to be with Alexander any more. We'd still do our bit in practical terms as well as financially. Alexander would have to get a part-time job and start paying his share towards the baby's upkeep. And if Emma didn't want to keep my first grandchild, well, I just hoped things wouldn't come to that. If that happened, I'd rather not have been told about the baby in the first place, thank you very much.

And then, when we'd made some headway in that little situation, I'd have to call my sisters (both living in

Sydney, Australia, did I say?) and tell them about Dad passing away. They hadn't seen him in ten years and I fretted that it would be too much for them to take in. Organising a funeral, grieving for the poor man and all the years he'd wasted listening to political talk shows on the radio. Not to mention, the expense of it all. I knew Dad wouldn't have subscribed to one of those nice and sensible 'Over-50' plans you see on the television, either.

"How depressing is that?" he used to say. "Saving up for your own friggin' funeral? Screwed for money, all your life. Right to the bitter end they're trying to wring it out of you. Well, they can stuff their Over-50 plan, so they can, the greedy bastards. They won't be getting ten quid a month out of me! They can chuck my carcass on the Halloween bonfire for all I care. Or feed me to the rats. Capitalist *fuckers*!"

Oh, yes.

You can't buy memories like that.

And I have no idea who to invite, I thought miserably. He has loads of relatives. *Had* loads of relatives. But none of them liked him very much. And he didn't like them. There didn't seem to be many frequent visitors to his home, at any rate. Like I say, he could be difficult. Maybe an informal stand-up buffet would be easier on all of us, I remember thinking as I bolted into the chippy a few doors down from our house, on the main road. I almost forgot to pay the taxi-driver, I was in such a state. Or would a buffet seem like we were scrimping?

"Two cod suppers, please."

"Nine quid. Cheers, love. Salt and vinegar?"

"Yes, please."

Nine quid for two cod suppers? Bloody 'ell, I thought, feeling ever-so-slightly robbed. The price had gone up by fifty pence since last time. What is the world coming to? Then it was a breathless dash up to our front door and thank goodness Alexander was still alive, his handsome face all swollen up with frightened tears. I hugged him to me for what seemed like an age but was probably twenty seconds. Together, we made our way to the kitchen, me softly rubbing his back the way I did when he was a baby and couldn't get a burp up. He was still sobbing too much to speak so I babbled on about the price of everything and we set the table together. Gary rang me as I was in the middle of unwrapping the cod suppers and telling Alexander that everything would be all right. Alexander loves fish and chips, you see. That's his favourite treat and I was trying to keep things as normal as possible for him while Emma made up her mind about their future. All three of them. Hers, Alexander's and the bambino's.

"Mags? What's happened to you?" Gary said crossly. "I'm standing here at the lighthouse and there's nobody in. I brought coffee and cakes. And you've got people waiting! They're awfully cross with you. Come all the way from Dublin, so they say."

"Oh God, that must be my three o'clock appointment, come early," I said, closing my eyes.

I'd forgotten all about them.

The couple from Dublin, not my eyes.

"The motorway's much improved," I added feebly. "Em, can I take a rain-check on the lunch, Gary? Sorry.

96

My father has *died* and my son needs to talk to me about something extremely important."

"Oh, I am sorry," he said at once, "to hear about your father."

"Thank you. Listen, I'll call you tonight if I have time, to talk about Julie. Okay? And by the way, could you please tell those people from Dublin I'll give them a buzz tomorrow evening and we'll arrange another appointment? Thanks, bye."

"Okay, Mags," he said. "How did he die?"

"Suddenly," I said. "His heart stopped."

Which was rather stating the obvious, I daresay. I mean, is there any other way of dying?

"I'm sorry for your trouble," Gary sighed.

What a gentleman.

Then I dropped my mobile on the stone floor and broke it.

"Shit!" I said, looking hopelessly at the pieces.

"Mum," said Alexander, somehow having managed to filter out the fact that his maternal grandfather had expired in rather tragic circumstances, "I love Emma so much, I don't think I can live without her. How long does it take if you swallow tablets? And do you go to sleep before it hurts?"

"What?"

My heart twanged in and out again, like a cartoon heart falling in love. Could my six-foot tall, *gorgeous*, first-born son really be this serious about that skinny little waif, I wondered? It seemed that he could. I was overwhelmed with fear.

"Don't even say something silly like that, my darling," I scolded him lightly, as if I thought he was only joking. "Of course you can live without her. She's always been very moody, I have to say. Moody little Emma and her designer shoes! Her feet pampered out of it and her poor wee tummy starved. Plenty more fish in the sea, love. That reminds me, have a small piece of this lovely cod before it gets cold. Where's the vinegar, darling? They didn't put enough on mine. Did you fetch it from the cupboard? I can't eat chips if they haven't got lashings of vinegar on them. No, you start eating. I'll get it. Oh, doesn't this smell lovely? Fancy a slice of bread and butter, love?"

Normality, you see?

Normality is everything in this life.

"But you got married when you were nineteen," Alexander said accusingly. "That's younger than I am now. And you said you knew my dad was the one for you, the minute you set eyes on him in the Limelight Club. Well, Emma is the one for me. I'm old enough to know when I'm in love."

I had to admit Alexander had a point.

"Yes, but that was years ago," I told him gently, struggling to find some way of lessening what heartbreak might be to come. "It was different then. The cost of living was lower. We didn't go to university, your dad and me. You're both so young, pet, far too young to settle down. You have years of study ahead of you, years of growing up still to do."

"If Emma doesn't want me, I can't go on living and

that's all there is to it," he said simply and we both sat there, arms round each other, watching the fish and chips turn cold on the plates. No point in telling Alexander he might have discussed the possibility of pregnancy with Emma before it was too late. I mean, Bill and I were no better but at least we knew for certain we loved each other. If Emma dropped Alexander and didn't carry their baby to full term, well, the poor boy would be mentally scarred for life. I just knew that. Alexander is incredibly sensitive for a boy.

Easy for me, huh?

Oh, Julie, if only you knew.

8

The Wake

WHAT WITH MY DAD'S FUNERAL TO SORT OUT, AND Alexander and Emma's baby-news to come to terms with, Julie's Galway escapade had to be moved to the back burner for a while. Gary called me several times that evening and in the end I simply told him Julie was having a holiday by herself and she didn't want any company. He was very upset but I assured him Julie was simply working through a few issues from her past and the best thing he could do was leave her alone.

"You know how she is," I reminded him. "She likes to handle things her own way."

He had no choice but to agree with me though I knew he was going to start looking for her right away. It wouldn't have surprised me if he'd hired a detective already. He's very determined, is Gary Devine.

"Where did you say she was again?" he tried, at the end of our conversation. Which was rather cunning of him but he was desperate, I suppose. And it was right on the tip of my tongue to tell him the name of the spa but I remembered just in time.

"I'm sorry, Gary. She didn't say."

Liar, liar.

I dialled Australia.

Oh God!

It's not easy telling your two beloved younger sisters the father you've all ignored for years has pegged out with his head on a supermarket loaf. I did my best to sweeten the pill. But still, they had to be told their father was alone when he left this life. Peaceful and quick, as it hopefully was. He was nonetheless alone in a shabby rented house, his last meal a humble can of chicken and mushroom soup. They were hysterical, needless to say. Their chirpy Australian accents disappeared in a heartbeat and their full-on Belfast snarls returned with a vengeance.

I had to cover the handset with my hand. It was nervous laughter, of course, but I felt bad about it. They said they'd be on the next flight and although I knew it would be hard for them, I was delighted. It was unsettling to think we hadn't been together for ten years. And flights have got so much cheaper recently but there was always something coming up and important things to be done, and too much on at work. And we never managed to arrange anything. But now, our father's premature passing was uniting us in our own hometown at last.

So Ann and Elizabeth were in the air somewhere as I identified Dad's body and liaised with the funeral director. Bill was on the phone for hours, informing the long list of relatives and acquaintances. I was hoping they'd all make their excuses and leave us in peace to grieve. But no, they all wanted to come to the wake. I watched Bill's face darken as he gave directions to Eglantine Avenue, over and over and over again. By the end, he was just saying, "Oh, you can't miss it!"

The house had taken on an eerie, still quality as if it was preparing itself for an important occasion. Alexander lay sobbing quietly in his room, still inconsolable over the temporary (or perhaps permanent) loss of Emma. But the other children were marvellous, tidying up at lightning speed. Which was a revelation for me, I can tell you, as it usually takes them several hours to put a pair of socks away. Bill was amazingly thoughtful. He did his best to get into the spirit of things even though I warned him it was going to get very weird. Well, Protestants are more formal about these things. I daresay it's the influence of the British Royals. Stiff upper lip, no matter what. And why not? Making a scene never did any good, did it? Bill's never been to a real belter of a wake, and I was worried for him and our precious children. But I knew in my heart there was nothing I could do to stop the momentum. So I went crazy with a duster and just let events unfold. Wakes are like that, anyway. They take on a life force of their own. (Pardon the pun.) Bill bought a huge bouquet of elegant white flowers for the hall and some pretty boxes of tissues to dot around the place. Then he did a rapid trolley-dash down the biscuit aisle in Marks & Spencer while I did an even quicker vacuum of the entire house. Bunging laundry into wardrobes and hiding my most expensive handbags in one of the hatboxes on top of our wardrobe. Well, you never know. Gatecrashers aren't bothered if it's a funeral or a 21st birthday party. Then the hearse was suddenly pulling up at our front door and that was a pantomime in itself.

My father's house was in no fit state for a wake, you see. Traditionally, in an Irish wake, the deceased person is laid out in an open coffin on their own bed in their own bedroom for two days and one night, and anyone who knew them (however briefly) comes to the house and pays their respects. And partakes of light refreshments (in truth, as much food and alcohol as they can stomach) and a 48-hour session of singing and storytelling. They mean well, naturally, the mourners. And all the Catholics I ever knew thought it was a great honour if the house was stuffed to bursting point, with hopefully a good number having to queue outside on the driveway as well. The more, the merrier. It's taken as a sign the family is popular in the community. But Dad's place hadn't been decorated since Mum left. He used to keep dogs and the furniture was scratched to bits. And he's a heavy smoker. *Was* a heavy smoker. And he was never very handy with a bottle of Mr Sheen even before the political stuff took over his soul. So it had to be my house on Eglantine.

But it only hit me then, as the ornately carved walnut-coloured coffin was being brought into the hall, what was actually happening. And I immediately decided I wasn't having my dead father displayed in any of the bedrooms. Oh no, I'm sorry, darling! I might adore the aesthetics of castles, cloaks and candlesticks but I'm not so keen on hauling the recently departed up and down my stairwell. I could never, you know, *undress* in a room if I knew it'd been used for a wake. I'm sorry, call me a twit if you like but I just couldn't. And obviously he couldn't be left in any of the children's rooms. That would have been cruel to them. And the boys' den is full of shelves of video games which wouldn't have looked respectful and anyway the atmosphere is all wrong in there, it's way too modern. And the guest room is right at the top of the house and far too small for a wake. The bed is tucked in underneath the eaves and the mourners would have knocked themselves out on the sloping ceiling.

So we put him in the good room at the front of the house that we only use at Christmas and on special occasions. The undertakers were pleased they didn't have so far to carry the coffin. The thing is, that room contained my collection of one hundred and forty-seven (outsized) Gothic candlesticks so it was all very 'Dracula's Castle' but there wasn't time to move stuff. I kept having this mental image of Christopher Lee appearing from behind the purple velvet curtains (complete with ruched swags and heavy gold fringing – the curtains, not Christopher Lee) and baring his fangs. And for the first time in my life I felt a bit silly being a post-Goth. But, I mean, what am I supposed to do? Keep one room of my home in a constant state of readiness for an 'open coffin and light refreshments' evening? Magnolia drapes and two dozen hard chairs? Tea urn and a choir in the corner?

There were about twenty actual candles in the

collection (thankfully ivory-coloured, not black) so I lit them all with a box of matches and hoped it would generally appear very 'churchy' and spiritual. The lid of the coffin was then removed and propped up against the wall. Whereupon, I collapsed and Bill carried me through to the kitchen for a brandy. The callers began to arrive before I'd even got my coat off (I'd been running some last-minute errands just prior to the hearse arriving). And that started me crying again because it reminded me of Dad and the hunger-strikers, and how he would start ranting the minute he answered the door to me.

I spoke in hushed tones to a lot of people I'd never met before and they told me they were sorry for my trouble, and then headed for the stairs. So we had to get Bill to act as usher. He deflected them politely but firmly into the good room and after an initial look of consternation they shuffled innocently into the candlestick forest. Many of the mourners were absolutely speechless when they emerged from my front room. They opened their mouths and tried to form some words of comfort but usually nothing came out and we just gave them a glass of whiskey and said: "Thanks for coming. It was all very sudden."

Well, they wanted death and I gave it to them with knobs on. Maybe we should have thrown a sheet over the biggest candlesticks (as Bill suggested) but I felt a dustsheet would have looked much worse than several rows of five-foot ornaments. And I daresay the massive stone gargoyle beside the fireplace was a bit intimidating for some but we couldn't lift it without doing our backs in. It was hard enough getting 'Goily' into the house in the first place, after Bill spotted him under a pile of doorframes in a reclamation yard and bought him for me for our tenth wedding anniversary.

At least Dad was actually having a wake, I consoled myself as I made a small mountain of turkey and ham sandwiches in the dining room, the designated buffet area. A death in the family is no time to impose your vegetarian beliefs on the viewers. I mean, the mourners. Yes, at least he was having a wake. No thanks to you, Mum, you crafty old skiver with your official divorce papers and your busy guesthouse in Devon. Oh yes, having a sensitive English lover with a relative in the UDR comes in very handy, doesn't it? Gets you out of all sorts of awkward family do's. And Dad's lot, they couldn't fault me; they never offered to host it. Nosy parkers, they came to my house all right but they didn't want him cluttering up *their* bedrooms. Some cheerful women in flowery blouses I'd never seen before in my life (the women not the blouses) took up position in my kitchen and proceeded to empty the cupboards of all cups, mugs and plates. They washed everything in the sink, ignoring the dishwasher completely and then served tea and coffee to the masses for twelve hours straight before telling me they'd had a lovely time. Who washes dishes *before* they are used? I've still got no idea who they were but they left my kitchen spotless. They even cleaned the crumbs out of the plastic seal round the fridge door. I'd been meaning to do that properly for several years. There was a queue for the main bathroom so we had to direct total strangers through to the en suites. I forgot to hide my best bras which were hanging out to dry on our shower door. (They have to be hand-washed, you see, good bras.) One of them went missing. The red balcony-bra with the black ribbons threaded through it. Bill loved that bra on me. It was a real nipple-skimmer.

Why do we put ourselves through these things? In this age of hi-tech everything, is it fair that we still have to observe such a centuries-old tradition? Children shouldn't have to see dead bodies, they really shouldn't, I don't care what anyone says. You can stuff your justifications in a sack, mister. Traditions? It used to be traditional to hang petty thieves in the town square. We don't do that any more.

Alicia-Rose was very upset when she saw my father's face. He was still looking pissed off, even in death.

Eleven tins of luxury chocolate biscuits we got through. Seventeen loaves of best white bread and two dozen jam-sponges. So many people, the doorbell never stopped ringing. In the end, we left the front door open. My dad's priest showed up around midnight. (The funeral director had tracked him down for us.) And that was hard work because he kept asking me what chapel we went to, and various queries about parish minutiae. Had I attended the *blessing* of this and the *veneration* of that, and whether I was a member of the *Legion of Mary*. God help him. I couldn't for the life of me remember what he was talking about. If you don't use it, you lose it, I suppose. I resorted to stuffing my face with shortcake biscuits and then pretending I'd remembered something vital, before dashing out of the room so I wouldn't have to answer him.

I think word got out in Dad's neighbourhood there was a great wake going down in Eglantine Avenue because we had hundreds of callers. I had to send Alicia-Rose to the shop for more toilet tissue (or as I call it, bog-roll) and liquid soap, twice. And somebody sat on the hall table (it was the only genuine antique we had) and broke it. But the wake was a great success and that was the main thing. At one point I fell asleep sitting in the laundry-room, folding a tea towel (hiding from the priest again) and only woke up when a draught slammed the back door shut.

I felt cold and tearful all the next day and when Ann and Elizabeth finally turned up the following evening I nearly collapsed with emotion.

And shock.

They'd changed so much, I nearly didn't recognise them. Yes, they'd sent photos over the years, but the pictures generally only showed their faces. In the flesh, it was a whole different story. When the pair of them had left Belfast, they looked just like me. Tall and awkward, pale as sheets, and very scruffy indeed. Cardigans and leather brogues, the legacy of a convent education.

But Ann, who was the first to appear on my doorstep, had gone all tanned and toned and glamorous in the intervening decade. She was sporting a short spiky crop of pink hair. Yes, pink! And wearing a fitted (very fitted) two-piece dress-suit with killer heels, and carrying a massive pink handbag with chunky gold chain-handles. She had a tiny little pink hat with feathers on it and her blusher could be seen from space. She was like the millionaire princess of Punk. I mean, she *is* an aerobics instructor at a very posh country club and no doubt has a glamorous image to uphold. But obviously she'd forgotten we still wear black to funerals in Belfast. Bill nudged me in the back because he knew I'd be struggling to say something kind about Ann's hat. And I knew that whatever I did say would be hopelessly inadequate so I just reached for Ann and hugged her until she couldn't breathe.

"Steady on, love," she laughed, her Australian accent having returned.

"Where's Elizabeth?" I said eventually.

"She's just paying the cab fare," Ann announced to the general company, swinging her handbag into Bill's chest. "Put that somewhere safe, love," she told him, winking crookedly. I supposed she'd had a few gins on the flight. Or maybe it was jet lag.

Elizabeth then lumbered into view. And I do mean, lumbered. She'd put on about ten stone since I'd last seen her! My God, she was big! Her face was still the same, though. The same colour of eyes as me (hazel) and the same pointy chin. But she really had been enjoying her food. She's a hotel manager, by the way. Elizabeth was dressed in a dark blue velvet jacket and wide blue slacks with yellow flowers on them. A yellow necklace with beads as big as eggs. And her long black hair was wound into a tiny bun at the nape of her neck. She was well made-up, though. And her fingernails were long and red and quite exquisite. Elizabeth was never very particular about her nails and make-up when she was living in Belfast.

"Oh, Elizabeth," I cried, doing my best to hug her. "I'm so glad you were able to make it. How've you been?"

"Well, I can tell you one thing, Mags, I've not been on a diet!"

Another discreet nudge from Bill.

"It's just so brilliant to see you both again," I wept.

And it was. I ushered them up to our bedroom so they could change their clothes and have a sit-down in peace, without half of the population of the city staring at them. Elizabeth could hardly get up the stairs, she was that puffed.

"Now you know why I didn't make it home sooner," she gasped, as I showed them into my ivory boudoir. "I wanted to lose weight first. This is nice, Mags love. I like your bed."

"You don't know what this means to me, thanks so much for coming," I said, kissing her bronzed cheek tenderly. "You're here now and we'll have a good long chat about life and everything when the funeral is over. Now do you want to see Daddy first thing? Or do you want to have something to eat first?"

"We had a bite of lunch on the plane," Ann sighed, "but I could murder a proper cup of tea, love. Really stewed, the way we used to make it in the old days."

"Okay then. You two get your breath back and I'll fetch a tray up. And you can come downstairs and wow the rest of them when you're ready. There's hundreds of people milling about down there and I think the novelty of my front room is beginning to wear off. I need a new attraction. So be prepared to chat until your jaw drops off!" They didn't let me down.

At dawn on the day of the funeral, the last cup of tea

had been drunk. The last biscuit had been swallowed. All the booze was gone, even the out-of-date liqueurs at the back of the dining-room cabinet. Any number of songs had been sung, including Dad's all-time C&W favourite, 'Are You Teasin' Me?' By the Louvin brothers, somebody said.

I'd been asked about ten thousand times how my mother was coping. The implication being, she didn't give a flying fig about her poor lonely dead husband.

"Oh, she's in despair," I said. "She's too upset to travel, actually."

Even though I knew she was merrily grilling organic pork sausages, and hand-stitching lavender sachets to hang on every handle and shelf of the guest-house.

Then the mourners gathered on the ground floor after they'd had a final peek round the rest of the house en route to the bathrooms and the priest began to say the Rosary. I saw my poor heathen children creeping down the hall towards the kitchen in case anyone noticed they didn't know the words to the prayers. It was only then it dawned on me how hard it must be for the first generation of secular children in a long line of devoutly religious ancestors. How strange it is for them when everybody else is blessing themselves and muttering ancient prayers and they're just standing there, clueless. I wanted to cry but I couldn't. Because I was the one who was supposed to be in charge.

The good room was then officially emptied of all persons except for Bill and myself. I didn't know what to do so I simply touched Dad's hands gently and said a brief goodbye to him. I didn't kiss his cheek – we were never a kissing sort of family. I did tell him I loved him, for the very first time in my life (though sadly, not his). Bill and I then left the room together, holding hands and feeling completely weirded-out. The undertakers screwed the lid down tight over my father's still-frowning face and it was over. Sixty-eight years of seething resentment and missed opportunities. And the woman who should have been there beside him was busy handing out plates of cooked breakfast to her guests in the B&B in Devon.

What a gold-medal skiver!

Pity they don't have it in the Olympics.

We Irish, we'd clean up in the 'Bizarre Funeral Rituals' and the 'Avoiding Painful Emotional Issues' categories.

So, there was me, Bill, our children, my sisters and several hundred strangers in the chapel that morning. And the priest finally understood I was an odd sort of Catholic when I refused point-blank to go up on the altar and read from the Bible. Not for any political reason in particular, mind you: I just couldn't face addressing an audience. And Bill and the kids wouldn't have known where to stand or how to walk off again so they couldn't do it. I mean, what are you supposed to do when your father croaks it, but reading in church has a laxative effect? So yes, I did actually decline to read at my own father's funeral Mass. Well, the crowd had never seen anything like it. You could hear the gasps of horror a mile away. Somebody actually said, "Sweet Jesus Christ, is the daughter not going to do the readin'?" out loud.

113

At the burial, I still couldn't cry. I was so angry with my father for ignoring me for forty years. And for letting my mother walk away from him without a backward glance. The two of them had cheated us out of a lifetime of happy family memories. Even though it wasn't their *fault* they were incompatible, I suppose? Ann and Elizabeth were too shell-shocked by the sea of mournful grey faces huddled together in long black coats, to cry either. Majestically turned out (Ann in a bright red trouser suit and matching pillbox hat, and Elizabeth in a sweeping purple cape and jaunty beret), they were the only spot of colour on the day.

I invited all the well-wishers to the post-burial dinner afterwards because I was too much of a coward not to. Mentally I was hoarding our savings for Emma's baby, but they'd given us good value as mourners and they deserved to be fed and watered. But I think they could tell it was a duty rather than a pleasure for Bill and myself when Bill did a rough head-count at the cemetery gates and called the hotel to let them know, all the while totting up costs on his pocket calculator. Needless to say, we were about as popular as dysentery in the hotel afterwards. (Sorry about all this lavatorial imagery, by the way.) They shook hands with us again but there was an unspoken accusation in the air. Middle-class know-it-alls, they seemed to say. I wore the biggest pair of dark glasses I could find and us Grimsdales skulked off into the residents' private bar as soon as the meal was over. Well, we weren't exactly residents but after stumping up for such a huge function, how could they refuse us? A glass or two of brandy beside that roaring (gas) fire in the dimly lit bar, and the chill began to leave my aching bones.

Poor Dad.

Poor me.

Dad's landlord wasn't so shy, however. When we phoned him the following day, he said could we please have the house cleared by the end of the week? As he wanted to redecorate and get some new tenants in. Also, we had to cancel Dad's pension, and the milk, and get the amenities disconnected. Mass cards were ordered and his heart medication was returned to the chemist for safe disposal.

There's a lot to do when someone dies.

We brought the leaning stacks of yellowing newspapers to the recycling depot. All of the furniture was knackered so I arranged for the council to take it to the dump. The rest of his stuff fitted into two black bags which we stored in our garden shed for the time being. Because Alicia-Rose is afraid of ghosts and she wouldn't let the black bags anywhere near our attic. And suddenly that was it. A life over and gone.

Oh yes, Emma turned up at the hotel later that evening and was reunited with Alexander. They were kissing tenderly in the lobby as the mourners were leaving and I thought to myself, there's a new life beginning as another one ends. It was the only hopeful moment in the day until we discovered two things. Firstly, Emma's own parents had thrown her out of the house and said they wouldn't be suckered into babysitting yet another illegitimate grandchild. They already had more than enough on their plates what with Emma's two sisters' offspring, and so on. And secondly, Emma said she *would* like to keep the baby but could we please pay for a planned Caesarean section as she was completely phobic about childbirth? And that was why she'd left Alexander in the first place.

Bill and I exchanged glances.

"Certainly, Emma," said Bill. "We'd be happy to."

What else could we do?

I said *of course* we would pay for Emma to have private healthcare and, in a burst of love and devotion, I added that Alexander and Emma could stay in our drawing room (perhaps converted into a cute little bed-sit) until they were qualified and on their feet financially. Which basically meant they could live with us for the next ten years or so. Rent free. Bill was so upset he had to have a double brandy in the hotel lobby. He didn't mind about the baby. He was delighted about the baby. But he was bitterly disappointed that Alexander was being so wet about the whole thing. We talked about it as we walked home from the hotel bar later that evening.

"Why didn't he kick down the front door of Emma's house the day she left him, push her father out of the way, call her mother a selfish bitch, get down on his knees and propose to the stupid girl?" he fumed. "Have I taught him nothing?"

Once a Punk, always a Punk.

And also, he was plastered drunk.

And then I had to remind my husband we were only sitting pretty in Eglantine Avenue ourselves because of the whip-round our relatives had organised for us, all those years ago.

"Still," Bill added lamely, "the boy could have thrown his bed through the window at least. Some well-intentioned, but ultimately futile, token-gesture of rebellion. How the hell did we raise such conservative children?"

With twenty-one years of bloody hard work, that's how.

9

The Coven

WE SAW ANN AND ELIZABETH OFF TO THE AIRPORT A
few days later, with many promises on both sides
to phone every week, without fail. And they said maybe
they'd come back again for Christmas if they could book
enough time off work. Neither one of them had settled
down yet with families of their own and I think they were
between romances too. So I supposed they simply fancied
a bit of company and companionship over the holiday
season. I told them they were more than welcome to stay at
our house. They were to visit whenever they liked and
stay for as long as they liked. Bill would have preferred it
to be just our own immediate family for Christmas but he
said nothing. I would have told him I loved him even
more that day, for being so understanding, but really that
wouldn't be possible! On the way home from the airport,
Bill and I nipped into town for lunch in Delaney's coffee
shop. It was the first time we'd been alone together for

weeks and we just sat quietly holding hands in a cosy little booth near the window. Revelling in having nothing to do for the rest of the day.

As we were leaving Delaney's, it began to pour. We scurried across the street to the shelter of the car, and bumped into none other than Gary Devine. Bill and Gary exchanged pleasant greetings and so on but I felt a bit frozen out. Gary was clearly not my biggest fan, that day. The conversation was very strained. I remembered he'd sent a gorgeous wreath of yellow roses and trailing ivy to the cemetery on the day of the funeral and I thanked him for it. I said he was very kind and thoughtful and he just nodded back, the hurt in his eyes plain as anything. Obviously, Gary knew I was holding out on him and he resented me for knowing where Julie was. But although I wanted to tell him about the spa I couldn't risk it in case he landed down there, saw Jay and Julie together (covered in bits of straw, no doubt) and went postal. There'd already been one funeral and I didn't want to have to go to another couple. I decided it was time to get The Coven on board.

I foolishly thought, they know Julie better than anyone. They'll know what to do. Julie's best friends and partners in crime, The Lisburn Road Coven. And by the way, they gave that grand title to themselves. Amanda and Rebecca are prosecution lawyers, Josephine owns a very expensive lingerie boutique (few of the bra and briefs sets cost less than £75) and Veronica and April run big, popular wine bars in the trendy Stranmillas district. They're a fearsome bunch at the best of times but absolutely terrifying when they're tanked up. They take no prisoners and they mean what they say. So I thought, if anyone can sort out this mess, it's The Coven. They won't tiptoe round Julie. They'll tell her she's being silly and fetch her home.

That was the plan anyway.

So, on the way back from Delaney's, I nipped into Josephine's staggeringly up-market boutique for a moment (all tiny gilt chairs and a real wool carpet), filled her in on the situation and gave her the gold-edged business card. Bill was waiting for me on the road outside and he thought I was just picking up some samples for Dream Weddings. Anyway, he'd never be caught dead in a lingerie shop so I knew I'd be able to have a private chat with Josephine. I told her about Jay O'Hanlon the Sean Bean look-alike and said I was worried something untoward might be about to happen in Galway. Julie was quite taken with this man, I said, or so it seemed to me. Well, I had to tell Josephine about Jay O'Hanlon. But I did warn her to keep it under her hat because it was paramount that Gary Devine didn't find out about him.

"I think she's having a bit of a crisis, Josephine," I ventured bravely. "I'd like to go down there and talk some sense into her but I've far too much going on in my own life at the moment."

Josephine looked incredibly sceptical. She thinks I'm the most boring person alive but then Josephine thinks nothing of having one-night stands with younger men. She claims it's only a spot of glorified market research into the pulling power of zebra-print thongs. Josephine's married to a wealthy estate agent but I know for a fact their handsome son was fathered by a male model from Berlin. They called him Franz because he was conceived in Germany. Obviously, Josephine's hubby doesn't know she was doing vertical gymnastics in the lift with a gorgeous stud half her age. She was on a biz-trip with her husband and there was a fashion-show going on in the hotel foyer. So Josephine nipped into one of the lifts with this male model and one gorgeous son turns up nine months later. Like I said, Josephine's quite a character. I should have known better than to go anywhere near her, that's the bottom line.

"Leave it with me, Mags," Josephine said, eyeing my genuine (if threadbare) 1920's vintage coat with some amusement. "I'll get on the blower to the girls right away."

And I went home feeling purged and at peace and collapsed into bed with Bill. I don't know what I'd do without that man – he's the only thing that keeps me sane sometimes. He kissed my neck and shoulders tenderly (classic Goth fetish, the neck and shoulders area) until I felt relaxed and then he just lay beside me, holding my hand. As I fell asleep I decided that if there was any money left after the birth of Alexander and Emma's baby (and maybe a spot of therapy for Emma to get her food issues under control) I'd pick out a nice Celtic headstone for Dad and I'd let my sisters decide what to have engraved on it. Even if it was something sentimental (in Irish), knowing them. I was feeling very generous that night. I didn't dwell on what Bill would say when I told him a big whack of our savings had been spent on the funeral. He thought the whole thing had cost two thousand pounds when really it had cost four. And that I was going to spend another five thousand on a massive lump of Irish granite. I mean, he's never raised his voice to me in twenty odd years but still . . . Once a Punk, always a Punk.

But telling Josephine about Julie's carry-on at the spa was the worst, worst, absolute worst thing I could have done. Don't read the next bit if you're easily offended. Honestly, just skip to the next chapter if you don't want to read about the saucy goings-on in a Galway hayloft. I could leave out the details but you might as well have it all, now you've got this far.

Oh, boy.

You see, Josephine knew lots of things about Julie that I didn't know. Up until that point, anyway. I mean, Julie told me all the emotional stuff about her parents fighting on the patio occasionally with two broom handles, and about Gary smothering her with his wedding ambitions and so on. But the spicy, sexual stuff she told to The Coven. The lovers she'd had, what they'd done in bed together, size of various manly appendages and expertise in lovemaking, et cetera. And that her top sexual fantasy of all time was that she'd bump into a Sean Bean look-alike (or even better, the real thing) and that he'd ravish her *in a hayloft*. Blimey Charlie, as Peter Kay is fond of saying. Blimey Charlie and bloody 'ell. The pieces of Julie's undoing were coming together like vultures circling in the desert.

So what did Josephine do? Did she gather The Coven together? Yes, she did. She phoned them all while I was resting in my lovely Victorian-style bed, still tired almost a week after the funeral. Did they collectively book into the spa full of shocking-pink armchairs without further ado and set off that very night in a brand-new people-carrier belonging to Josephine's sister? Yes. Oh yes, they did. Did they talk some sense into Julie and get her to come home to Gary and stop her toy-boy nonsense? No, they did not! They decided to give old Julie a treat so they looked up a picture of Sean Bean (as Sharpe) on the internet and printed it out. They picked up a similar period military costume complete with sword, on the way to Galway (from a second-hand army surplus store in East Belfast) and they went down there and they gave it to Jay. And they also gave him some interesting suggestions as to what he should do with it.

It was easy enough to find Jay as he was the head barman at the spa. He was an open-minded sort of chap and well up for a bit of fantasy and fun, no problem to him. He wasn't at all offended that Julie's mates wanted him to dress up in a moth-eaten bit of navy-blue felt and pretend to be another man. Actually, he told them he'd been mistaken for Sean Bean lots of times already so it was no big leap of the imagination for him to get into character. And he could ride a horse. Excellent. So, off Jay went with the jacket and the sword in a glossy carrier bag, and the girls checked into their rooms for a few days of relaxation and pampering.

Lucky for some.

And so, next morning, The Coven were slipping into the heated pool with trayloads of exotic cocktails being ferried to them, and Jay was slipping into the military jacket in order to surprise Julie before she even knew that her friends were in the building. Jay sent Julie a text asking her to dress like a gypsy-girl and meet him by the hayloft as soon as possible and then he saddled up one of his father's horses (they owned the biggest retired donkey and horse sanctuary in the country) and galloped off to give Julie the surprise of her life.

You can imagine the rest, can't you?

She called me that night and told me all the gory details but I'd say what happened next was inevitable. There was Julie in her white linen ruffle skirt and peasant top, huge hoop earrings and dainty leather sandals. Waiting by the hayloft in the sweltering July sunshine when she heard a horse's hooves come clattering down the cobbled lane. She thought her eyes were deceiving her when she saw Jay in the military jacket with the gold buttons, his tousled blond hair hanging in his eyes and a long narrow sword bouncing beside his thigh. She told me afterwards that she had a mini-blackout there and then. Her legs simply folded beneath her and she half-fell against the rough walls of the barn. And that was only the first of several moments of ecstasy that afternoon as Jay slid to the ground, gathered Julie up in his arms and carried her inside to the barn's dusty shadows. He kicked some loose straw and farm tools out of his way and Julie whimpered with delight. He laid her gently down onto a bale and stood looking intensely at her as he hastily unbuckled his jacket and pulled off his sword. Julie said she could almost hear the sounds of a battle going on in the background, gunpowder explosions and the clang of metal on metal. But that was clearly just her blood pressure hitting the jackpot. Then Jay eased her peasant top (and balcony bra) down off her shoulders and kissed her hard on the mouth.

Fools rush in where angels fear to tread.

"You know you want me, so stop pretending you don't," Jay said gruffly and poor Julie thought she was in heaven.

She forgot all about Gary Devine and how kind and gentle he always was. She forgot about her reputation and her dignity and who she would spend her retirement years with. Julie and Jay almost rocked that humble hayloft to its very foundations. She told me she couldn't remember her own name for a while and if she hadn't had some ID in her handbag she might be wandering the roads of Galway still. No foreplay, she didn't need any. Ten seconds after that first kiss, they were lovers. They did it on the hay-bales, on the floor, with him on top, with her on top. With their clothes on, then half-off, then completely naked. Standing up against the door, in the water trough and finally with her hands tied to the wheel of a wooden handcart. Oh yes, our Jay was into a bit of harmless bondage, and Julie was a willing convert. He slapped her smartly on the bum at one point. Not too hard but hard enough to leave a red mark. And he told her she was too uptight and snobbish and she needed the attentions of a real man to tame her. And he left teethmarks on her ankle. Which I thought was a bit of a liberty. Call me old-fashioned but I definitely wouldn't fancy a smack on the rear and a good telling-off during the inaugural lovemaking session. And of course, Julie was dicing with danger. Dicing with death, really, allowing a man she didn't know from Adam to tie her up like that. But she was thrilled. Incoherent with delight, she was. Jay snagged his collarbone on a rusty nail when he was releasing her from the cartwheel afterwards and a trickle of blood ran down his bare chest. It all added to the general air of hedonistic abandonment. Julie said she thought her heart was going to stop with sheer pleasure.

"I actually screamed out loud at one point," she told me. "I've never screamed in twenty-three years of sexual adventure and experimentation. It was when he was throwing me into the trough, Mags. It was such a hot day but that water was stone-cold. And his legs!" she whispered into her mobile, from the comfort of a bubble-bath later that evening. "Mags, you should have seen his legs! When he tore off his jeans the buttons broke, by the way. The muscles on his thighs were incredible! All covered with soft blond hairs. *Massive* doo-da, needless to say! Perfect shape! And his kisses! So rough yet so good! I honestly thought I was going to die."

No mention of that particular service on the spa itinerary, I'll wager. *Heart-stopping sex provided in all the rooms by our gorgeous gigolo. Reasonable surcharge for the use of a nearby hayloft.*

Jay was incredibly strong and Julie wasn't in her right mind. A perfect combination. She had the best sex of her life that afternoon, so she told me. Afterwards he held her in his arms and they both wept a little and then Jay told Julie he loved her and he would always love her, no matter what. Of course, she had to tell him she loved him too though she didn't mean it. She was only being polite, Your Honour. And by the time she discovered who had set her up, it was far too late to worry about Gary Devine. That particular ship had well and truly sailed.

The Coven was helpless with laughter in the mezzanine bar that afternoon when they saw Julie limping into the foyer with a piece of straw sticking out of her platinum-white bob, her peasant top ripped to shreds and one of her sandals missing. Amanda laughed so hard one of her contact lenses went round the back of her eye. Josephine accidentally swallowed a whole wedge of lemon in one go and almost choked to death but Amanda gave her a mighty thump on the back and it popped right out again. They were all very impressed with Jay when they met him, it has to be said. Very impressed indeed. And let me tell you, those girls are hard to please. They said Julie could pass him on to the rest of them when she was finished with him. That's if there was any mileage left in the poor lad. What a laugh! And Julie's place as Grand High Witch of the Lisburn Road Coven was set in stone forever.

10

Blue Days

THERE'S A PRICE TO BE PAID FOR WANTING TOO MUCH. There's a price to be paid for thinking you can handle life's various tribulations by yourself. And I paid it a few days later when I finally told Bill I was going to book plane tickets for my sisters so they could come home again at Christmas and we could visit our father's grave together. Without the stress of several hundred mourners looking on. I'd promised Ann and Elizabeth (or as Bill calls them, A&E) I would make the arrangements for their visit and also a short layover so they could see Mum in Devon. And that I was also forking out for a massive granite Celtic cross for my father, to make up for not really bothering with the poor unfortunate man when he was alive. Bill looked at me like I'd gone soft in the head.

"Your sisters have both got good jobs," he pointed out straightaway. "Why can't they pay for their own plane tickets?"

"Because I'm the eldest."

"That's not a proper reason, Mags. It's bad enough I'll not have you all to myself this Christmas without having to pay for two plane tickets. And why the big headstone for your dad? You know it was his obsession with politics that made him such a distant father, always. Wouldn't something smaller be more in keeping with the other graves? Some bigoted nutcase will only smash it to bits anyway if it's going to be that noticeable. You know how cemeteries get vandalised in this city."

"I can't say where the idea came from, my love. Guilt, I suppose? I've told Ann and Elizabeth about it now in any case and they're very taken with the notion."

"Are they going to help pay for it, then?"

"I doubt it. At least, they didn't offer."

The debate staggered on for some time in this fashion. Me telling Bill all my big plans and him pointing out the even bigger, nay massive, flaws in them. I told him I'd booked some expensive private healthcare for Emma and also requested an elective C-section for her because of her childbirth phobia, which would be sorted out when she'd discussed various options with her new doctor. He didn't appear to be very sympathetic, I must say. Bill, that is, not the doctor. The doctor was all public-school charm and heavy gold bracelets. *He* sounded like he went to bed each night and slept under a duvet stuffed with £100 notes.

"But that was the only way I could convince Emma to keep the baby," I added, barely pausing for breath. Well, Bill knew that much already but he was rather shocked that the wheels were already in motion. And that Emma was registered with such an expensive doctor. When I explained that this consultant was the only one Emma could find to see her at short notice, Bill looked unconvinced.

"I'll bet," was all he said. Meaning moody little Emma likes the best of everything. Doctors, as well as shoes.

Like I said, I can read Bill's thoughts.

"Yes, indeed she does like the best of everything," I told him. "Which is why she's going out with our son."

Checkmate!

Consequently, the drawing room was soon to be converted into a bed-sit for Emma and Alexander with a small bathroom in one corner and a dinky kitchenette in the other. Bill knew I'd offered to have them stay in the house with us, of course, but he'd been thinking that Alexander and Emma would prefer to find a place of their own and get married. He'd not actually gone along with the idea that any son of his would agree to move into the family drawing room and live off his parents.

"I don't think they'll need their own bathroom, though," said Bill, looking at the walls doubtfully. "We have four bathrooms already. The water pressure will be adversely affected. Can't she just sleep with Alexander in his room? He's got a double bed."

"Oh Bill, Alexander's room is tiny, it's far too small for a cot and the baby stuff. That's why I'm doing this because otherwise there'll be toys and equipment all over the house. The drawing room is thirty feet long."

SHARON OWENS

"Well, the baby can have the guest-room, then. It's next door to Alexander's."

"But I've already asked a builder to make plans."

"What builder? Tell me his name and I'll cancel the plans, don't you worry about that."

"Oh, Bill!"

"No, honestly, we don't want them to get too cosy, Mags."

"Yes, we do."

"No, we don't."

And finally, I told him that Julie was having 'an episode of some kind' in County Galway and was currently enjoying lively sex in a rural setting with a handsome young barman called Jay O'Hanlon, while I was lying through my teeth about her actions to Gary Devine. But the good side of *that* particular situation was, it was costing us nothing whatsoever. Just some extra responsibilities for me at Dream Weddings until Julie returned, of course. And it looked like she would be down in Galway for a few days yet. She was having the time of her life there.

"Sex for breakfast, sex for lunch and sex for dinner," I said, trying to make the whole thing sound hilarious. Hoping the Punk in him would be impressed with Julie's utter abandonment of the normal rules and conventions of society. Then I sat rubbing a blob of vanilla hand cream into my dry knuckles while my gorgeous husband pondered the tangled web I'd spun for myself.

"Julie's off her rocker, isn't she?" I prompted him. "I never knew she had it in her. Mind you, neither did Gary!

I hope neither one of us has a crazy affair one day, Bill. I don't think I could cope with any more excitement."

But Bill wasn't amused at all. He was absolutely bewildered. I've never seen him so flustered. Normally, he's cool as a cucumber. In fact, I was always teasing him and comparing him with Mr Spock from *Star Trek*. (I don't tease Bill quite so much these days. I think he's been through enough.) He paced up and down the bedroom with his head in his hands like Robert de Niro in that disturbing movie with Jodie Foster.

"We'll still have some money left," I told him in desperation. "And God knows Julie owes me one heck of a bonus."

"Don't talk daft, Mags. It's not the money, pet," he kept saying. "It's not the money!"

"Really, Bill? You don't mind?"

"Not about the funeral, no. I might have known you'd be left to pick up the tab when your father died. He never did have any sense with money. It's the *secrecy* I can't understand. Why didn't you tell me about Julie going off like that? The real reason Julie left you on your own to deal with Janine Smith's wedding? Why did you lie to Gary about Julie's whereabouts? If you'd told him she was in Galway the same day she set off, he might have caught up with her and sorted all this before it got out of hand. I mean, *why?* You've made it so much worse. Why did you bottle all this up, Mags? Why didn't you tell me? We're supposed to be best friends. Or have you forgotten?"

All the while I could feel hot tears springing up and

my nose was on fire with shame. I knew I was going to sneeze all night with sheer embarrassment – it's a funny tic I have.

"Because you're always there for me," I sobbed. "Because you always decide what to do for the best and I always take your advice."

"But aren't I usually right? Well?"

He really didn't get it.

"Yes, you are! I can't remember the last time you really messed up. And that's the only annoying thing about you, Bill. Sometimes, you get on my goat, you're so bloody perfect and sensible."

Bill picked up the portable television then and, honestly, I thought he was going to throw it through the window. There were big veins bulging on his forehead that I'd never seen before. But he just raised the telly and lowered it again a few times and then set it back on its silver stand. Eventually, he sat down on the bed beside me and sighed deeply.

"I don't understand, Mags. You said you loved me being sensible. You said, if only every other man was more like me, the world would be perfect. If you didn't want me to be sensible any more, why didn't you say something?"

"But I do want you to be sensible! I do, Bill."

"Then, how am I supposed to know when to be sensible and when not to be? Can you perhaps give me a list of the situations I am not allowed to get involved in?"

"But these were personal issues, don't you see, my love? It wasn't a case of leaving you out deliberately. Julie is my friend and it was my father's funeral. I wanted to sort them both out by myself. How can you know more about my relationships than I do? It's not fair. I honestly thought Julie's fling would blow over in a few days and it was her business and nobody else's. I thought she'd flirt with this guy and maybe kiss him goodnight or something. I never thought she would throw caution to the winds like she has. And my father! He didn't tell me he was on heart tablets. Why didn't he tell me about the heart tablets instead of his usual blow-by-blow accounts of the irrelevant political blusterings in this dump?"

Even though it's not a dump at all. It's very beautiful for the most part but I was in a fouler of a mood. And when I'm in a bad mood, Belfast is automatically a dump. And everybody in it is a thieving rascal.

"Look, you're all upset over this and there's no need for it! You should have told Gary that Julie had gone away to that fancy spa in Galway for a soul-searching holiday. And organised a modest funeral for your father with no fancy dinner afterwards. And your sisters should have stumped up their share of the cost. Yes, they're great girls but fair's fair, Mags. We have four children to support."

"Hindsight is a wonderful thing," I said, barely able to get the words out because I was in such a rotten sulk. Easy for Bill to tell me what I should have done. Casually tell my sisters they had to drop everything and fly halfway round the world for a funeral. And bring their cheque books with them, while they were at it. And just as casually tell Gary Devine that Julie didn't want to see him any more. Mind you, he would have done it for me.

I know that. Bill would have made the phone calls for me. But I didn't *want* him to. I wanted a little bit of independence, for once in my life. Well, be careful what you wish for, I suppose.

"And while we're on the subject, Mags, I don't mind about Alexander and Emma moving in together but it's up to them what they do with the rest of their lives. I'd prefer it if they got their own place and, really, you should have let Emma decide what to do about the baby. It was her decision. Not yours and mine, not even Alexander's. He would have had to deal with it, Mags, if Emma didn't want him or the baby. They've got to grow up sometime. You can't look after them like they're some sort of pet project, like two hamsters in a cage. They're adults, Mags. Plus, it will cause a lot of disruption in the house for Andrew and Christopher and they've got exams coming up in school. Fat lot of revision they'll get done with a baby crying half the night."

(Andrew and Christopher were in the same year at school, being born only eight months apart. Christopher was a month premature, you see.)

"I know, Bill! I know all of that."

"You don't know. Look, Mags, honey, I've seen this happen to other people our age. They start minding the grandchildren on a full-time basis and suddenly they find themselves trapped. Their children get used to the convenience of a built-in nanny and the grandchildren get used to the routine and the old-fashioned dinners. Mashed potatoes and gravy, birthday parties with jelly and ice cream. Next thing, the parents are off to Spain for a fortnight on their own and the grandparents are down at the GP's waiting for MMR jabs."

"That won't happen with Alexander and Emma."

"Are you sure? Because I think that's exactly what'll happen. I know you, you can't stop yourself from taking over. You'll be up and down the stairs with tea and toast and piles of laundry, and tidying up toys non-stop."

"I won't."

"You will. Emma's obsession with her weight takes up all her spare time – she won't lift a finger to help you. We'll never get rid of them, Mags. If they have another baby they'll be back on the penniless song-and-dance routine, forcing us to pay for everything. We can't afford it, love. Alexander should be taking charge of this situation, not you and me. It's his baby now, not ours."

"But he's still at university, Bill. Have a heart. He's penniless. And so is Emma. I just didn't know what to say to them. How could I leave Emma on the street? She had nowhere else to go!"

"Oh, Mags. You just don't understand, do you? They're *adults*."

"I can't believe you're being so logical about this. It's our first grandchild, Bill and you know as well as I do, Emma is far too skinny and that's probably why her own parents can't cope with the pregnancy. Already she's talking about being off her food with morning sickness. She's eating nothing, nothing at all. She needs help. Bill, I was only trying to help the girl."

"Don't worry about that," Bill said then, shaking his head with resignation. "You'll be helping Alexander and

Emma out no end for the next twenty years. And so will I. Even though I'm totally opposed to all of this interference, I can't stand by and let you do everything, now can I?"

Oh dear.

It's a horrible desolate feeling when you know you've got things wrong. But even then I was still convinced there was nothing else I could have done to salvage the various situations. Julie really shouldn't have had that hayloft spanking session with Jay O'Hanlon, I thought bitterly. Gary will really blow his top now. And maybe if I hadn't told Josephine about the Sean Bean look-alike, it would never have happened. And yes, I should have asked Ann and Elizabeth to contribute towards the funeral but they've been working so hard in Australia, and trying to cope with their homesickness and I just hadn't the heart to do it to them. And I thought to myself, they'll never forgive me if I cancel the headstone. Not really. It'll come up every time we get together. Not out of any malice on their part, no: it'll simply go into family folklore. They'll say, "Do you remember the time you promised our wee daddy a Celtic cross and we got all excited about the engraving, and then you changed your mind? Aw, Mags, you're some kid!" To top it all, Bill thought I was making life far too easy for Alexander and Emma and that we'd end up babysitting for years while he and Emma just carried on regardless with their lives. Going to gigs and getting legless drunk in the students' union. Travelling round the world with their backpacks and their arty novels. Enjoying the next decade doing exciting things together, instead of Bill and me. We'd still be reading bedtime stories to the grandchildren and ironing endless piles of laundry, according to Bill. And letting our other children think we were running a free nursery of some kind. So they were free to procreate at will and just give the stork our address on Eglantine.

It was all such a holy mess.

And Bill was being so decent about it, really. He was being his usual loving and understanding self. Patting me on the head for trying so hard and failing miserably. I couldn't stand it. It was like Dad's shocking death and Julie's mad affair and even Emma's surprise baby were all my fault but he was still going to be nice about it because he loved me. That made me so angry I couldn't breathe. None of it was my fault, *none of it*. My father was an impossible man and my sisters may have loved him but they've never liked him. They were always a bit scared of his temper to tell you the truth, he used to get that mad when the DUP party political broadcasts came on the telly.

"Ah, would you look at the cut of them auld so-and-so's!" he used to yell at the screen. "Look at them, smug as all-get-out with their big red faces! Children, you can always tell a Unionist by his big red face. Look there! Stuffed to the eyeballs with the very best of meat and drink! Lining their pockets with money they stole off the Catholics! Easy to talk about the democratic process when you're up to your big fat red neck in stolen goods. *Bastards*, the whole lot of them! Ah, would you get back to Scotland where you belong and give us a bit of peace?

Planter trash! Get to fuck out of it and then we'll talk about the democratic fuckin' process. God bless Ireland! Ah, turn it off, my head's thumpin'!"

And so on.

We used to leave the room when the British National Anthem started up at the end of the night's programming, in case he went ballistic and started lashing out. Ann and Elizabeth could have visited him whenever they wanted to but instead they called me from Sydney once a month and asked me how he was getting on. Like I was his officially appointed carer and they wanted a progress report. Like I should have taken him to the zoo or something in a wheelchair and bought him an ice cream. He was well able to cook and clean for himself, my father, and I will not be made to feel guilty that I didn't keep house for him. I'm not a skivvy and this isn't the 1940's. I hadn't got the time to call round there every day with a packet of J-Cloths and a lamb chop and that's the honest truth. Feminist principles aside. So it was an even bigger mystery to me, than it was to Bill, why I was going to so much trouble and expense now that my father was dead.

And Julie had no right to involve me in her messy love life either. I was beginning to feel quite cross with Julie, I must say. She was forty-one years of age for pity's sake. She was old enough to leave her own fella. He was a good man, was Gary Devine. She was lucky to have him in my opinion. But then again, to The Coven I'm just a boring old housewife with chunky ankles and a baggy black cardigan. I'd like to tell them that Bill and I have a red-hot sex life but they'd never believe me. Sometimes

I have three orgasms in one night. Those erotic massages Bill gives to me, well, money simply couldn't buy them. There's not a fancy spa in this whole wide world could make me feel the way Bill does when the notion takes him. And besides, if they knew what Bill was really like in bed they'd be after him themselves. They're ruthless. I've told you that before.

Speaking of sex, I'd told Alexander enough times to wear a condom. I couldn't think how or why he managed to get that stick-insect girlfriend of his pregnant in the first place. Oh, I don't mean to be abusive when Emma couldn't help the way she was. I know anorexia's a proper illness like depression. I *know* that. But I couldn't stand it when they went to bed together in our house, in case I heard Emma's pelvis snapping in half in the dead of night. Oh, the very sight of her hobbling up and down the stairs made me want to eat all the Danish pastries in Marks & Spencer and then get stuck into the party nuts and crisps. Bill's right, you know. There's nothing as nice as a lovely round bottom.

"Don't cry," Bill said softly. "Get into bed and I'll fetch you a big mug of tea and some chocolate biscuits to cheer you up. Do you want a few gossip magazines from the shop? Is the latest copy of *Heat* out yet?"

"No, leave it! Leave me alone!" I cried. "Don't tell me I've made a mess of everything and then patronise me on top of it. Poor old Mags! She does her best, you know but she's such an idiot. Hasn't a clue what to do in an emergency! And they say George Bush is stupid! At least he doesn't dress like a middle-aged witch in clumpy shoes and stupid flared trousers. I'm a fool, my darling. You can't sort me out this time with a chocolate digestive and a brew, Bill, no matter how much you claim to love me."

And even that was embarrassing because we don't say 'brew' in this part of the world. We say 'a cuppa' or 'a cup of cha'. That was the Peter Kay influence, I'm afraid. He says 'brew' all the time. I wonder what Peter Kay would do in my situation, I thought miserably. He'd probably write a hit series and make another ten million. Me? I couldn't give it away fast enough. "Maybe I should just sell the house and give the money to charity?" I wept. "And then we won't have to open the Eglantine branch of Suckers' Nursery?"

"Now, Mags, please don't get yourself in a state," Bill said again, starting to look quite worried.

"I can't help it, Bill," I said. "I *am* in a bloody state. I think my head is going to explode with all this worry and tension. I didn't mean to make such a bags of everything, Bill. Do you think I'm doing all this on purpose to irritate you? Do you think I've gone completely mad? I'm only trying to help my son because I'm afraid if I don't take control of the situation, he'll fall apart."

"Come on, darling, calm down. Are you hormonal at all? Let's check the calendar and you can take some Primrose Oil and Vitamin B-complex. Yeah?"

Oh, it would have to be *complex*, wouldn't it?

So he went to check that chart we keep on the inside of the wardrobe door with my PMT days blocked out in blue marker. On 'blue days' I try not to do anything silly like punching people (who might happen to annoy me in some way) hard in the face. I felt like a monkey in a science lab. No wonder Josephine and the others thought I was pathetic. My own husband thought I needed to be monitored. And sedated with sour worms and pictures of drunken celebrities lying in the gutter with their knickers on display. Or not. And that was when I really saw red. As red as our bedroom curtains, actually. Toffee-apple red. Fire-engine red. *Lava* red.

So what did I do?

Did I do the sensible thing and get into bed with a cup of tea and try to forget my bad mood by pouring scorn on the photo-shopped pictures of Z-list celebrities?

Did I, bog-roll!

"I won't get into bed, Bill my darling! I'm going out for a walk!" I shouted into his stunned face. "And don't you dare come after me! I'm capable of going for a walk by myself. I can do that at least! And I can order granite headstones and drawing-room conversions if I want to. And I can cover up my boss's affairs if I want to. And *you* can't tell *me* what to do! I'm not mentally retarded even if the whole lot of you think I am!"

I shouldn't have said that.

It's 'learning difficulties', isn't it? Or 'special needs'? I have special needs all right, I thought to myself, because I'm a married woman with four children, a massive house to keep clean and tidy, a recently dead father, a long-term uninterested mother, an important and demanding job and an emotionally damaged boss who's cracking up.

"Mags? Are you feeling all right? Crikey, this is a bad

143

one! Eh? You only get PMT this bad once in a decade."
And he consulted my chart, his finger running down the
page, his forehead creased into a massive frown.

"Shut up! You're badgering me and I can't stand it! I
won't stand for it, do you hear me, Bill Grimsdale? Oh!
Leave me alone!"

Well, Bill ran out of the room and downstairs to the
yard, accidentally dislodging one of his precious guitars as
he went. He started kicking the back gate and swearing
like I don't know what. I knew he needed some air and
he was only going down there to stop himself from calling
me some names I richly deserved but I couldn't go after
him and say sorry because I was erupting like a volcano
myself. I wanted to thump him for being such a sensible
Spock-like male! My own darling husband and I was
furious with him! Jealous, really. I was jealous of him and
his logical brain and his trim figure and his calm
personality. Bill will never have fashion dilemmas and
blue days. He has beautiful ankles. And he never makes
a lot of extravagant promises he'll never be able to keep,
to ungrateful people who don't even appreciate his
kindness. He has no idea what it's like to be a woman on
the verge.

I slammed out of the house in an absolutely stinking
mood and I marched straight down the road into a hair
salon that I'd never set foot in before because it looked so
expensive and I told the stylist to give me a chin-length,
raven-black bob with a peacock-blue streak down the
front. Sorted, I thought smugly. Julie's not the only one
who can do mad things. I'm crazy myself, don't you

know? Every bit as barmy as she is. I nearly had a heart attack, though, halfway through the colour-process when I thought I'd left my credit card in the house but thank goodness it was tucked safely into my cardigan pocket. I keep it on my person, if I can, in case my handbag is grabbed in the street. I loved that credit card more than life itself, the moment I felt its tiny flat body against my fingers. I kept my hand on it until I was offered a cappuccino and biscuits, in fact. Oh, but it's a great feeling when you have eight grand's worth of spending power on your actual person. You could almost do anything if you only had the imagination. Two solid hours I sat in that red leather chair, mesmerised by the drone of the hairdryers and the glamour of the teenage stylists. No wonder some celebrities are as thick as two short planks, mind you. How can they possibly keep up-to-date with current affairs when it takes so long for a plain old haircut? Enjoyable and all as it was. I tried to read a newspaper but the dye fumes kept putting me off my train of thought.

However.

In for a penny, in for a pound. The black bob with the blue streak in it looked utterly fabulous when it was finished. I told myself it would be no bother at all to have to use straightening balm and straightening irons on it every morning from now on and I paid up, leaving a huge tip. But the new look only went part of the way to dispelling my boiling rage so I'd no option but to keep going. I needed to do something big, something really big to channel my anger. Something *painful*. To punish myself for being such a total idiot.

SHARON OWENS

The tattoo I'd always wanted! A set of angel's wings on my back . . . a small set of angel's wings. Bill didn't like tattoos. He said they inevitably turned into hopeless green smudges after twenty years. And that only very reckless and shortsighted people went in for them. Not literally shortsighted, you know what I mean.

Cheeks flushing with fear, I took a taxi into the city centre and without hesitation I had the angel's wings done on my back, in a little tattoo parlour beside the Linenhall Library. Twenty-three years after first deciding I wanted them. Just a tiny set of wings, mind you, not a Robbie Williams-sized one. That would have been vulgar on a lady. But hey, it was bloody sore all the same. I knew Bill would go mental worrying about contaminated needles but it all looked very respectable and sterile in there and honestly, I was past caring. I thought, if I do cark it at least I won't have to worry about turning into a boring old granny with that stick-insect Emma lording it over me in my own house. And then, blood from the tattoo sticking to my T-shirt, I went into a fancy boutique nearby and I bought this *designer* pair of midnight-black, real suede, pointy-toed boots for an amount of money that would normally make me spit with disgust. World Vision could have built a decent-size school in Ethiopia for the money I spent on those boots. I don't know what came over me. I was far too old for a blue streak in my hair and pointy-toed boots, not to mention a tattoo but I wanted to spoil myself for a few hours. I was projecting ahead, I suppose. Seeing my forties going the way of my twenties and thirties. Endless walks to and from the

146

school gates, making costumes for school plays, pinning messy drawings to the fridge, having no nights out. Which didn't make any sense because I love my children more than anything and I have never cared for fripperies like blue hair and designer boots but maybe I was feeling guilty about Bill's and my savings going up in smoke?

Anyway, it was done. If I'd lived in London I would have looked like a kick-ass fashion designer or a top columnist in some sassy magazine. They'd probably have stopped me in the street to ask my opinion on something topical and shown it on the ITN news. In Belfast, however, I resembled a bit of a sad case. I walked round the shops for a while, feeling too cross to go home but too shy to sit in a coffee house by myself. Some teenage Goths saw me loitering in the park and they said "cool hair" and I thought I still had an edge to me and I was all delighted. But then they spoiled the compliment by laughing rather loudly when they'd walked on. I was tempted to buy some cigarettes and sit on a wall smoking them but I have never even liked the smell of tobacco so that was a non-starter. I went into the Palmhouse and thought of the night Bill and I made our first baby and I wept for a while beside the hyacinth display until some tourists came in the other door and I backed out again, mortified.

Eventually I got hammered drunk (it only takes three gin and tonics) in our local pub off Larkspur Avenue and, to cap it all, I called Gary on my mobile and told him what was going on in the Galway spa. I told him everything, nearly. That Julie was terrified of getting married because her own mother and father were bonkers, and that

Charlotte had had a protracted breakdown and that Sidney had taken his own life. And also, there was this handsome young guy called Jay O'Hanlon who worked in the spa and he was a bit of a looker and Julie was feeling very vulnerable and was possibly attracted to him and might even have *kissed* him already. Just kissed him, mind. But it meant nothing if she had, she was only having a harmless little dalliance to bolster her fragile self-esteem. And I did stress Julie's vulnerability because I didn't want Gary to be cross with her. So, I 'fessed up, big time. Except for the small details of the hayloft romp and the multiple orgasms and the handcart bondage, obviously. And Julie's screams of delight in the ice-cold water trough and the fact that she's infertile. Well, you'd need to be heartless altogether to mention that lot, wouldn't you? I didn't want Gary Devine to crash his car on the way down to Galway. By all accounts, the traffic over the border is chronic at the best of times. Well, they don't have as many cops as we do here in the north. Gary was so furious he ran out of the farmhouse without even replacing the receiver. I heard it clattering onto the maple floorboards and then Gary roaring his head off in the background.

"Joo-leeeeeeee!"

Oh dear.

I had another gin. And then another.

Next thing I knew, I was being shaken awake at closing time. It felt really weird to be walking home in the dark with blue hair in my eyes and brand new boots on my feet. I kept missing my step because the boots were so soft I couldn't feel the pavement through them. It must be heaven to live like this all the time, I thought. To never feel hard cheap shoes cutting into your toes and heels. No wonder rich people seem so relaxed and confident all the time. They don't have to keep patching up their crippled feet with sticking-plasters. I was talking to myself as I turned into our avenue, like a hormonal drunken teenager or something. I almost expected my mother and father to tell me off when I got home. But then I remembered my father wouldn't be shouting at me or the DUP political broadcasts ever again.

"Oops, don't think about that or you'll be off caterwauling again," I whispered to myself, finger laid against my lips. "Crying forever and a day like the legendary Mrs Charlotte Sultana."

I hoped Bill wasn't going to lecture me about liver-damage. I'd completely forgotten about the tattoo even though my back was definitely a little tender. I kept thinking I must have bumped up against a hand-dryer or something in the ladies' room.

But no, the hall was deserted and silent. I stole in like a cat burglar and immediately tripped over something big and flat, fell headlong onto the rug and hurt my knee.

When I switched on the lights, Emma's stuff was piled up in the hall. All thirty-nine boxes of it (I counted them – though I might have been out by a box or two because of my blurred vision) and she and Alexander were in bed together in his room. I could hear them chatting away, nineteen to the dozen. I thought, at least I don't have to worry about Emma getting pregnant now because she's pregnant already. And it was kind of comforting to have the suspense taken away like that. The kitchen was strewn with dirty dishes as the other kids had made their own supper but not tidied up. The grill was greasy and there were crumbs everywhere. Bacon sandwiches. No doubt they'd taken advantage of me going AWOL to buy a packet of bacon slices at the corner shop and devour it. I don't cook meat very often, you see, what with Bill and myself being vegetarian. I'm more of a salads and sandwiches person.

Bill . . .

Had he left me? Of course not. As he often says, at times like these, he has nowhere else to go. But I know he's only teasing me. Bill was in our bedroom playing his favourite bass guitar with the volume turned down very low. You can't play the guitar loud in a terraced house anyway or the neighbours will call the police but somehow the softness of the notes seemed ominous to me. I think it was Joy Division, and he plays that when he's really down which is about once in a decade. Bill didn't see me because he was facing out of the window as I tiptoed up the stairs. I watched him for a while from the doorway, thinking how handsome he was and how he might have been famous if he hadn't married me and had four children. I started to cry again, then. Only this time I knew it was going to be a proper, headache-inducing marathon of crying so I bolted myself into the main bathroom and pressed my face into a folded bath towel so nobody in the house would hear me.

A few moments after that, Julie called my mobile to say that Jay was lying asleep beside her in her room at the spa, and that he'd lost his job for shagging a client. Julie's words, not mine. They'd been caught doing the wild thing in the showers, apparently, but Julie wasn't annoyed in the least. She said Jay was far too good for the place anyway and he never should have been working in a bar in the middle of nowhere in the first place. She told me she'd tied Jay's ankles together in the ladies' changing rooms when they thought the last swimmer had left the pool area, but then one of the cleaners came in and caught them mid-climax. And that Jay had leapt up, over-balanced (always a risk with bondage) and fell heavily onto the bench, bruising his world-class appendage. Poor Jay! Maybe if he'd kept his family jewels in his shorts a little more often, they wouldn't have come a cropper over a wooden bench. But anyway, he'd got his marching orders and then Julie said she'd be home soon because she was missing the lighthouse terribly and had I told Gary they were finished yet?

I didn't reply. I couldn't speak because the room was spinning. God, I was pissed that night. I forgot to tell Julie that Gary was on his way down to Galway. I felt a bit sick to be honest so I just said I'd talk to her some other time, and best wishes to Jay O'Hanlon, and cheerio. And then I switched off the phone and went on crying. It hadn't even dawned on me that Gary might be almost at the spa by then. I mean, it takes about seven hours to drive from Belfast to Galway. And you could knock two hours off that, easily, if you thought the woman you were going to marry was making a fool of herself with a handsome toy boy. Poor Gary. But anyway, there was a big pile of fresh towels on the mat beside the radiator and they were all nice and warm, and to tell you the truth I think I dozed off for a bit. Well, half-dozing and half-sobbing, I suppose. I really was very tired.

Of course, my big sob scene was ruined twenty minutes later when I attempted to subdue my swollen red eyes with cold water from the mixer-tap. Bill heard the gurgling in our ancient copper pipes and he knew I'd come home. Or at least that was my interpretation. In fact, he knew already that I'd returned. He'd been tracking my movements all day.

"Mags, love?" he said, knocking lightly on the door. "Mags, are you okay in there?"

I thought of ignoring him but really, how long could I stay locked in my own bathroom with no food or bedding? And besides, I was so weary I would have sold my soul to the devil for twelve hours' unbroken sleep in my lovely ivory bedroom. I unbolted the door and stood there, refusing to look up at him. I couldn't bear for Bill to see my puffy old eyes beneath such a beautiful silken curtain of blue hair.

"Wow, that's beautiful," he said after an initial slow intake of breath and I knew he was turned on like never before. He's always had a little thing for Toyah Wilcox, you see.

Once a Punk, always a Punk.

He touched my fringe with the back of his hand and whistled softly. The silence between us was charged with electricity, just like in the Limelight Club twenty-odd years before. But of course I'd messed that up too, hadn't

I? Because now we couldn't celebrate my new hairstyle with a bit of a Punky romp because we'd had a fight earlier in the day and he wasn't sure of me any more. I'm a sulker, I'm ashamed to admit, and when I'm in a bad mood it takes me days to drag my libido out of the doghouse. Bill knows this. The moment passed and we both sighed heavily.

"I'm sorry I shouted at you," I said. "I didn't mean a word of it, you know I didn't. I'm just so tired, darling. I'm wrecked, actually."

"That's okay. I'm just glad you're back in one piece," Bill said softly and he put his arms around me and kissed the top of my head. "You smell of cigarette smoke," he said, smiling. "Off boozing on your own? What am I going to do with you?"

"I'm sorry, darling. I had a few drinks in the pub. The funeral, you know, and saying goodbye to my sisters again, and the worry over Emma and Alexander . . ."

"I know. It's okay. Forget it. Can you remember how many gins you had? Should we be on our way to the hospital?"

"No, I think I'll survive. I had three, I think. Or five, maybe . . . definitely no more than five. Were you worried about me when I took off?"

"Well, yeah, I was. Obviously. But I followed you and saw you going into that fancy salon. Then I lost track of you for a few hours. Later, I phoned the pub and they told me you were there. I asked them to let me know when you were on your way home and I was looking out for you from the bay window."

"So you did see me coming in?"

"Yes, I did. I thought you might want to take a moment to compose yourself before apologising to me."

You see? I told you! The man is Spock's long-lost twin!

"Actually, Bill, I missed you. The minute I stormed out of the house I missed you but I was in such a rotten mood I just had to keep going. I won't do it again, I promise."

He smiled a kind of lopsided smile then, as if he wanted to believe me but couldn't quite bring himself to.

"Do you want that cup of tea now?" he asked then, reasonable to the last.

I nodded and shuffled past him into our bedroom. "That would be heaven," I sighed, "and then I'll have a nice hot shower and get this awful smoke out of my lovely new hair. I can't wait till they ban smoking in the North."

After which, I collapsed onto the covers and fell asleep before the kettle was even boiled.

Next morning, Bill had gone to work by the time I woke up, my head throbbing with a massive hangover. My clothes had been taken off and laid on the dressing-table chair. My lovely new boots were side by side under the bed. Not a mark on them after the day I'd had. I guess that shows you what top-quality boots they were. I was wearing my slinky black PJ's and there was a big glass of water on the bedside cabinet. And a basin on the floor alongside a box of tissues and a couple of old towels spread over the carpet. Memories came filtering back to me slowly, very slowly. Oh dear, I had asked for double gins the night before and I'd had five of them! Ten gins! And I'd been moaning about my woes to the barman like some middle-aged man having a mid-life crisis. What a madwoman, I thought with a flash of burning shame before convincing myself that pub measures were tiny and therefore I'd only had about five proper gins. Which wasn't too bad considering the pressure I'd been under in recent days. And I daresay the staff have heard it all before and they only half-listen anyway. There was a note from Bill on the pillow beside me. Yawning, I opened it.

Bad news.

Gary *had* crashed his car on the way down to Galway. I really shouldn't have told him like that, I thought, feeling a severe twinge of guilt. Luckily he hadn't been badly hurt, just a broken leg and a spot of concussion. A lorry had pulled out in front of him and he'd hit a telegraph pole swerving and ended up on his side in a field of potatoes. He'd phoned Bill from the hospital first thing that morning to let us know he was okay. I thought it was strange of Gary to phone our house but likely he wanted me to pass the message on to Julie. Poor Gary, still trying to make contact with Julie even from the misery of his hospital bed. He'd been taken to Drogheda General at the time but was being transferred to Belfast soon by ambulance. The car was a write-off. Bill said he would leave it up to me whether Julie was notified or not. He seemed to think it would be a good idea to leave a message for her at reception in the spa but he didn't think we should get involved beyond that. I immediately phoned the spa and left a message for Julie and then, it being a Saturday, I crawled out of bed and ventured downstairs to see what my family were up to.

More bad news.

Alicia-Rose was dancing round the kitchen waving a letter in her hand. Singing a pop song by Men At Work. Turns out, she'd secretly applied for a year's student-exchange programme in Australia and had just been accepted. Oh, goody. One of my precious, gorgeous children was leaving home for the first time. The start of the end of my perfect family life. No, no no! Suddenly I stopped caring about Julie altogether.

11

A Souvenir from County Galway

OH JULIE! JULIE SULTANA, WHAT WERE YOU THINKING of? I mean, I'd almost stopped caring about Julie. But because of the shock and anxiety caused by Alicia-Rose's proposed trip to the Land Down Under, any interest in my boss's personal life from that point onwards was purely academic. Well, that was the plan anyway.

Get this.

Julie got my message all right about Gary's car accident and in a rare fit of compassion she decided to come home to Belfast and make it up with him. For a while. Just until his leg mended. I couldn't believe it when I heard. If Julie was ever going to leave Gary Devine, she should have done it that day. It made no sense at all for her to cosy up to Gary again when she'd cheated on him with Jay O'Hanlon with such energy and enthusiasm. After all the hoopla she made about me telling him it was over between them, I ask you! But no,

Julie must have decided her life wasn't complicated enough at that point. So, she made it up with Gary and he was delighted. According to Julie, she just felt too sorry for Gary to dump him when his leg was broken. But I thought that she knew, deep-down in her soul, that he was the man for her. Anyway, they patched things up quite easily.

I mean, Gary didn't know about Julie *sleeping* with Jay and he didn't know that Julie had told me to break it off with him, so there wasn't much explaining to do, really. Just an apology (over the phone) for taking off to Galway without him in the first place and another apology for not filling him in years ago on the 'Charlotte & Sidney Marital Meltdown Roadshow'. But to add a little twist to the proceedings, Julie brought Jay O'Hanlon back to Belfast with her in the white Mercedes convertible and she installed him in the all-mod-cons apartment in the converted flour mill in Saintfield. A souvenir of her stay at the spa in Galway with the shocking-pink armchairs in the foyer.

As you do.

And then she drove on over to Gary's house, had a lovely hot bubble bath and collapsed into their rustic-style bed, exhausted.

"Love the hair," Julie said to me when she popped into the lighthouse to open her mail next morning. It was her first day back at work since meeting Jay.

"Do you think I'm too old for a blue fringe?" I asked nervously. Julie doesn't flatter me, as a rule. She thinks I look like 'a gypsy matriarch in mourning for her wild-card husband', most of the time. But she doesn't mind because I make her look so good, by comparison.

"Na. Go for it, kiddo. Forty is the new thirty, Mags. Or in my case, twenty-five! Oh, I shouldn't tell you this but my thighs are so stiff I can barely walk. It's not easy doing the splits on a glass coffee table. I'm telling you, those lighthouse steps nearly killed me this morning."

Poor Julie.

She was so proud of herself.

"We take naughty pictures of each other," she said then, winking at me.

I didn't say anything. But I sincerely hoped she was storing the Polaroids in a safe place. We didn't want a sex-scandal on our hands, after all. It would have been very bad for business. Or maybe not but then we can't all be Paris Hilton.

"I'll put the kettle on," I said, shaking my head. "I have about a million things to ask you about these latest bookings."

And for a few blissful hours it was business as usual. Except with Jay safely settled in front of the flat-screen telly in the Saintfield apartment, and a giant pepperoni heating through in Julie's formerly pristine designer oven. Julie had left her toy boy some money and a copy of the *Yellow Pages* and told him just to phone out for a takeaway whenever he was hungry. There was a video store nearby and a small supermarket where he could buy milk and bread, cigarettes and magazines. Julie had any amount of CDs and DVDs in the sitting room and a few pieces of gym equipment in the second bedroom. So hopefully her new lover wouldn't be bored. Well, not a bit of him! Jay took to Belfast life like a duck to water. He must have thought he was in heaven as he'd recently been evicted from his digs in Galway and had been kipping on a friend's (broken) couch. He knew how to turn on the power shower in Julie's luxury bathroom and he knew where the pretty glass mugs and the Earl Grey tea bags were kept. And he didn't know a sinner in the city. So there was no way he could get himself into any trouble while Julie wasn't there. So far, so good.

Then, after lunch Julie popped into the Royal Victoria Hospital on the infamous Falls Road in Belfast and prepared to wrap Gary round her little finger. She'd bought him a huge bunch of pink roses and a heart-shaped box of chocolate and champagne truffles. She told him she'd been a bit silly and yes, she'd flirted with one of the barmen at the spa in a fit of crazy desperation (related to her being forty-one and only just coming to terms with it) but nothing serious had happened between them. The engagement was still on and there was nothing to worry about. Which was amazingly brass neck of Julie considering she still had bite marks on her bottom from her latest Sharpe-inspired role-playing afternoon with Jay. That old military jacket was seeing more action in 2005 than it ever had in its heyday, I can tell you.

Poor Gary was so love-bombed in his hospital bed he said he would give Julie the benefit of the doubt and they'd say no more about it. She kissed him tenderly and said she would go straight back to the farmhouse after work and make sure it was all shipshape. Arrange some extended staff-cover for the horses and so on, as Gary wouldn't be able to ride for a while. Which she did do, I have to say, and then she nipped back to Jay for a quick spanking session on the corner sofa (during which he used her bare back as a plate from which to eat his leftover pizza) before spending the night at Gary's house, alone. Just in case Gary rang her there on the land-line. And he did indeed call her, eight times to be exact. Once an hour, on the hour. For fifteen minutes, exactly.

I suppose he was becoming paranoid.

Julie told me she was having the best of both worlds at that point in her life. She had Gary's enormous bed all to herself every night and she was happily lying in it, watching *Sex & The City* videos and eating microwave curries, while Gary was safely confined to the hospital. And Jay was neatly tucked away in the exclusive apartment in Saintfield. Resting up his massive doo-da for the next installment of Sharpe-inspired antics, no doubt. Jay knew about Julie's plan to be nice to Gary for a while but of course Gary was in complete ignorance of the cuckoo in his nest and to be honest with you, I had no inclination to enlighten him. As I said, I was far too busy having nightmares about my beautiful daughter being hurt or harmed in a foreign country, and I'd more or less washed my hands of Julie's rollercoaster love-life.

Emma was still refusing to eat anything except fresh fruit and stinky raw fish (some celeb-inspired crackpot diet, I expect), and she and Alexander were arguing non-stop about their future. Her thirty-nine-plus boxes of stuff had been stored in the guest room for the time

SHARON OWENS

being but she said she wouldn't unpack properly till the drawing room bed-sit had been finished. I was a little bit shocked at Emma's eagerness to live with us in a self-contained 'flat'. Even though it'd been my idea to begin with. But then Emma let slip that her own parents had given her bedroom to her sister's twin baby girls. So she really did have nowhere else to go. And that rankled with me, too, because she made it somehow seem like she was the one doing *me* a favour. If you know what I mean?

"It won't be a dream home," she said more than once. "But it'll do for the time being. Once I get it fixed up and some of my own accessories on display, it could actually be quite nice."

I suppose Bill was right (yet again) when he said they'd never stand on their own two feet while we offered them a cushy alternative. Bill and I still hadn't decided exactly what to do about the bed-sit plan at that point, incidentally: whether we'd apply for another bathroom and a fully operational kitchen and so on. And some top-notch soundproofing so we couldn't hear our own son having noisy sex. There was a general feeling of restlessness in the house as a result of all these deliberations. I said we should give them the full Monty so Emma could feed and bathe the baby on her own. And hopefully learn some mothering skills early on, without me taking over. Bill worried about the rates going up and said we might be registered somewhere as taking in lodgers. And should we charge them a nominal rent to cover electricity and so on? And would they be allowed to use the phone without paying? It was all very complicated.

162

Meanwhile, Emma and Alexander were up and down the stairs like yo-yo's. Fighting, slamming doors, making up, having *noisy sex* in Alexander's room. Emma liked to moan at the top of her voice during these make-up sessions (it did actually sound as if she was being stretched on a rack and burned with hot irons) which is all very well if you live alone in a detached house. You can articulate all you like if you don't have a party wall. But they weren't living in a detached house, or even on their own, and Andrew and Christopher were absolutely fascinated by their bedroom business. I overheard them talking about it in the kitchen one morning, wondering what Alexander was doing to Emma and how they could learn to do it too. Not to Emma, no, dear! To some other poor creatures they had yet to meet. Bill started playing *The Last Man In Europe* constantly and frequently went to bed wearing headphones. We never got around to celebrating the blue fringe.

In my 'spare' time, I prepared the most delicious meals I could think of. Caesar salad with the croûtons tossed in a home-made dressing to soften them up. Honeydew melon slices served with cubes of cooked chicken and garlic potatoes. Fresh cherries (individually stoned by myself) and perfect 'school-dinner scoops' of vanilla ice cream. Emma rejected the lot with barely a flicker of her false eyelashes and Alexander was often cross with me for trying to force-feed her.

"Stop it, Mum, you're upsetting her," he would hiss at me on the stairs. "She's on a special diet this week."

What of, I wondered. Water and air?

Two weeks passed in this bizarre fashion. I could feel a massive sulk descending on me and I couldn't stop it. It felt like a brick getting lodged in my windpipe and it hurt to breathe. People who never sulk don't understand this phenomenon. True sulking is not a choice you make. Sometimes, the sulk is bigger than the sulker. It takes you over, much as I imagine class A drugs do. I decided I would just sit back and watch it all unfold with my fingers over my eyes, like you do when they're blowing up a tall chimney on the television. I spent a lot of time in the bath and a lot of money on wine and downmarket gossip magazines. I'll say this for the so-called Z-listers (poor mites), they do make you realise you're not the only idiot in the world and that's a good thing. I was so disappointed, you see. I was still smarting that my efforts to help had only made everything worse so I was keeping my mitts off and my gob shut.

I still hadn't met Jay at this point and I was glad about that. I worried he might be some sort of alien come to earth to mate with 'mature' women and I was afraid he'd have hypnotic laser beams for eyes. But then Julie rang me from Gary Devine's farmhouse on the first Monday morning in August and asked me to drop off some cash to Jay on my way home from work, so he could go shopping for food. She couldn't go herself as Gary was getting out of hospital that evening and she was up to her eyes in homecoming preparations. Not to mention trying to cover up a bruise on her wrist (that pesky bondage again) with heavy make-up and a handful of bangles.

"They use the euro, you see, in the Irish Republic

while we Northerners still have the British pound," she told me.

"Like, yeah, I know that, Julie. I'm not as stupid as I look."

"And poor Jay's broke, in any case," she added.

"Surprise, surprise," I muttered under my breath. "He ought to charge you for sex, then he'd be rich." But of course, she heard me.

"What's up with you, Mags Grimsdale?"

"Nothing. Can't he wait till you see him tomorrow?" I said. "I'm too tired for a run out to Saintfield in the back of a taxi."

"No, Mags, he can't wait! There's no food in the fridge and no vodka either."

Oh dear, I thought. Can't have Jay going without his vodka.

"Look, do me this favour now and you can come in to work an hour late tomorrow, okay? Please, Mags? My very dearest friend in all the world, pretty please with ribbons on?"

"Oh, Julie!"

So I had no choice but to raid the petty-cash tin in the lighthouse and take a taxi out to the converted flour mill in Saintfield, and give it to him. As it were.

Interesting experience.

Jay answered the door with beads of water all over his olive skin and wearing nothing but a *very* small pair of black underpants. Light-reflecting Gigolo underpants. I was embarrassed for him, to tell you the truth. Clearly he was just out of the shower. And yes, he did have a massive doo-da even when it wasn't reporting for duty, Sergeant, if you know what I mean. And yes, he did look like Sean Bean when he was twenty-five and yes, I could definitely see the attraction. I could kind of understand why Julie was risking everything to sleep with him though I still thought it would end in tears. But I wasn't hanging around to fall under the spell of those laser-beam eyes and besides, Bill would have hit the roof if he'd known what was going on. Not that he's a prude, you understand. But he doesn't believe in pulling other people into your own difficulties. So I explained the money situation to Julie's lover and then I scarpered 'pronto', politely turning down his invitation to stay for coffee. He probably thought the lot of us were as promiscuous as Julie, I seethed inwardly. Us heathen Nordies with our loose morals, the direct result of the influence of King Henry VIII, don't you know? No bother to us to casually drop our knickers and bend over the kitchen table for a two-minute quickie with a stranger from the south. Why, it passes the time till the coffee is stewed, don't you know? And it's easier than finding something to talk about in these days of political correctness gone mad. Anyway, it was very rude of Jay not to wear a robe, wasn't it? I can't be doing with people who walk about in the nip. Such total narcissism, it's positively offensive. I think I must have made a mean face at Jay O'Hanlon behind his back. In fact, I know I did – I realised with (mild) shame that he'd seen me in the mirror beside the front door. As I left the apartment we both knew I thoroughly disapproved of the whole situation. That was probably why he waved goodbye to me from the sitting-room window, standing up against the glass with his legs wide open. Really, that man could have made a fortune in the porn industry. Shameless isn't the word. The taxi-driver nearly reversed over a bollard with shock. I said, "Don't mind him, he's from Galway."

As if that explained everything.

"Things have fairly changed down south since they got the bit of money," he said quietly as we set off for town again.

I just nodded.

I didn't bother telling Julie about Jay flaunting himself before me that day. That's probably what he wanted me to do, I reckoned. Have a catty row and fall out with her. Then he'd have had Julie all to himself. The crafty weasel. But I was smarter than that. I'd read thousands of women's magazines over the years and I knew the first thing a bully does is isolate his woman from her friends and family so she loses her perspective and becomes more submissive to his authority. Well, I had a fourteen-year start on Jay O'Hanlon and he wasn't getting rid of me that easily. And I didn't want to get into the whole 'are you after my fella?' thing with Julie either. That's another curiosity about people having affairs – they always think everyone else is lusting after their paramour, don't they? No point in telling Julie I wouldn't want Jay O'Hanlon in my bed if he was quite literally the last man in Europe. If there's one thing that turns me off a man, it's arrogance.

I had a lot on my mind in any case, because the

following morning I was going in to the university to have a chat with Emma about her suspected eating disorder. Well, she didn't know we were going to be talking about anorexia and how bad it would be for the baby. And I'd already decided I wasn't going to interfere in her life or Alexander's to any great extent. It was just a little nudge in the right direction. Some helpful hints and ideas, that's all it was. We'd arranged to meet for coffee in the snack bar to finalise plans for the drawing-room conversion. She couldn't decide on a country-cottage kitchenette theme or modern beech units and a concealed sink. I didn't want to talk about it at home because Bill was so uncomfortable with the whole thing. He wanted them to live independently from 'the mother ship' and pay their own gas bill and peel their own spuds. Fat chance. Young people today are worse than useless at keeping house. They think all meals begin with the words, 'remove lid and pierce film'. If the washing-machine goes on the blink they just lie daydreaming on the sofa and gaze at the ceiling until help arrives. My kids do anyway and they're *good* kids. I thought I might get Emma to compromise a little on the bed-sit – maybe just go for the bathroom but not the kitchenette? Well, she doesn't eat much, does she, I thought spitefully.

So, Emma had a diet cola with lots of ice and an under-ripe green apple. I had a messy cappuccino with three sugars, two sausage rolls bursting out of their pastry at both ends (plastered with salt and HP sauce) and a rather lopsided giant chocolate muffin with a soft chocolate centre which I didn't actually want but I was trying to make a point. By the way, that canteen could do with a new manager; they're far too free and easy with the presentation. We found a clean-ish table and sat down. Emma looked as if she was going to gag as I ate every last crumb of my food. I even scooped up the last drop of brown sauce with my forefinger and licked it off. Then I wished I hadn't as I'd just been jangling loose change in my pocket but there you go.

"So, Emma," I said, red in the face from my fatty feast, "tell me, how is the world treating you?"

"Oh, I've found this amazing new exercise video," she said, sucking an ice-cube. "It's so cool. It really minimises your thighs."

I thought, so does breast-feeding.

In my opinion, exercise videos were invented for people who don't do enough housework. But I let her prattle on about stretches and abs for half an hour while I smiled until my face ached. Eventually, pleasantries out of the way, I tried to convince her to go into therapy for her countless food issues. Then, I suggested she ought to gain roughly three stone for her own sake as well as the baby's. Not to mention, marry my son as soon as possible so they'd all have the same name, come the birth.

"No matter what they say," I advised her, "I do believe you get to see a doctor earlier on in the labour stages if you're a married woman." And to that end, I wanted Emma to allow me to arrange an unusual and highly romantic (i.e. Very Low Budget) civil wedding for the two of them. With an outdoor setting perhaps and a home-made buffet which I would serve picnic-style at Dunluce

Castle, for example? Or we could have had chilled salmon steaks and a medley of salads at the Giant's Causeway? On an off-peak day when there were no tourists about. Or even just back at our house with fairy lights on the chandelier and white ribbons everywhere.

Yes, well.

It did all seem very reasonable and sensible to me at the time. If she'd truly loved Alexander, she'd have married him anywhere. That was my opinion but I'd been thinking of love 1984-style. Back then, people didn't think about the future or how they'd cope for money and a roof over their heads after they were wed. Not like now when girls didn't want to get married until they were nearly forty and their ovaries were already battening down the hatches and preparing to submerge. But at least they had a designer fridge, a pension plan and a company car of their own by then. Or maybe young women nowadays have simply lost their faith in a man's ability or willingness to support them for sixty years. Take your pick.

Basically Emma wasn't interested in any of my brilliant ideas.

"Now, Emma," I told her, "you know this media career of yours is going to be, at best, a long shot. You've got to be practical and I've a lifetime's experience in putting on family events on a tight budget."

A few petty accusations and nasty counter-accusations, and a lot of tears later, Emma stormed off in a white-hot rage. After telling me I was a fat interfering fat old dragon with *fat* legs (note, she called me fat three times in the one sentence) and that I had 'über-weird' fashion sense. Which was really too outrageous for words because she wears old-men scruffy shirts over Lycra cycling shorts all the time, presumably to make her stick-thin figure look even more skinny than it does already. At least I make an effort to accessorise my hair clips to my handbag. And her knees! I've seen better legs hanging out of a nest. (That's what cheeky lads in Belfast say to particularly thin girls.) But Emma said I only wanted them to get married because I was afraid of what the neighbours might think. That I was an old fogey and a bossy witch! Me! And that she would not be going into therapy, would not in a million years be gaining three stone, would under no circumstances be marrying 'a Mummy's Boy' like my Alexander and would definitely not be getting spliced to anybody beside a cheapskate buffet of iced buns and coronation chicken in some 'weird' ruined castle.

Uppity little madam, I thought to myself.

We'd all like to live the life of Reilly but we can't afford it, can we, darling?

No, dear.

We can't.

If wishes were horses then beggars could ride. Or some other such nonsense.

I wanted to shake her hard but you simply can't go around manhandling pregnant women, can you? It just wouldn't look right, no matter that she deserved a good gonk. Gonk is what we in Belfast call a shock, by the way. I said, if she'd set her heart on Ashford Castle (which is very far from being ruined, it's the most lavish hotel in

Ireland) she should have said something sooner. And we'd get The Killers to provide the music at the reception while we were at it and she could have a gown made by elves out of spun gold She told me to get stuffed (or words to that effect) and she raced off into the corridor as fast as her feeble hunched-over frame would allow. I mean, she could hardly pull the glass door of the canteen open but once she was past that particular obstacle, she moved at quite a fast pace.

I ran after her, though, right into the English Department lecture theatre and I shouted, "Why are you sleeping with my son, then, if you don't love him? Tell me that! He seems to think the two of you are getting married!"

"Leave me alone."

"Were you only passing the time with Alexander until Mr Right came along? Why didn't you use birth control if you don't love him? Why did you bother to tell Alexander about the baby if you weren't going to stay with him? Why are you breaking his heart, Emma?"

"Leave me alone, I said!"

"You've got to eat properly when you're pregnant, Emma. I thought all you university students were supposed to be intelligent? I'm going to have to tell your doctor you've got an eating disorder, you know. You need help, pet."

"Would you bloody well go away? Nutcase!"

"Is this why the suffragettes fought for the vote? Is it? So you girls could all become a bunch of anorexic flibbertigibbets? Honestly, you've got no end of freedom in this country nowadays and all you can be bothered doing is vomiting up your dinner and starving yourselves into an early grave and sleeping around with disrespectful layabouts and having nervous breakdowns. I'm absolutely fed up to the back teeth with all of this carry-on, I really am. I'm fucking sick and tired of it!"

Which was totally out of order, to be fair to Emma. To fling out the family secrets like that in front of a hundred or so stunned students who were innocently sitting there, waiting for a class to begin. And she wasn't a flibberti-gibbet, either. She was very ill indeed. But I was confused beyond reason at that point. Come on now, don't be so quick to judge me. What would you do in my (designer) shoes? Support for my side was almost entirely male, I have to say. The boys were nodding slowly in tacit agreement, while the girls looked at me like I was dirt on the sole of their shoes.

"Leave it, Mrs Grimsdale," Emma said, crimson with embarrassment. "I'm far too young to get married. I want to have a life first. I don't want to give up my studies and become a domestic drudge."

A drudge like me, I thought. I suppose that's what she means? The girls in the room began to clap their support. As if Emma could ever have matched my efficiency with a floor-cloth. She wishes! Talk about delusions of grandeur.

"I won't leave it," I said. "Don't *you* think you can move thirty-nine boxes of stuff into my house and let my son wait on you hand-and-foot, and then tell me you don't want to marry him! Is he not good enough for you, then? Is the name Grimsdale not good enough for you? Is that it?"

Cue, sniggers from the audience. I mean, the class.

"Well, don't think you've got it all figured, Emma my dear, because I'm going straight home to cancel the builders. I'll tell you that for nothing," I added venomously. "And you can traipse back to your own family and stop using my home as a hotel and storage depot. I'll give you too young to get married! You can forget about the beechwood doors and the kitchenette now, lady! There'll be a concealed sink over my dead body!"

More sniggers.

"And you can start showing some gratitude towards my husband and myself for paying your medical fees while you're at it. Right? We're not made of money! Little Miss Independent still needs a handout from the boring old fogeys, it would seem? Not too proud to let a plumber and a PA pay for your fancy consultant! Eh? And don't you fucking call me a drudge! I'm a fucking *home-maker* and proud of it."

Yes, I know. I swore at Emma. And I'm not a big fan of swearing at the best of times. Even if it is labelled 'Alternative Comedy' on the telly and it wins loads of awards now instead of being censored. So yes, I actually swore at a pregnant anorexic girl in front of a hundred or more witnesses. It's pretty hard to defend that so I won't even try.

"Shove it, then," she said quietly.

I expect she didn't have the energy to shout at me after pulling open that big glass door all by herself. I thought, wait till the labour pains kick in, Emma love, then you'll know the meaning of the word 'work-out'.

Then again, she won't have to go through labour, I thought suddenly. What with the planned C-section and all (thanks to Bill's and my life savings). But no, it seemed Emma was fed up with me and my charity. "Shove your money where the sun doesn't shine," she said, adding sadly, "I'll take my chances on the NHS."

Immediately, I felt contrite.

"Look, it doesn't matter about the money, really it doesn't. That was just me losing my rag, forget it. The main thing is your health, Emma. You need to start eating, pet. You might harm the baby if you don't eat properly. The baby gets all its nutrition from your body. Think of the baby and please be reasonable. I'm only trying to help you."

At which point the tutor showed up and asked me to leave the building before he called the police. He actually pulled me over to the lecture theatre door by the elbow. Very aggressively, I might add. Emma was already sobbing onto the shoulder of some girl with long hair and a check shirt. I staggered, shaking, to the foyer where I took out my frustration on two hippy-type women sitting chatting behind a trestle table. They were handing out pro-abortion leaflets. I'm ashamed to say I put my heel to the table and kicked it clean over, scattering leaflets and cups of cold coffee all over the floor. Not noticing that someone had taken a sneaky snap of me kicking the table over, on their mobile phone.

"Will you stop tormenting these poor girls with your have-it-all balderdash?" I gasped when the tabletop had stopped reverberating. "Have you any idea how young they are? How vulnerable? They shouldn't be having sex at all. It's the boys you should be targeting with your information leaflets: tell them to sort themselves out with a bit of hand-relief, and leave the girls alone. They're barely into puberty now and you're recommending oral sex. It's outrageous!"

"Right-wing nutcase," they said calmly, starting to tidy up. (I suppose they get this sort of reaction on a daily basis.) "It's people like you have left the world in the state it's in."

"I am not and have never been a right-wing nutcase," I retorted at once. "I'm a vegetarian for your information. I'm all for freedom of choice and women's rights. Just not when it's my first grandchild and my son is suicidal. There's a girl in there who doesn't know what she's doing. She's killing herself with an eating disorder and we're all supposed to stand politely by and do nothing. Somebody needs to take control."

Yes, well, in retrospect I can see how that might have sounded. Just a teensy bit bossy?

"Please go away," they said, ignoring my obvious distress. "You've clearly got some serious issues to deal with. We're counsellors, not psychiatrists." And they gave my blue fringe a strange look. One of the women whispered something to the other one and they both laughed uproariously.

I was deeply offended.

"What was that? What did you say? What exactly are you insinuating?"

I had no idea what they meant unless it was to suggest

I was hoping to cop off with a younger man or something, with my blue hair.

"I'm a happily married woman," I declared. "I'm forty and proud of it. So you two can keep your smutty insinuations to yourself."

And I pointed at them several times for good measure. A few bystanders started to giggle. Some of them saluted me in a sarcastic way. Honestly, I didn't know where to look. I ran out of the building in floods of tears.

On the way home I made a detour into the expensive salon and had the blue fringe dyed black to match the rest of my hair. Just so nobody from the university would recognise me again and not because I felt I looked like a saddo of some kind.

The table-kicking picture ended up in the back pages of a local free newspaper two days later under the title, *Mystery Rebel Disrupts University Life*. But nobody in my family noticed because by then Emma had broken up 'for good' with Alexander and we were taking it in turns to keep suicide-watch on him. I'd only been half-serious about Alexander's low mood when I had a go at the two women in the foyer but sadly it turned out to be anything but an exaggeration. Bill took two weeks off work, and father and son went out on long walks together in the countryside. Alicia-Rose washed all the painkillers in the house down the sink. Ditto the bleach, weedkiller and rat poison. Andrew and Christopher stayed up late every night to make sure Alexander didn't sneak out to the 24-hour garage to buy more. Bill was very depressed when he saw my blue fringe had disappeared. He still hadn't seen the tattoo because I'd been changing into my pyjamas every night while he was brushing his teeth. All in all, a stressful period.

Oh, don't look at me like that.

I was only trying to help.

12

Emma

WHY DO AN AWFUL LOT OF ACTRESSES AND POP TARTS these days talk like five-year-old girls? You know what I mean? Little breathless whispery voices like cartoon characters. All wide-eyed innocence and perfect teeth and shy eyelash-fluttering. Yet they still have vulgar great breast implants which they flaunt, caress and cram into uplift bras every chance they get. Thongs on show, come-to-bed eyes. Pelvises vibrating like clockwork toys. What does it all mean? That the guy won't even have to do the thrusting once they get into bed together because they're more than qualified to do it for him? Never mind bed, now I come to think of it, anywhere will do. I won't name names but they know who they are. All but shoving the camera up their vaginas on MTV and then having to be shielded from countless sex-mad stalkers by twenty-stone bodyguards, every time they leave the house. All right for them, they can afford bodyguards. What are the rest of us supposed to do? I am utterly, utterly bored of it to tell you the truth. It's nothing but sex, sex and more sex on the television. The girls are no age, either. The younger the better, it seems. I bet most of them don't know their capital cities from a smack in the mouth. I'm no Mary Whitehouse, no, dear, but I really am exhausted to the point of nausea (actual nausea) of wannabe starlets in ripped denim shorts whispering on the television about their new video or movie or whatever. And then, said video or movie shows them feeling themselves up with their tongue hanging out and some himbo covered in body oil sniffing round their crotch. While they stare into the lens like some bewildered crazy crack-whore of fifty-five. Is it the pop industry managers' fault, is it the consumers' fault or what?

"It was such a lot of fun," they always say about the making of the video or the movie or whatever. Everything nowadays is either fun, hot, wicked or cool. That's it! Only four adjectives are necessary any more. Nothing is crushingly boring or supremely tedious or mildly amusing or downright hilarious. None of them ever says, "Do you know what, mister? I think I'm too rich. I'm going to give it all away and spend some time reading actual *real* books in my local library."

We lap it up, we really do. The more extravagant and spoilt our stars become, the more money we want to throw at them. Five million quid on an engagement ring? Fabulous diamond, sweetie! Here's another ten million for flogging any old tat you like, and don't spend it all in the one shop. Fantastic! I blame this vacuous showbiz nonsense for what happened to Emma after she moved her stuff out of our home. Oh yes, she'd broken up with Alexander again, I did say. She had some idea she was going to be a famous TV presenter or something, you see, so she stuck rigidly to her daily regime of diet cola and green apples and she went down to six stone and she lost the baby. Our first little grandchild. A week later, her weight dropped by another four pounds and her parents finally faced facts and had her sectioned into a private clinic in London. They took her over there on the plane. She didn't want to go but she was too weak to hold onto her bedroom door handle so off she went to the clinic, in the clothes she stood up in. Her father had to remortgage their house to pay the fees.

We were all numb with sadness. Emma's own mother wept with abandon when they came round to Eglantine to tell us the awful news.

"I'm so sorry I had a go at her in the snack bar," I said quietly during a gap between sobs. "Was all of this something to do with me? Did I trigger it?"

"What have *you* done?" Alexander asked me, his eyes blinking non-stop to hold back the tears.

"Did she not say?" I muttered, trying to sound all innocent and clueless.

I hadn't told Alexander about the disastrous meeting with Emma at the university. I hadn't told anyone. Secrecy again, you see. I was becoming very secretive. That's one of the peculiar things about getting older – you simply don't feel any great need to explain your actions to other people. Younger women will blab everything to anyone who'll listen, but we more than make up for it when we hit forty.

"I tried to persuade her to start eating normally, son," I told him in a soothing voice.

"You what?" he yelped.

"I said she needed to focus on the pregnancy and that we'd support her any way we could, and we'd help her to find a good therapist. I had no choice, Alexander. She was in denial about her anorexia."

"No, she wasn't anorexic," he said crossly. "She was doing her best to be healthy, that's all. She was eating crackers and soup instead of fast food. Sometimes when she'd been working out more than usual, she ate a whole salad."

Bill and I exchanged looks. Alexander was in denial too by the sounds of it. I wondered how he'd ever found Emma attractive in the first place but I daresay the boys are affected by all this 'heroin-chic' bunkum as much as the girls are.

"Thank you so much for coming over to tell us," I said to Emma's parents, after we'd just had the longest cup of tea in history. I'll never forget the strangled gulps we all made as we sat around staring at my Gothic candlestick collection. Now I was fidgeting to get them out of the house so I could mull over my own thoughts in private. "We all hope she gets better soon."

"Can I visit her?" Alexander said as they were getting into their car.

It had begun to pour with rain and there was even a touch of thunder and lightning.

"I'm sorry, Alexander," said Emma's father sadly.

182

"Emma doesn't want to see anyone at the moment. She says she's too fat for visitors."

Fat?

Bill closed his eyes.

"Oh," Alexander said lamely. "I see. Well, tell her I said hello, won't you? And do tell her I love her more than anything in the world. And if she wants to get back with me, she can still live here in the drawing room as we planned. Mum and Dad won't mind. Will you?"

He looked at us with tears in his eyes. We both nodded enthusiastically.

"Thanks, Mum. Thanks, Dad."

Alexander looked so pleased. As if he was giving Emma the moon on a stick. With his parents' permission, too! As if our drawing room was the equivalent of a four-bed villa with sea views, and the sheer luxury of it all would bounce Emma clean out of her eating disorder.

Bill hung his head in shame. I knew what he was thinking: if it were him, he would have got the address of the clinic out of Emma's dad at knife-point, if need be. And gone straight over to London and got himself arrested, trying to break in.

"The thing is," Emma's father said, "the doctors don't want Emma to see anyone she cares about for the time being. She's channelling all her energy into telling lies, they say. And really, she ought to be given 'time out' to realise that telling lies to everyone about her food intake won't actually save her from starving to death. Neither will wearing baggy shirts or drinking lots of water before she's weighed."

I could have told them all that months ago. I was out a fortune on bottled water when Emma and Alexander first got together. Emma wouldn't drink tap water in our house in case it was contaminated with chemicals or even worse, sugar. The rain was coming down in sheets by this stage so Bill dragged Alexander and me back to the house. We stood in the doorway and waved Emma's parents off like it had all been a jolly-old, happy-old, ordinary visit.

"Cheerio and drive carefully! By-eee!"

I tidied away cups and saucers and wiped crumbs off my nice blue butler's tray, far too upset to cry or give out to anyone. Wishing with all my heart I hadn't got our old cot down from the attic and cleaned it up a few weeks earlier. Maybe I'd cursed the pregnancy by preparing the cot in advance, I thought to myself. Like the wicked fairy in one of those hackneyed old storybooks they keep printing because the copyright ran out centuries ago. But I didn't say anything to Bill about my superstitions. He would have thought I was crazy. After all, he is a 'no-silly-nonsense' Protestant.

Alexander was flat-lining with depression that night and, strangely enough, so was Bill. He wept and wept for hours in our ivory bedroom and said it was all his fault for not being more supportive at the time. If only he'd bought the mini-kitchen and the compact bathroom sooner, Emma might have calmed down a bit, Bill said. If only we'd all left her alone and not watched every mouthful of food she ate, he fretted. I told him it was inevitable Emma would lose the baby when she wasn't eating properly and it was a miracle she ever got pregnant in the first place.

"There was nothing we could have done to help her," I said sadly. "You can't command a person to stop thinking they're fat when their ribs are sticking out like plates. Can you? It's just not going to work. I don't know why I even bothered trying to talk to her in the university canteen that day. She should have had professional help a long time ago, darling, and at least now she's in a safe place and hopefully she can start to make some progress."

"Do you think the pregnancy would have made her even weaker?" said Bill.

"I really don't know. I expect it would have been very tiring."

And so on. But the truth was, the baby was gone and Emma might soon be going the same way herself. And for what? Fashion? So she could fit into a pair of jeans designed for a seven-year-old child? God almighty, it's pathetic. What sort of an achievement is that, for heaven's sake? Is it really the so-called fashionistas that are to blame for this nightmare trend? Or was Emma just depressed and stressed out with life in general? And she'd channelled her anxiety into food issues when really it could have been anything. OCD, shoplifting, alcohol, premium-rate psychic chatlines? God be with the days when all you had to do was scrape a couple of 'C' grades in your A-levels and fill in the entrance form for Manchester Polytechnic. And remember to line your stomach with a lamb kebab before downing seven pints of cider in the Students' Union. I mean, we had stress back then too, but there was more of a feeling of camaraderie. You know, more 'power to the people'? Now, everything has become so disjointed.

Bill and I climbed into bed and he laid his head on my chest and cried until he fell asleep. It's quite alarming when a man cries, isn't it? I mean, really lets rip and sobs his heart out? Women can go psycho every day of the week and nobody bats an eyelid. We're all used to it. But grown men gasping for breath between racking great wails? No way. We're not used to seeing our menfolk displaying raw grief in this country. I kept telling Bill everything would be all right but we both knew I was bluffing. I massaged his lovely, dome-shaped head and his shoulders too and after a while he calmed down and drifted off. I lay awake for hours though, with a worrying sensation in my heart as if it might stop beating if I stopped concentrating on it. Eventually, as the dawn was filtering through the bedroom curtains I fell asleep too.

Alexander went to our family GP for anti-depressants a day or two later but the doctor told him his depression was reactionary, not clinical, and that time would heal him instead. Wise words from the good doctor but unfortunately Alexander decided he'd had enough stress for the time being. There was a bout of work experience coming up and he said he just couldn't face it. He dropped out of university the following week, saying what was the point in designing beautiful buildings when the world was so messed-up and horrible? Bill told him that was okay. Alexander could give up his architecture degree if he wanted but would he mind going along on a plumbing job now and then to help out? It was Bill's way of reaching out to his eldest son, I suppose. And so began Alexander's apprenticeship as a plumber.

Grimsdale & Son.

It has a nice ring to it, don't you think?

13

Rock Chicks & Vampires

SO WHILE ALEXANDER WAS FIGHTING OFF BLACK despair and Alicia-Rose was making her plans to fly the nest, what was Julie doing? Well, you might ask! She was diligently nursing Gary in the farmhouse each evening, working mornings in the lighthouse with me and spending her afternoons asleep in a multiple orgasm-induced coma at her all-mod-cons apartment in Saintfield. She and Jay were completely obsessed with one another by then.

"We did it standing up in Castle Court shopping centre yesterday afternoon," she told me one day, carefully unwrapping a cinnamon bagel.

"Did you?" I said. "Was Jay overcome with lust in La Senza?"

"Yeah, he was, actually. How did you know? In the car- park, it was. In a darkened corner on the fourth floor. There was no-one about and we just thought, why not?" They'd only gone in to buy a new duvet.

"We're just like you and your Bill when you first got together," she kept saying.

Like it was a competition or something.

"Maybe you are," I said, thinking, *if* we'd had a luxury shag-pad of our own back then. Which we hadn't, sadly. I didn't see Bill naked until we were already married and living in that little terrace on the Ormeau Road. I was eight months pregnant. I remember it like it was yesterday.

However.

Whereas previously Julie had always spared me the gory details of her love life, saving them for The Coven, she now became quite vocal concerning her affair with Jay O'Hanlon even though I didn't say or do anything to encourage her. She was determined, it seemed, to tell me everything. For example, in the middle of lunch or when we were on a buying-trip, she would just drop a saucy detail into the conversation. And then study my face to see what my reaction was. I think she was trying to shock me. It's not like she had anything to prove. I mean, I knew from the start she was a woman of the world and I didn't care one way or the other. There's worse things you can be than a lady of a certain age who's lived and loved and can tell you a few tales about it. But Julie seemed to think it was important I knew what she was up to.

"Very nice touch," I said, nodding my head, when she told me he'd covered her nipples in melted chocolate and eaten it all off again when it'd dried. Or, "Did he really? How interesting," over the revelation he'd once left her tied to the bed (both ankles and wrists) while he nipped to the nearest pub for a pint of Guinness. I mean, what would've happened if there'd been a fire in the apartment? Or a burglar? Or if Jay'd been knocked down and killed on the way back? She might have starved to death on her own luxury mattress. But I'd go on sprinkling salt on my soup or whatever and say nothing about the risks she was taking. And Julie would smile back at me like we were two crazy chicks sharing some wild adventure.

They spent hours lying in the outsize bath together drinking ice-cold champagne, she told me. Listening to The Strokes, Jay's favourite band. Kissing softly under the shower spray, sleeping naked on the fluffy rug in the sitting room with the gas fire keeping them warm, feeding each other chocolate ice cream and fresh strawberries, or salty fish and chips. Watching saucy films together in bed. Taking photographs of each other in various states of undress, various states of bondage. Their best effort was a shot of Julie lying topless on the bed, her wrists tied with a polka-dot silk scarf and Jay's antique sword laid across her throat.

Utopia, really.

"This isn't a Hollywood movie, Julie," I said occasionally. When I forgot I was pretending I didn't care what she got up to with Jay.

"Yes, it is, Mags," she'd say. "It's better."

"Don't you feel guilty *at all* about the way you're treating Gary?" I asked her once. And only once. Remember this was Julie Sultana I was dealing with.

"No, Mags," she said. "It's only a bit of fun, kiddo. Lighten up."

"But don't you worry Gary will find out about Jay and your secret apartment?"

"No, why would he? Gary thinks I'm at work all day. And Jay rarely leaves the building."

"But you said you were black and blue from falling out of the shower last week."

(Jay had squirted an entire bottle of luxury shower gel over Julie's wet skin and when he grabbed her, she went shooting out of the shower like a torpedo.)

"Gary never sees me naked these days," she said. "We can't canoodle yet because his leg is so tender, still. And I don't undress in front of him because that would be teasing."

"Oh, that's all right then," I sighed.

Well, you've got to admire the woman's logic. I remember thinking to myself, men have been getting away with this kind of thing for centuries. Tasty bit on the side, tucked away in some cosy love nest on the outskirts. Someone interesting enough to chat to after sex but not smart enough to know they're being taken for a ride. And now Julie was doing it too. Except I felt her affair with Jay was somehow unworthy of her. Simple as that. She's a very clever woman, is Julie, and she was only wasting her many talents ducking and diving between her two lovers. It wasn't as if she was the one in control, it seemed to me. She was trying to please both of them, in a way. Being the brazen love siren Jay expected her to be, doing the splits on a glass coffee table in the afternoon. Then running home to Gary afterwards with a basket full of food shopping and Get Well wishes. Cooking pies for him and plumping cushions for his sore leg. I thought it was all a bit degrading. But then she *had* given me the chance to break it off with Gary and I hadn't taken it.

Still, Julie seemed happy and that was the main thing.

Meanwhile I had given up crying in the family bathroom and was feeling strangely calm. I think I finally understood Bill's life-long theory that tears are a waste of energy and that emergencies require meticulous planning instead of pointless tantrums. I didn't remind him of the night he'd cried until three in the morning about Emma's lost baby. He was trying to block it out of his mind and, to be honest, so was I.

We were also trying to convince ourselves that our beloved only daughter Alicia-Rose wasn't really going to leave us for a year and go to Australia. We told each other she would back out at the last minute and say she'd changed her mind. After all, we said, how could she leave her palest pink bedroom with the dinky bathroom hidden behind silver shutters, and the white curly iron bedstead with the yellow fairy lights draped above it. And most of all, how could she ever leave my 5-star laundry service and home-cooked dinners every night of the week? And so, each time she brought home another funky bikini or pair of trendy flip-flops, we cooed over her latest purchase and said how lovely she would look on the beach. We never thought for one second she would actually get on the plane and fly away.

But she did.

Halfway through September she calmly bought her ticket and traveller's cheques and off she went. Waving goodbye to her felt like an out-of-body experience. Bill and I just about managed to hold it together in the airport until she was safely through the Departures gate. Then we limped out to the car and Bill sat silent for half an hour while I kept saying, "Did she really board the plane, Bill? I can't believe it. Should we go back inside and check that she actually did board the plane? I mean, she might be sitting in there, afraid to come home and tell us she bottled out? I can't believe it. I can't believe it, Bill. I just can't *believe* it."

And so on.

While Bill told me to hush, and that he'd drive home in a minute when his hands had stopped shaking and sweating so much they slid off the steering wheel. In the end, we sat there for three hours listening to Radio 1 with our mouths open. Then we went back into the airport terminus and asked after our beautiful daughter at the information desk. But there was no sign of her. Yes, she had been on the flight. Yes, it had set off on time with no problems or delays. Our Alicia-Rose had grown up and left us and we were both in a profound state of shock for several days. I tried drinking a few nightcaps of gin and tonic to block out the pain but it didn't work. I just woke up in the middle of the night with a raging hangover and murderous abdominal cramps. So much for lapsing into a lovely alcoholic oblivion, I thought sadly. Clearly, my adult metabolism had moved on from the Pernod-and-chips diet of my youth. A future of stone-cold sobriety stared me in the face and there was no escape from my stomach-churning sense of loss. I didn't like it one bit.

I went into Alicia-Rose's bedroom once and switched on her bedside lamp for a few minutes, knelt down by the side of her bed and said a prayer for her safety. Bill saw me kneeling there and he didn't even laugh. That's how serious it was.

"Say one for me while you're at it," he said gently and I just nodded. It was around that time I started going back to church. Not to attend Sunday service, no. I don't really like kneeling in crowds, I must say. A bit claustrophobic. It's years since I've been to Mass (apart from weddings and funerals) because I prefer to pray in private. But in the quiet times between services I would go in, sit at the back of the church and think about things in general for half an hour or so. Maybe light a candle occasionally if there was nobody else about to see me. And I thought, maybe if I'm sitting here, God will give me a little feeling of reassurance, he'll let me know that Alicia-Rose and Emma and everyone is going to be all right. Well, I said to myself, there must be more to life than just getting by? There must be some point to all of this struggle and heartbreak and pain and love and loss? Why do I love Bill and my children so much if all we are is a bunch of living things competing with one another for food and shelter? And though it absolutely kills me to admit this, I enjoyed the atmosphere in the church. It's an old one, very Gothic in style, lovely stained-glass windows. Shafts of coloured light streaming down onto the long wooden benches when the sun came out. So even though I've seen *The Da Vinci Code* and I'm a fervent supporter of birth control being made freely available in developing countries and all that liberal stuff (and by the way, where did they raise the money for all these fabulously beautiful churches in Ireland in the seventeenth century when so many of the people were dying of hunger?), I decided to put my commonsense head away for a few minutes each week. And just concentrate on being spiritual and praying for Alicia-Rose out in Australia with the poisonous spiders and the crocodiles and the blistering sunshine. I mean, you worry about your children all the time anyway but somehow the fear is a lot worse when your precious child is on the other side of the world. I even knelt to pray at the ridiculous outdoor grotto dedicated to Saint Bernadette which is something I always swore I would never do. And I'd even told Bill that if he ever caught me doing it, even caught me looking sideways at that neon-painted grotto, he was to shoot me. Or failing that, take me to the Royal Victoria Hospital for an urgent brain scan.

What can I say?

It was a difficult period in my life.

I was lonely.

There, I've said it.

I had a full and busy life with a full-time job and a husband to love and four children to worry about and I was still lonely. Bill was busy training Alexander to be a plumber and teaching him to drive because you can't be a plumber if you can't drive yourself to call-outs. So he didn't phone me during the day any more, like he used to. And Julie was busy telling lies to Gary on a full-time basis and spending every minute she could merrily mounting and dismounting the bold Jay O'Hanlon. He was insatiable, she told me. He never got tired. Well, I thought, how would he? He has all day to lie about, relaxing and showering and resting-up his mighty doo-da at Julie's expense. Ten minutes after a frantic 'wreck-the-flat' bout of sweaty animal-sex, she said, he was ready to begin again. She was chuffed with herself for teaming up with such a devoted stud. Even when Jay got her name tattooed on his arm one day (incidentally in the same parlour I'd gone to though I hadn't told Julie about it yet) she thought it was all some kind of major joke. She laughed and laughed at the fact her name was written in black ink on a barman's arm. I took Jay's tattoo as an alarm bell, though. A red flag of warning but Julie didn't flinch. I mean, tattoos are pretty permanent, aren't they?

"He can get it covered over when we split up," she said casually, tucking into a ready-made pasta salad from Marks, one lunchtime in the lighthouse.

I was munching my favourite snack, their sour cream pretzels. I have no idea how much money Julie and me have spent in that store over the years. An absolute fortune no doubt but it was worth every penny. Sometimes, it's only the promise of a lemon drizzle cake or a stone-baked pizza that stops you from signing yourself in somewhere.

Anyway.

"He can have it disguised with leaves or roses or something when we go our separate ways. Keep your wig on, Mags. Honestly, he's such a nutcase!"

As if being a nutcase was a good thing.

I wondered if Julie was subconsciously falling for Jay

because he was so 'off-the-wall'. Because she'd been brought up by a couple of 'eccentrics' and that's why it felt so normal for her to be with Jay. I mean, he didn't work at all and he didn't go out of the flat much and he rarely got dressed. But then again neither did Julie's mother when she decided to drop out of the real world for ten years.

I was sure it was only a matter of time before Gary was up and about again and then he'd find out about Jay, and the whole thing would end in tears. Belfast is a very small town. There are no secrets here. But unfortunately, that means if you *do* grass somebody up there's nowhere to hide. So we generally keep our mouths shut. Therefore I was pretty sure nobody would actually *tell* Gary that Julie was doing the dirty on him. But he was bound to clock them himself in a café or bar or just sitting at the traffic lights somewhere. I worried about it more than she did but even I didn't think Julie Sultana's toy-boy tryst would end up in a shocking outburst of violence in the Café Vaudeville! Oh well, as Julie said during our little stint in A&E at the City Hospital (which made a pleasant change from the Royal Victoria), nobody could possibly accuse her of being dull and boring. She was a lot of things but she wasn't dull and boring. Every cloud.

We'll get to the Café Vaudeville incident in a little while.

October arrived and the nights began to draw in.

And then we got our biggest commission of all time. The people from Dublin turned up again at the lighthouse. Poor Gary, he'd been so distracted the day he called to take me out for lunch, he hadn't recognised them. It turned out the guy was a major rock star and I do mean *major*. He was a fully paid-up, by-the-book, larger-than-life, eyeliner-and-platform-heels American rock star who was living in Ireland for a while. Enjoying the good life on his country estate in County Kildare. Or until the novelty of being off heroin wore thin, at any rate. His doe-eyed girlfriend was a top French model, about ten inches taller and four stone lighter than he was. Your classic 'bucket and spade' combination. And they wanted to use a wedding planner that none of their friends or acquaintances had used before. So they'd chosen us from the *Yellow Pages* and all I can say is, thank goodness Julie happened to be at work that day because I would've passed out on the stairs if she hadn't. It's not that I get star-struck, not really. I just think most celebrities come from another planet. It's kind of hard to relate to a person who goes to the corner-shop for caviar and crackers in their own helicopter. Well, maybe not the corner-shop but you know what I mean. And it's impossible to know what to say to them. You can't exactly waffle on about the price of home-heating oil, can you? When they own an island in the Caribbean. Now I come to think of it, if it wasn't for celebrity gossip, what would we even talk about with one another? You know, I must be getting older or something but I'm beginning to think Peter Andre seems like a lovely person. I don't even mind his perma-tan.

Julie was magnificent, the way she handled those multi-millionaire cooler-than-cool dudes. She didn't bat an eyelash throughout the entire meeting. It was amazing. Me? I had three hot flushes, my mind went blank twice and I almost said *fuck me* when the rock star described his budget. Not because I fancied him, no, dear. But because I was totally stunned by his extravagance. A heck of a lot more than it cost Bill and myself for a civil wedding and two beanburgers in 1985, I'll tell you that! I can't reveal their names because we had to sign a secrecy clause. But I'm sure you can guess who I'm talking about. The photographs were already promised to a glossy magazine and none of the guests was going to be allowed to take a camera into the venue. It was so secret we had to arrange the entire thing without any of the guests finding out there was even going to be a wedding (until about 24 hours beforehand), never mind the tabloid press getting tipped off. Heavens, no. They would have ruined everything by hovering above the ceremony in some light aircraft and whipping up a sandstorm. Well, a gravel-and-cigarettes storm, maybe? However, I can tell you some of the details.

They wanted their wedding ceremony to be held in the grounds of a ruined Irish castle, and the reception in a luxury marquee which would be erected nearby. What ruined castle exactly, we didn't establish on our first meeting. Somewhere remote enough to be considered terribly private and exclusive but not so remote the guests couldn't actually find it. Right away, I knew there'd be a muddy swamp of regulations to wade through – some of our by-laws date back to the Stone Age. Ditto, a good few of the local council die-hards. Still, I hoped they'd be so besotted with the idea of a celebrity wedding taking place in their backyard, they might be prepared to compromise a little on the details. Money talks, isn't it the truth?

The marriage ceremony itself? Well, they fancied something whimsical and poetic specially composed just for them. And for the wedding to be co-celebrated by a Pagan Druid in full regalia and an open-minded magistrate who didn't mind being upstaged by a Pagan Druid. Again, a little money would probably go a long way towards easing any misgivings the magistrate might have, we decided. Wondering to ourselves, who do we know needs a new roof on their local community centre and do they happen to have a ruined castle nearby? You know how it is when you're working backwards? Oh dear, now this kooky little arrangement could lead to all sorts of problems, I thought to myself. But of course I smiled politely and so did Julie, as if we get Druids and open-minded magistrates traipsing in and out of the lighthouse on a regular basis.

I knew the papers would have a field day whipping up fears of a Pagan Revival and condemning the worship of false gods and all manner of jiggery-pokery. No doubt, we'd be invited onto UTV Live and asked to explain ourselves to some fire-and-brimstone religious minister. I'm sure Julie was relishing the prospect of so much free advertising for Dream Weddings but I (being the practical one) feared the loss of our more conservative clients. And they do tend to be the ones with the healthiest bank balances.

Needless to say, the rock star and his French-model

SHARON OWENS

girlfriend didn't have to worry about any of that. Their main concern was making sure they had enough room for their entourage near the altar. Apparently, they couldn't get married without five personal assistants, three make-up artists, two hair-stylists, one fashion-designer, one nutritionist, four pet-minders and a lighting-expert from Norway within hand's reach. (They'd hired the Norwegian themselves because they knew it gets pretty dark in Ireland when the clouds roll in, thus requiring a lighting-expert from a Nordic background.)

Things went from bad to worse after that. The loved-up lovebirds mistook our politeness to indicate that NI was a happening sort of place where anything was possible. Next up on the agenda, the guest list. Brace yourself, ladies and gentlemen! There were exactly 666 guests on the list. The happy couple had to plunder their old phone books to scrape together the last few dozen, and distant relatives were going to be flying in from the four corners of the globe. But the final tally was 666 and they'd even invited a few diehard fans to make up the numbers if any of the relatives got lost en route to the ruined castle. Now, don't worry, this devilish number had no real significance other than to impress the rocker's fellow musicians and full-time hellraisers. That's what he told us anyway. But still, I knew there'd be a bit of a ruckus when the press found out. Especially if it'd been a slow week for real news stories.

I'm sure you're getting the general idea by now, of where this wedding was going. And you'd be right. It was 'Halloween Meets Bling' on a grand scale. The wedding cake? Oh, yes. The bride-to-be wanted her wedding cake to stand five feet tall and take the form of a haunted mansion. Complete with twisty-pointy turrets, overhanging balconies, iron railings on the overhanging balconies, trailing ivy on the iron railings on the overhanging balconies. Actual electric lights in the windows if it could be arranged. She said she had always, always, *always* wanted such a wedding cake. All her life, it was "all she had ever dreamed of". Well, you need to get out more, my dear, I thought to myself. Even though I have a solid stone gargoyle in my front room and a rather big collection of giant candlesticks. But, at least I don't make a song and dance about my fetishes, I keep them to myself. I was slightly puzzled at the model's request for a haunted-mansion cake because she didn't seem to be into serious rock music but I suppose she wanted to impress her husband-to-be. And it was his money paying the bill so we said we'd do our best to find a baker who'd be willing to try. I had serious doubts we'd find a local baker, though. I said I'd find out how much it would cost to have a top chef kidnapped in Paris, flown to this country and forced to bake a haunted-mansion cake at gunpoint. And I was only half-joking.

The meeting wore on and the requests got sillier. The groom-to-be fancied a red velvet frock coat with skulls embroidered on it and a red silk top hat to go with it. We didn't envisage any huge problems there as Ireland is coming down with fashion designers since the Celtic Tiger woke up and began to roar. But could they make top hats, I wondered. Julie saw the shadow of doubt flicker across my eyes and inclined her head at me to say nothing. So I didn't. I measured the guy's head circumference and told him his aftershave was lovely. Shame about the halitosis but then sustained drug-use can really bugger up your molars, so I've heard.

The bats! Oh, I nearly forgot to tell you about the bats. The groom-to-be also thought it would be nice to have real live bats released at dusk, just before the dancing and the serious boozing got under way. Julie and I exchanged glances at that one. There was no way the government, either north or south of the border, was going to allow such an infringement of animal rights but we said nothing. We knew we'd come up with some less-controversial alternative and convince him it was fabulous and groovy when the time came. We discussed staging the ruins with lights and props. At one point I just knew Julie was about to volunteer the loan of my stone gargoyle but I interrupted her by offering tea or coffee or indeed a glass of champagne to our guests. I couldn't take the risk of the pair of them or someone in their hefty entourage making off with my most prized possession at the end of the day. Which seems laughable now in the light of what actually happened but life is like that, isn't it? Full of surprises, is life.

Back to the doe-eyed bride: she wanted a fireworks display as night fell. Obviously not too close to the bats being deployed, for obvious humanitarian reasons. Although it would have been rather hilarious to release thousands of fluttery little bats over the heads of the crowd and then disorientate the bejaysus out of all of them with a few tons of gunpowder. Worth a clip on *You've Been Framed*, I imagine. Oh God. So yes, she wanted red, white and blue fireworks to symbolise both her native France and her beloved's home country, the USA. That seemed okay with us although again we said we would have to consult ancient rules and regulations regarding local council etiquette and we weren't exactly sure how much a bespoke fireworks display would cost. I didn't think we'd be allowed to make a lot of noise near birds and wildlife but of course we didn't mention anything awkward at the time. That's why we get paid a lot of money, Julie and me. Because we do all the boring stuff like making endless phone calls to reference libraries and police stations. And flattering stuffy old town mayors and vacuuming up any stray confetti before the next wedding begins.

My head was splitting by this stage and we hadn't even touched on the catering. Julie knows some top chefs specialising in mini-bowls of Irish stew and best Irish seafood platters but of course it wasn't going to be that easy, was it? Oh no. Our happy couple wanted to go all New Age and forward-looking. Or at least, that was the image they wanted to project to the rest of the world. The menu was to be entirely vegetarian if not vegan. Julie looked at me when the two of them began a short sermon on vegetarianism. Julie can't abide veggie sermons, she loves a nice fillet steak cooked rare. But we said it was a super idea and we'd look into pricing a top vegetarian chef right away. I joked about kidnapping another chef from Paris but nobody laughed. It's a serious business, getting married nowadays. Slight problem with the food: vegetarian cuisine in this neck of the woods seems to consist of a few strips of soggy aubergine, deep-fat fried and served on a bed of under-cooked brown lentils. Yuck! We'd really have our work cut out to find a decent chef willing to work in the open air.

"Leave it with us," Julie purred, fluttering her eyelashes at the rock-star and admiring his girlfriend's enormous pink rocks.

And that's not a euphemism. There were three pink diamonds the size of golf-balls on her engagement ring. It occurred to me then, and not for the first time, if it wouldn't be easier to get myself a part-time job in our local chippy. Or even open a chippy of my own? The prices they charge, I'd be a millionaire in six months. But of course, I'd never do that. I must admit, I do enjoy my work most of the time, there's always something exciting going on. Today is just a blip, I told myself. A little bit over-the-top and ridiculous but surely as the preparations progressed, some of the more outlandish requests could be downsized or dropped altogether? I mean, I couldn't help wondering if this media-circus was going to damage the general image of getting married. I hoped the whole thing could be shoehorned into something more tasteful as the months went by. Well, no harm in hoping.

Next up, the invitations! Pop-up invitations, to be exact. To be hand-made, naturally. A little paper vampire was to leap out of the card, they said, complete with a red-lined paper cape and fangs dripping paper blood. Nice. There'd be lots of information on the back of the invites, too. The guests were to be told of the secrecy surrounding the location, the no-cameras rule and the *dress code*. Here we go, I thought. This will be good. And it was. The dress code for the wedding of the century was to be Rock Chicks & Vampires. And no exceptions were to be made, not even for the guests who were knocking on a bit. Or the forty-three relatives of the happy couple who were bona fide pensioners already.

Julie laughed her head off and said they were the wildest pair she'd ever met in her life, which cheered them up no end. I wondered how much dosh they were getting from selling the photographs. But still, there's an awful lot of unhappiness in the world, I said to myself and at least this 'wacky' wedding will give the readers something to talk about. So, yes, Julie said we'd have some spare Vampire & Rock Chick costumes made up and stored in the marquee in case any of the guests didn't get round to renting or making their own. I had an upsetting vision of some old dears staggering across the lawn of an ancient castle wearing fishnet stockings and satin bustiers but luckily our clients didn't see me making a face. Another potential *You've Been Framed* moment, I think you'll agree: when the cloaked-up grannies and granddads went wading into a bunch of fresh cowpats. Note to self! I made a mental note to get the 'house-keeping' staff to remove any cowpats and wash down the grass well before the wedding began.

Thankfully, we were almost at the end of the meeting by this point.

Last up on the agenda: the goody bags. Our clients

said they said they wanted to give out the 'coolest freakin' gift bags in the entire world' at the end of the night. Well, that was no problem for our Julie. She was probably born clutching a goody bag, she told them. She had dozens of ideas for Rock Chick & Vampire gift bags, as it transpired. Vouchers for designer lingerie from Josephine's boutique in the city centre. Lucky old Josephine, she always does well out of Dream Weddings. By the way, Josephine offers a mail-order service for the really hot stuff so customers can buy all the gear they want without having to ask for it face-to-face. So Julie said she would pop a brochure and a voucher into every bag, for starters. Then there'd be lots of other lovely things. Red scented candles, toffee apples bearing the date of the wedding, black leather mobile phone covers. Pots of scented face-and-body glitter, silver fountain pens and bottles of black ink. Semi-precious skull cufflinks, strawberry-centre truffles in a black cardboard box, mini-bottles of pink champagne. Letter-openers shaped like daggers. The list was endless. So was the string of zeros on the end of the rock-star's budget. Each individual goody bag (and remember there were 666 invited guests) was going to be worth £200 alone. That's £133,200 on goody bags, I told them, whipping out the office calculator. Our man didn't look surprised in the least. In fact, he looked thoughtful for a moment and then said, make it £300 as he didn't want to look cheap. £200K on gifts, well, that's an awful lot of money, isn't it?

Rock & Roll, babe.

His words, not mine.

I had to excuse myself and stagger up to the kitchenette for a glass of water when I heard how much moola they'd set aside to pay for this 'for-the-glossies' wedding. I daresay the magazine was going to finance most of it. And it wouldn't do either of their careers any harm. But still, the sheer scale of the event was very daunting to me. The expense of it all, the organisation involved. Keeping the media at bay but still interested, the countless health and safety restrictions we'd have to get round. But Julie carried on like we get this sort of brief every day of the week. I was very impressed with Julie in spite of my various doubts and misgivings about her relationship with Jay. For a while in that meeting, she was the same old Julie I'd grown so fond of. Her 'I can do anything' attitude was an inspiration.

The rock star and his lovely lady refused our offer of coffee and pastries when the meeting was over. They were just on their way to the airport, as it happened. Fashion show in Milan, they said. Julie air-kissed them both several times and said she had so many ideas she didn't know where to start. They handed over the cheque and we all swapped contact numbers. I saw them safely down the lighthouse stairs and waved them off in their blacked-out limousine. When I got back up to the office, Julie was casually checking her make-up before going to visit Jay.

"Start making preliminary calls, Mags," she said slowly, crayoning on red lipstick. "But don't confirm anything until I okay it. Right? I'm just nipping out for a couple of hours. And if Gary phones tell him I'm having my nails done. He'd never dream of ringing the salon."

Julie's second home, the salon. It's called The Beauty Spot.

Lovely little place.

"Actually, Jay quite fancies me having a Brazilian wax. Or a Hollywood, isn't he outrageous? You know, I might just pop into The Beauty Spot on my way to Saintfield and see if they can fit me in. Hope it doesn't hurt too much!"

And off she went skipping down the steps of the lighthouse, singing some sugary pop tune and happily swinging her big white handbag with the heavy bunch of glass and silver charms attached. There was no point reasoning with her so I didn't bother. I just sighed heavily, made a pot of tea in the kitchenette and prepared for a strange afternoon researching fantasy cake design, the collecting and releasing of live bats (bound to be a law against the releasing of live bats for fun, I thought), red velvet suits, health and safety issues regarding ancient ruins and the hiring of busloads of security staff. All of it very vexing. Particularly the security staff. We didn't want to go hiring the wrong sort who might cause more trouble than they were being hired to prevent. After two hours on the phone, I hadn't come up with an awful lot so I did three things. I took a taxi into town to lodge the massive cheque in the bank for safekeeping and I bought some emulsion paint and various things to fix up the office in the lighthouse. And I sent Emma a massive bouquet of pink and white roses with a nice message attached. Since we now knew where the clinic was. They said it would be helpful if Emma got some cards and letters each week.)

The message said how truly sorry I was about everything.

Really sorry for hurting Emma's feelings, and best wishes from all of us.

Well, I was sorry. I couldn't believe Emma was actually close to death that day in the lecture theatre and only weeks before I'd hated her so much, I wanted to shove her down the stairs for tormenting my Alexander into giving up his architecture degree. I hoped the clinic would let Emma keep the roses when they arrived because they were very expensive indeed. Gosh, but I'm very good at spending money. Once you get started and over the initial guilt it's very hard to stop. Then, fingers crossed, I went back to the lighthouse and set out my paint-roller and tray in the office. I'm very quick at painting walls: years of practice, I suppose. I fervently hoped Julie wouldn't land back to work when I was only halfway through and be cross with me for wasting time. But then I remembered her Brazilian/ Hollywood surprise for Jay and I knew she'd be fully occupied for the rest of the day.

As it were.

It's so good for taking your mind off your worries, painting walls with a gentle shade of chocolate. If you take it nice and slowly and really concentrate on getting the edges crisp and clean, you can *almost* forget your only daughter is in Australia and your boss is making a fool of herself with a younger man. Just before the shops closed, I nipped into town once more for some new light-bulbs and a few decorative sachets of cinnamon and mixed spice. And then home to pick up our old sofa-bed. By the time Julie did show up at the lighthouse the following afternoon, the office had been completely transformed. The walls were a luxurious pale chocolate colour and there was a matching rug on the floor. The desks had been placed closer to the window and there was a big tasselly lamp standing on each of them. Lovely boudoir lamps with feathers and beads round the edges of the shade. And the bases were made of mottled brown glass. I'd brought in some dried grasses and twigs, and pots from home to fill up the empty spaces and there was a length of cream muslin wrapped round a small pole above the window. A big bunch of fake white lilies stood in a tall glass vase by the door and our small sofa-bed (it was fine with a cream throw over it) was squeezed in too, for good measure. Luckily it's very light and comes apart easily so I was able to trail it up the stairs in three pieces. There were comfy beige velvet cushions on the office chairs and a small gold starburst mirror on the wall. It was thoroughly gorgeous, I have to say: very sophisticated and comfortable. The acoustics were softened, too. My voice on the telephone even sounded different, more sexy and authoritative somehow. There was enough paint left over to give the kitchenette a coat of Truffle Delight and I also put a bunch of twigs in there, on the counter beside the kettle and mugs. Oh, it was so much nicer than before, I can't tell you. And with the cinnamon sachets dotted round the room, it smelled lovely as well. I dared Julie to say it wasn't gorgeous and she didn't disappoint me.

"It's *gorgeous*, Mags," she said, taking it all in. "Really it is. Absolutely gorgeous. You *have* been busy, thanks very much. The clients will love this, I suppose we should have done it years ago."

"Oh great! Ta, Julie! You're not just saying that to humour me?"

"No, I love it. It's very cosy. I've been spending a lot more time at my flat than before and all-white is a bit tiring on the retinas, I'll be honest with you."

She did look exhausted.

"What is it, Julie?" I said then. "Has Jay done a bunk with your DVD-player?"

I can't resist saying that word – DVD-player. It's about the only gadget I can remember the name of.

"No, Jay has not done a bunk with anything," Julie said crossly. "Why would you say something nasty and mean to me like that?"

"I'm sorry, Julie," I said at once. "I meant it to sound funny. What's the matter?"

"It's worse than Jay scarpering with the hi-fi, actually," she suddenly admitted, slumping heavily onto the sofa-bed and closing her eyes. I noticed she'd trowelled on the foundation that day, presumably to cover her under-eye shadows. "I think I could cope if Jay left me. I never thought he wouldn't leave me some day. But that bikini wax I had yesterday drove him clean wild. We didn't sleep once, not for a single minute. He was on his knees for hours. He said he loved me."

I was a bit shocked, both with the mental image this confession conjured up and also with Jay's insistence he was in love with Julie.

TMI, dear! I was trying not to get involved.

"I forgot to tell you, Julie, we're nearly out of envelopes," I said, interrupting her mid-flight. "Should I get onto our supplier and order some more? What about changing the shade to buff? That's very *in* right now. And it would go with our new interior. We could have business cards made up with a little picture of the office on them? You know, like the card you got from the spa in Galway?"

"Whatever you like! For heaven's sake, it's only stationery. Are you not listening to me, woman? Jay said he loved me, Mags. He must have said it a hundred times yesterday. He wants us, oh, you won't believe this but he wants us to get married. He knows I can't have children but he wants us to get married straightaway."

"Oh, Julie!"

"I mean, the age gap is silly and we've only known each other two minutes but Jay said he's found his soul mate. And that would be bad enough but so does Gary. I mean, Gary wants us to get married as soon as possible. All last night he was going on and on about the meaning of life, et cetera. He says he doesn't want a big expensive wedding now after the trauma of the car accident and all. And he forgives me for having a silly little flirtation in Galway. Thanks for telling him about that, Mags, by the way. Not! He says the car crash made him realise life is short and we should live every day as if it's going to be our last. He wants us to get married in a quiet ceremony and go away on an extended honeymoon as soon as we can arrange it. And until his leg is better he can't work with the horses anyway so what are we waiting for?"

"Oh, Julie."

"Is that all you can say? Advice please, Margaret! I have two men wanting to marry me and proposing to me on a daily basis. What should I do, Mags? I'm getting all confused and I'm never out of the shower these days, what with all the hanky-panky. My hands are shrivelled away to raisins, look!" She showed them to me. "What will I *do*? My engagement ring keeps falling off. Is that a sign I should leave Gary, do you think? I mean, I only stayed with him out of sympathy, and guilt. I mean, he only broke his leg because he was speeding down to Galway to rescue me from having an affair."

"Julie Sultana," I said carefully, "I have absolutely no idea what you should do. No idea at all. No idea *whatsoever*."

"Oh now, Margaret Grimsdale, don't be coy. You must have some opinion! You're the most opinionated person I've ever met in my entire life. You've often said you could set the world to rights if you were left in charge for just one day. So come on, advise me. Should I be clever and agree to marry sensible-head Gary and go straight out to Saintfield and finish with Jay today? Or should I leave Gary for good like I originally planned, and live with Jay in the apartment for a while and get to know him better? Or should I go completely mad and marry Jay and just see what happens? Although I'll make him sign a pre-nup first, of course. I'm quite a wealthy woman, you know. Or should I leave both of them and stay single for a while? You know, live a celibate existence? That's very zen right now. Get into meditation? Give my bits and pieces a chance to recover? I'm starting to chafe down below. How on earth do prozzies manage, I wonder? I suppose they go a bit numb after a while and the drink's bound to be a comfort?" And she made a face at me to show she was in considerable discomfort in the 'intimate feminine area' as they always describe it on advertisements for sanitary towels, tampons, panty-liners, moist wipes and so on.

God, I do wish they'd stop all this in-your-face 'bodily-function' advertising. And ban the babies' nappies and that silly blue water, while they're at it. Most upsetting to see ads that remind you of blood and urine (and the rest) when you're trying to relax of an evening. They irritate me, those ads. Which is why I probably spoke out-of-turn to Julie.

"Celibacy would be a tough call for you, Julie," I said quietly, thumping some keys on my computer. "Your nether regions might go into shock."

"What do you mean by that, you cheeky monkey? Are you implying I'm some sort of bad woman? Are you, Mags? You're not going all saintly on me, are you? Because I couldn't stand that, I'll tell you now. I'm not working with a moralistic bore. I couldn't bear it!"

"No, actually, I'm not a moralistic bore, Julie. You can do what you like with Gary and Jay. Introduce them to one another and have a threesome, if you fancy a change. It's a free country. Mind you, I don't think pre-nups are valid in the UK. Each case is tested on its own merits, so I believe. So you might want to make an appointment with a good solicitor before you run off and marry your toy boy. Just give me a bit of notice, will you? Because

I'm going to book myself two weeks' holiday on a desert island to get away from Gary Devine. He'll blame me for all of this, you know? For not telling him."

"Mags, are you cross with me?" Julie asked then, her lovely face creased with hurt and confusion. Maybe I'd been a bit too sharp with her, I decided, remembering Charlotte and Sidney's crazy antics many years before. "Have I done something to annoy you?"

"Now, Julie, you listen to me," I said kindly but firmly. "You're my best and dearest friend and I love you like a sister. More than a sister, actually. Because my sisters can be a bit touchy sometimes on the subject of marriage and children. And I can talk to you without worrying about saying the wrong thing every time. But I am not, repeat *not* getting emotionally involved in this situation with yourself and Jay O'Hanlon and Gary Devine. I've just buried my father and seen Alicia-Rose off to Australia, and my eldest son's girlfriend is in a psychiatric hospital at death's door from anorexia. And he's dropped out of a top course at university and is now spending his days putting toilets together, wearing Bill's old overalls. I'm missing my sisters like mad, and Bill and me are almost broke after forking out in advance for a stonking-great Celtic headstone complete with Gaelic engraving. Basically, I have more than enough to contend with at the moment and I'm worn out styling this blessed bob properly every morning because, if I don't style it, it looks like a wild hedge in a storm. So you do what you think is best regarding Gary and Jay but please, please, *please* don't ask me for advice. Because whatever I say

217

will be wrong, total rubbish, absolutely irrelevant and I'll get the blame if anything disastrous happens. All I'll say is this: we cannot legally release live bats at the wedding of the century. So I'm planning to commission some art students to make fake ones and we'll get some puppeteers to raise them up on invisible threads from a purpose-built platform, which will have to be concealed behind a round tower or whatever high wall we can find when we *eventually* select a venue. Okay?"

Meaning, when Julie stopped bunking off work to shag Jay O'Hanlon, and helped me for a change.

"So you're not going to give me any advice at all, then?"

"I'm sorry, Julie, but no, I'm not."

"Right," she said, flinging her handbag onto the desk. "Let's get down to business. If that's the way you want to play it! Double-check with our clients they don't mind having fake bats at their wedding, then give the students the go-ahead and make sure you get receipts for the materials, construction of the platform and the puppeteers' expenses. And do make sure you get planning permission for the platform before you do anything else. I'll go through these brochures again and settle on a venue today, right?"

"Right," I said. "You do that."

"Right," she said. "I will."

And a grim silence descended upon us.

14

Gary

I KNOW IT MAKES NO SENSE NOW IN THE COLD LIGHT OF day but as October and November drifted into December and the nights were getting long and icy and full of Christmas promise, I got rather used to Julie's 'juggling-two-set-of-balls' routine. Logic dictates it couldn't have gone on like that forever but sometimes living in a fantasy world of your own creation is a hell of a lot easier than being a grown-up. I treated Jay O'Hanlon like a sitcom on the telly. He was always *there* in the background but he wasn't really *real*, if you know what I mean? On a day-to-day basis work was running relatively smoothly. Julie was pulling her weight in the lighthouse (we were taking more wedding bookings than ever) and we hadn't had a single snag or complaint. She didn't tell me quite so many of the intimate details of her love life with Jay and I didn't ask her searching questions any more, like, where will it all end? I suppose we both became complacent.

I was expecting a full house for Christmas, what with the terrific news my two sisters would definitely be jetting in from Sydney for the holidays. They said they fancied spending a bit of time with me and the family, and that they hadn't had enough time to see us properly during the funeral and all. And thank God, Alicia-Rose was coming home too. I'd paid for her ticket with a second credit card Bill knew nothing about. Well, men do get a bee in their bonnet about personal debt, don't they? Whereas women know that some things are far more important than sky-high interest rates. Like seeing your beautiful daughter again and being able to put your arms round her and squeeze her like a cobra. And besides, I thought to myself, the way global warming is going I might not live long enough to have to pay the credit-card company back.

I'd bought a new luxury sofa-bed for the drawing room, for Ann and Elizabeth. And Bill had covered the shelves of video games with French shutters to make the space seem more homely. Emma was also being granted Christmas leave from the clinic and she'd surprised us all by writing to Alexander to ask if she could come to us for the holiday fortnight. She said she didn't want to go to her own home because her two sisters had three babies between them and she didn't want to be reminded of the miscarriage. Of course, Alexander was only too happy to have the chance to spend some time with Emma again. Though Bill did warn him not to get his hopes up, that Emma might just want to be friends with him this time. We decided she should have the guest room so she could have some space and privacy. (Which is why my sisters were going to be sleeping in the drawing room.) We made Emma's room as nice as we could, with a portable television and a small floral armchair and matching footstool. There was a pale blue patchwork throw on the bed, some novels and magazines in a wicker basket, and a cute little pink radio on the bedside cabinet. The room was also fully stocked with brand new towels and toiletries, and there were some pink paper tulips in a wire basket on the windowsill. I'd bought those tulips for my own bedroom but what can you do? I wanted Emma to feel at home after all the horrible things I'd said to her in the university.

The house was decorated from top to bottom with bunches of gold twigs in all the fireplaces, gold ribbons tied along the banisters, and some cheap plastic apples sprayed gold and displayed in a glass bowl on the dining-room table. We had a real tree in the hall, hung with Shaker-style angels and ceramic cookies we've had for years and years. They're quite tatty now but they still look very charming. I did it all on a non-existent budget but it was nice and homely, all the same. The secret of good decorating is to keep the house absolutely tidy at all times and have one unusual piece in every room. Not easy with a big family and no spare cash but still, my home was all I had to express myself with so I stayed up late most nights, dusting shelves and folding tea towels into baskets, and washing plates and cups that wouldn't fit into the dishwasher. I did end up losing a few pounds which was nice as I was able to fit into a good pinstripe

suit I hadn't worn for years. And even Bill was amazed
when my chunky ankles slimmed down a bit and you
could see the beginnings of a tendon (or whatever it's
called) sticking out the back. Trying to maintain the
façade of being middle class is a very tiring occupation,
that's the truth of it. Sometimes I wish I had the courage
to sport a greasy ponytail and a pink velour tracksuit and
just lie about the house eating multipack biscuits and
watching Jerry Springer being wise on the telly. But I
know I'd rather die trying to be genteel than go down
that particular road. By the looks of it, once things start to
slide it's very hard to get back on track. So I did my
Christmas shopping, albeit mostly in the one shop (book
tokens and leather-bound diaries: what a lifesaver for the
time-poor) and spent a blissful hour one night wrapping
them nicely in brown paper and attaching orange raffia
ribbons and pretty cardboard gift tags. Because you've
got to match your gift-wrapping to your Christmas tree
theme, haven't you? I have a big wicker hamper in the
hall where we store any glitzy-looking prezzies that don't
tie in with our simple Shaker theme. If the hamper is full,
I have a hessian sack with a Shaker angel printed on it, on
standby. Bill thinks it's hilarious but he goes along with it.

Then Julie took the notion of popping into the Café
Vaudeville for lunch with me on Christmas Eve just to
see what sort of Christmas atmosphere they'd managed to
rustle up. You know, to see how they could possibly
improve on the enormous red-glass chandeliers. I was
delighted to oblige her and as high as a kite anyway
because Alicia-Rose and my sisters were due in Arrivals at

5pm and Julie said she would drive me out there and pick them up in her white Mercedes. So off we went to the Café Vaudeville, plastered in glittery make-up and laughing fit to beat the band over nothing at all. We were sublimely happy. Which just goes to show, you never know what's round the corner. Because that's where it all went pear-shaped. As pear-shaped as a whole tree full of pears, never mind the partridge. Well, that's where it all *began* to go pear-shaped. There was much worse to come unfortunately but we didn't know it then.

Fools rush in where angels fear to tread.

I think I've said that before.

Ought to be Dream Weddings' new logo, I thought to myself later that afternoon in the cafeteria next to A&E. As we sat shivering over two watery teas. I said to Julie, I must have that saying printed on our new buff envelopes. She didn't see the funny side, I have to admit.

Jay was there, you see? Jay O'Hanlon, in the flesh. Barman and doo-da owner extra-ordinaire. Right there in the Café Vaudeville. Being interviewed for a job as, well, as barman. Which he'd applied for without telling Julie because he wanted to 'contribute to the relationship' and also because he feared he might become agoraphobic in the all-mod-cons apartment in Saintfield if he didn't start getting out more. He'd seen the job-ad in a free newspaper that gets delivered out Saintfield way, phoned for an interview, tidied himself up and caught a bus into the city centre. Which was all very admirable and enterprising, really. I mean, at least he wasn't intending to go on being a kept man forever.

So just seconds after Julie and me had admired the amazing Christmas decorations and ordered our starters, Jay came out strolling out of the office, spotted us and joined us on the sofa with the lovely draped canopy over it. It was kind of funny for me, seeing Jay with his clothes on. Up until then I'd only seen him in his gigolo-kecks but there he was in a black shirt and faded blue jeans and a pair of brand-new Converse sneakers. Dirty-blond hair nicely blow-dried and a couple of days' stubble on his chin. Looking all casual and sexy and gorgeous. He'd been offered the job on the spot and he wanted to celebrate by buying cocktails for the three of us. We shook his hand warmly and he sat down between us and put one arm round Julie's shoulders and the other arm on the back of the sofa behind me. I felt a shadow of concern flicker across my consciousness but I told myself there wasn't anyone who knew Julie in the Café Vaudeville that day. Anyway, like I said, I was counting the minutes till I saw my Alicia-Rose again so my danger-radar wasn't working at full strength. Julie snuggled into Jay and kissed his cheek and he kissed her hand and then they kissed properly for twenty minutes. Whispering sweet nothings and giggling like teenagers. I felt a right gooseberry but I ate my goat's cheese tartlet (Julie left hers untouched) and we ordered the salmon for mains. It was very nice, I must say. Jay didn't order any food for himself but Julie fed him little bits and pieces off her fork. They ate a few chips together, taking one end each in their mouths, and licked the salt off each other's lips when they got to the middle bit. If it hadn't been for the canopy hanging over our seat, I think they'd have been asked to leave the premises.

"Get a room, you two," I joked at one point. "You're making a show of me."

They apologised and made a great effort to be well-behaved but Jay started kissing Julie again the moment I went to the ladies' room to check my make-up after polishing off a giant lemon sorbet. Julie and Jay hadn't had dessert – they were too busy eating each other. But they had three more cocktails apiece even though I did warn them the cocktails at the Café Vaudeville are quite strong, but they took no heed. Unfortunately the alcohol made both of them a little bit randy and more than a little forgetful. According to Julie, (I was still in the powder room at this point) Jay slipped one hand under her white linen skirt and gave her a quick but fabulously tender and erotic little thrill. Which delighted Julie so much she forgot to be cross with him for leaving the flat in Saintfield without permission. Yes, it was an outrageous thing to have done in a public place but Julie said afterwards that the lights were turned down very low and as far as she knew, herself and Jay could not be seen by anybody on the ground floor. She'd forgotten completely about the VIP area because we never go up there. I don't even know to this day how you go about gaining access to the upper level. And I don't expect I'll ever find out now because I'm too embarrassed to darken the door these days.

However.

By the time I returned to our table Julie was slumped

against Jay's chest, half-asleep with a big grin on her face. The bar was warm and dark and full of the scent of Christmas dinner and brandy. Jay said something about Belfast not being nearly as bad as people he knew always made it out to be and that he could really see himself settling north of the border some day. I just smiled at him. Well, I was only two hours away from seeing my Alicia-Rose again and I could almost smell her coconut shampoo if I closed my eyes and wished hard enough. If Jay'd told me he was having a sex-change and entering an enclosed convent I would have thought it was a brilliant idea and given him my blessing. So there we were, the three of us. All content and pleased with ourselves, stuffed full of Christmas fare and listening to a selection of cheesy Christmas Number Ones on the in-house stereo.

A perfect day.

Well, nearly perfect.

It was just a pity that Gary Devine saw everything (and I do mean *everything*) from his upstairs table in the VIP area, to which he'd been invited by a corporate client. He could see right down the back of the canopy hanging over our table. And as soon as the shock of seeing his beloved girlfriend having sex with a stranger had worn off, he limped downstairs and shouldered his way through the crowds towards Julie, Jay and myself. And just stood looking down at us for what seemed like an eternity.

"I'm Gary Devine," he said quietly to Jay. "I'm Julie's long-term boyfriend and fiancé. Who the fuck are you?"

"Gary! Jesus! Listen, we can explain," I began, but it

was far too late for explanations. I still had no idea what Jay had just done to Julie under the table but anyway it was all desperately uncomfortable.

"You should have told me about Julie and this guy, Mags," Gary said sadly. "I thought you were better than this, I really did. Don't you ever speak to me again. I mean, *ever*."

And I knew by the low and despairing way he said it that he meant it.

I nodded my head and said nothing more. I didn't blame Gary one bit for hating me. I'd have felt the same in his shoes. It's all very well looking the other way when your friends have affairs but who's to blame when somebody gets heartbroken and humiliated or beaten to a pulp?

The atmosphere was awful. Gary was making painful gasping sounds. I think he was crying but I didn't want to glance up at him. I looked away and tried to think of a good excuse to leave the building. A bomb-scare would have been welcome at that point which is an absolutely evil and criminal thing to say but that just shows you how bad it was. However I sensed Julie didn't want me to abandon her there alone with the two of them. So for the sake of friendship I stayed where I was.

"Gary, we have to talk. It's about time we were honest with each other," Julie said then, pulling her designer cardigan closed and attempting to put a positive spin on having a showdown in a public place. "The thing is, I'm not quite ready to make the sort of commitment you'd like me to. This is nothing to do with Jay so don't blame him. It's all my fault. Jay wanted me to tell you about us from the very beginning."

"How noble of him – you've got yourself quite a catch there," Gary spat at Julie, disgust and anger dripping from every word. "Though he's barely out of school by the looks of him." Then he turned to Jay and said, "Does your mother know the kind of thing you get up in a public place, young man?"

"Please, Gary, please try to understand. I just wasn't ready to get married. I don't believe in marriage –"

"Save it," Gary said. "Never mind marriage, Julie. It's over. I'm a patient man and I can put up with a lot of things but God knows I will not tolerate you treating me like a piece of dirt. You just don't get it, do you? *I loved you.* I loved you the way you were. We didn't have to make it official. You could have told me how you felt. Now, I don't know what I ever saw in you. You were so beautiful to me . . . Come to think of it, beauty is only skin-deep. Isn't that the truth? I hope you'll be very happy with your pretty little toy boy. Another five years and you could be his mother."

Ouch.

"Gary, listen to me!" she said gently. "This doesn't mean I still don't have feelings for you. We can talk it through?"

"What the hell for? So you can string the two of us along and blame your crazy parents instead of your own selfishness? You lying bitch! It's over between us. Didn't you hear me the first time?"

Then Gary suddenly and without any hint of warning

whatsoever, head-butted Jay (who'd just stood up to shake hands manfully with the losing side) and knocked him out cold. Broke his nose, it has to be said. I could hear it snapping. Oh, it was blood-curdling to witness. Julie sprang to her feet and told Gary to calm down and stop acting like a playground bully. Whereupon he slapped her face hard, called her a worthless slut and shuffled out of the bar on his gammy leg before the door staff even knew what was going on.

"Don't bother coming home tonight!" Gary shouted over his shoulder.

"I won't!" she cried. "I still have my apartment in Saintfield. So there!"

"I'm throwing your stuff in the bin!"

"Go on, then. I don't care!"

Oh dear.

Cue, pandemonium. Jay'd hit his head on the edge of the table when he was going down and split his forehead open just above the eye. There was blood everywhere and Julie had to call an ambulance when Jay hadn't come round two minutes later. Poor lad was in an awful state. Not to mention the lovely white bohemian canopy which now resembled a makeshift field-hospital from World War I. Everybody was staring at us like they'd never seen a head-butt before. Jay was carried out to Arthur Street by a couple of waiters and helped into the back of a mini-ambulance. I apologised over and over to the manager about the damage we'd caused to the furniture and fixings but he said not to worry, and hopefully our friend wasn't seriously injured. Julie went with Jay to the hospital and she made me go, too. We were all mortified. Even my knees were blushing. I joked to the ambulance-driver that we'd been bare-knuckle-fighting round the pubs for pints but he didn't laugh. He just said Jay's nose was badly swollen and hopefully his lungs weren't filling up with blood. Then Julie began to freak out and the driver jumped two sets of red lights and mounted the footpath to get past a bus. It was so utterly awful, I can't tell you. Julie thought Jay was going to die and as she said to me later that day in the cafeteria, she really didn't know anything about him. Apart from the donkey sanctuary that his family owned, she wouldn't even have known who to contact. It was only in the A&E waiting-room that she discovered Jay was short for James. It was written on a bankcard in his wallet. Up until then, she'd never thought to ask if Jay was his proper name or a shortened version of it.

Meanwhile, Gary went out to Julie's apartment in Saintfield and trashed the place from top to bottom with a baseball bat. Totally ruined it. He must have been incandescent with rage. Because, as I said before, Gary is an animal-lover and as gentle a soul as you'd ever hope to meet. He poured a large tin of white gloss paint (there was one under the kitchen sink) into the outsize bath, over the pure wool carpets and across an entire rack of Julie's beautiful clothes. He broke the smaller pieces of furniture into bits, smashed three sinks and both toilets. He jammed a tin of crabmeat down the waste-disposal unit and wrote SLUT all over the walls with lipstick and squeezy brown sauce. Finally he thrust the baseball bat right through the headboard of Julie's French hand-painted bed and left it there. It was horrible. I cried when I saw it and it wasn't even my apartment. But it was so upsetting to see Julie's beautiful home violated like that because it was just like her, all pale colours and elegant lines. And Julie wasn't a slut, not really. She was confused, that's all. She didn't want to get married and then Jay O'Hanlon turned her head with his sex-bomb ways and his rugged Galway accent. It could have happened to anyone.

So anyway, Jay and Julie took refuge in the lighthouse when Jay was fit enough to leave hospital and actually I was quite glad about that (at the time) because the lighthouse has a solid steel door and no windows for the first forty feet and it was probably the only place in Belfast that would have been safe for them. Gary was in a murderous mood. I mean, he could have killed Jay with that head-butt. The nose-bone can penetrate right into the brain if you get hit hard enough, Bill says. Men! They always have to hurt each other, don't they? So Julie and Jay were driven out to the lighthouse on Lagan Road in an ambulance and I stayed behind to fill out some forms, and give a short statement to the police. Jay decided not to press charges but we still had to say what happened. Lordy, lordy!

In the end, Bill collected me from the hospital and we drove out to the airport in silence. There was nothing left to say, was there? I knew Bill was thinking I should have left the table the minute Jay sat down with us but even platonic relationships are so complicated these days. If

I'd walked out on her, it would've driven a wedge between Julie and me. And besides, I didn't want to be done out of my lovely Christmas lunch in the Café Vaudeville because of Jay O'Hanlon, of all people. Call me shallow but I so wanted to enjoy that lunch, knowing I'd soon be chained to my own kitchen sink for two solid weeks.

"I'm sorry, Bill," I said as we sat in gridlock on the motorway.

"It's okay," he said, smiling at me. "It's not your fault. But I did say it would end in tears. It gives me no pleasure to know I was right."

"Not half, it doesn't," I muttered under my breath. "Yes, Bill Grimsdale was right, once again!"

Because of the rush-hour traffic, Bill and I were over an hour late getting to the airport and my sisters weren't too pleased about the delay after such a long and tiring flight. We found them sitting with Alicia-Rose in the bar, all sipping Irish coffees, wearing thick scarves and complaining loudly about the bitterly cold weather. We told them we were so sorry, there'd been an emergency with a friend of Julie's taken ill, and the great reunion with Alicia-Rose and my sisters went ahead. I was overwhelmed with happiness when I held them all in my arms. I felt like anything was possible and we'd have the best Christmas ever. Singing carols round the (gas) fire, watching feel-good movies on the television and eating mountains of festive food.

And so we did.

I spent most of the holiday in the kitchen cooking and

making tea and being a mother-figure to my sisters: well, our biological mother had skipped off to the Maldives with Tone for 'a bit of a rest'. Skiver! Still, I thanked my lucky stars my name wasn't Julie Sultana. I kept thinking of her sitting up in the lighthouse with Jay, like some kind of latter-day fairytale. Jay with his lovely face ruined and Julie with her personal life in tatters. Bill relented on Christmas Day and invited the two of them over to Eglantine for their dinner but Julie said they would prefer to rest in the lighthouse and thanks anyway. So we dropped them off a basket of food and a small telly and a bottle of rum. She was delighted, I have to say, when she answered the door to myself and Bill. There was blood all over the front of her sweater which she told me had happened when Jay tried to make love to her, and it brought on another nosebleed. Poor Julie. It wasn't the best Christmas she'd ever had.

But it probably was the best one I can remember.

Even when my sisters insisted on going out to Dad's grave on New Year's Eve afternoon to see the newly-erected headstone and sing 'Are You Teasin' Me?' at the tops of their voices (and lay an Irish tricolour over the white marble chippings), I was still glad I was boring old Mags Grimsdale, second-in-command. It was unbelievably cold and the wind chill made it worse. I could barely think, it was that bad. Bill waited in the car, looking rather smug with the heat turned on. The rough-finish Celtic cross did look fabulous against a stormy black sky and the three of us girls had a right good laugh at the inscription, which read (in Gaelic): *'Beloved Husband,*

Father and Grandfather. Love Never Dies.' Well, we reasoned, why not? Our mother would likely never come to see the grave so what was the harm in giving the old man a nice inscription? And even if she did make the effort some day in the far-distant future, she couldn't read Irish anyway and she'd be far too proud to ask a passer-by to translate. I whipped the Irish flag off again though, the second Ann and Elizabeth were finished singing.

"What are you doing? Don't take it off!" Ann said crossly. "We had that made specially by a master-flagmaker, and blessed by a bishop before we left home. We want to leave it on the ground until it rots."

"We haven't poured the holy water and the Irish whiskey on our wee daddy yet, either," Elizabeth said, rooting in her enormous mock-croc handbag for the bottles.

"You two've been away from Belfast for too long," I told them bossily. "We're trying to tone down all this kind of thing in the interests of peace and security. And anyway, there's a few hoods hanging about down the far end and I don't know where they're from. Now get back in the bloody car before the lot of us are lynched."

Bill drove out of the cemetery so fast the hoods wouldn't have had time to blink, let alone take down our registration.

Honestly, ex-pats take the biscuit, don't they?

There was quite a strained atmosphere at dinner that evening but then Ann had the great idea of ringing round all her and Elizabeth's old schoolmates and organising an impromptu knees-up at the Wellington Park Hotel disco.

They managed to contact eleven of their chums from their schooldays on Rosetta Road and I was very touched when they said to me, "Come on, Mags, get your coat on."

And they didn't add their usual joke afterwards, about me getting my coat on because they were turning off the gas fire in the living room!

"Really?" I said, almost surprised they'd asked me to join them, after I'd spoiled their graveside ceremony with a lecture on peace and harmony.

"Aye," said Elizabeth, warming up her Belfast brogue for the night ahead. "Sure, the way you dance, we'll need something to laugh at if the talk dries up!"

So, after a frantic 'girls-getting-ready' session in my bedroom, off we went down the street, arms linked and singing our heads off. Something glam-rock and daft by Van Halen but I didn't care because I'd had a couple of gins by then and I was wearing my lovely new suede boots. I asked Bill if he wanted to come too but he said he'd rather stay at home and laze in front of the Christmas tree. And also that he'd rather face a pack of hungry wolves than take part in an old girls' reunion with the three of us. He waved us off at the front door and I blew him a kiss and said I'd be home by midnight for another kiss with him under the mistletoe.

"Crikey, Mags, give the poor fella a rest!" said Ann and we all laughed.

"Don't wait up for us two, though, Bill. We could be anywhere by midnight," Elizabeth added with a mischievous twinkle in her eyes. "With any luck, we'll be engaged to a couple of gorgeous, twenty-year-old millionaires and sailing off to Cannes in their yacht!"

They were only joking, naturally. We'd already decided to come home at 11.30 and see in the New Year at home with Bill and the rest of the family. But it was still fun to pretend. For a second, it seemed like we were all eighteen again and I felt a lump of happiness in my throat. Some moments in time you know will never come again and that was one of them.

"Come on," I said suddenly. "Hurry up or we'll not even find standing room in the Welly. And don't let me get too squiffy, will you?"

And this time I made sure I left my credit card at home. One tattoo is enough for any girl.

15

The Lighthouse

WE WERE WELL INTO JANUARY AND MY SISTERS HAD gone back to Australia again. After having some of the 'best nights of their lives' gadding about the city centre and blowing kisses to any good-looking guys they happened to see in the various clubs and pubs. At one point, they nearly ended up in a catfight when some possessive girlfriends got the wrong idea in a glamorous Indian restaurant. But it was thankfully sorted out when Ann convinced them that she and Elizabeth were a lesbian couple, just having a laugh. Which wasn't exactly hard to do, considering Elizabeth was wearing my old Reefer jacket at the time and was smoking a cigar.

I cried my eyes out at the airport, needless to say, when they left. And again two days later when Alicia-Rose boarded her plane. Even though I'd promised Bill I wouldn't cry. I couldn't help it. My beautiful daughter with the big blue eyes and the long white hair was all independent and organised at last. And she looked every inch the professional traveller by then, with all her 'permitted items' safely packed in her hand luggage and her big shiny suitcase-on-wheels checked in within two minutes of entering the building.

"Thank God for Dream Weddings," I said to Bill constantly that night, or so it seemed. "Because without Dream Weddings to keep me busy I could honestly see myself becoming very hard to live with."

"No comment," Bill said guardedly.

And we both laughed for ages.

⚭

It wasn't easy trying to plan for the wedding of the century with Julie and Jay living in the lighthouse. They were under my feet constantly like the children used to be when they were younger. I bitterly regretted moving that old sofa-bed of ours into the office, I can tell you, because Jay and Julie made themselves quite at home on it, barely bothering to get up when I arrived for work each morning. And the air in the room was stale and there were plates and cups left on the desks and on the lovely new rug. A circular rug that I'd spent hours tracking down so's it would echo the shape of the office. And now it was strewn with Jay's unwashed socks and bandages (his broken nose) and Julie's dainty bras. The first thing I'd have to do each day was open the windows, gather up the mess and wash the dishes. A woman's work is never done. Julie would scamper off to the bathroom to get herself smartened up as best she could in the miniature sink with a flannel and a bar of soap.

"It was good enough for people in the old days," she'd say stubbornly when I told her she could do with a shower at my house.

And Mr Wonderful would just lie there while she was out of the room, his head resting on the lovely cushions I'd bought in town. And he'd say I was just to ignore him and work away. Which was well-nigh impossible in a twelve-foot-wide space. Every time I had to step over the edge of the bed to get to the files, he'd say, "Watch yourself now." Like he was doing me a big favour. It was infuriating. Even though I felt sorry for him with his two black eyes and his obvious pain and discomfort.

And Julie was no better. She made no effort to rent another apartment. I think she was actually wallowing in her new bedsit-drama lifestyle. You get that sometimes with people who've never been to university, who've never lived in a HMO (House of Multiple Occupancy). They seem to think living in a mess, knee-deep in chip wrappers is a bit of a laugh. Well, it isn't hip and trendy. It's lazy and silly, that's what it is. I told Julie the housing market was coming down with buy-to-let opportunists. Now that houses have become so expensive in Belfast, only landlords can afford to purchase them. Which is bad news for buyers but very good news for renters. She said when the big fancy rock-star wedding was over she'd take her time to look properly and she'd buy another place, and until then she wasn't going to be reduced to renting.

"I am many things," she said crossly over morning coffee, "but I am nobody's *tenant*."

Julie decided not to press charges against Gary for destroying her lovely home. She said she didn't want any fuss and commotion and really, I didn't blame her for that. Dream Weddings didn't need the media intrusion and poor Gary had suffered enough. He hadn't touched Julie's white Mercedes though, which was parked outside the lighthouse every night so we decided he must have calmed down a little bit. Julie sent her engagement ring back to him by recorded delivery and then she had the flat in Saintfield cleaned and restored by professionals and put up for sale. She said she didn't want to live there any more and anyway the neighbours had filed a complaint against her for making too much noise after midnight. The estate agent who came out to assess the property, valued the apartment at a staggering half a million pounds! For a two-bedroom, two-bathroom flat. Can you believe it? Albeit with a landscaped patio-area and top-notch tiling in the showers. This country really has lost the run of itself. He said it would sell in no time despite the management fees which were a thinly veiled form of daylight robbery.

I was counting the days until they moved out because Jay had bought a deep-fat fryer for the lighthouse kitchen and he was in there most days, merrily cooking banana fritters and singing songs by Bruce Springsteen. And hanging his sexy faded jeans out to dry on the balcony railings. I found myself resenting him, despite his bruises and his nosebleeds. Easy to lie about doing nothing all day when the rest of us are working ourselves silly. I mean, where would Jay have been without the lighthouse? In a shop doorway, that's where. At least that's what I thought at the time. But canny old Jay wasn't quite the innocent he seemed. Oh no. I bet he planned everything, right from the very start. Julie Sultana was only a stepping-stone to the main prize, in the end. So there we were, the three of us, stuck in that tiny office at the top of the lighthouse. Me and Julie trying to locate vegetarian chefs, trustworthy security guards, red top hats and designer mobile-phone covers. While Jay spent most of his time lying on his back reading the papers and looking for another job, the Café Vaudeville having decided to terminate his employment rather abruptly. It seemed they'd made a mistake and didn't need another barman after all. I can't say he was really putting much energy into the search, though. He kept saying he'd love to open his own restaurant some day if he could only find a financial backer willing to put their faith in him. No doubt he had his handsome green eyes firmly trained on Julie's half a million pounds' equity. She must have known what he was hinting at but she didn't pick up on it. I suppose she hadn't decided yet what she was going to do with him. And you don't want to go into business with a toy-boy lover, do you? So she just said a restaurant sounded lovely and what a pity she would need all the money from the sale of her flat to buy another property, prices being the way they were. Otherwise she'd have jumped at the chance to go into the restaurant business. I couldn't prevent a delighted smirk or two from crossing my chops when Julie said that. At least she hasn't gone so crazy she's giving Jay O'Hanlon access to her finances, I thought to myself. Good for you, Julie.

Then Jay took up smoking again. Cigars to be precise. I think he did it to spite us because neither Julie nor myself are big fans of the deadly weed. And he started getting a bit moody with Julie, not answering her sometimes when she asked him a question or pulling away from her whenever she kissed him. Then she'd be whispering to me, had I noticed anything different about Jay and what did I think was wrong with him and what should she do about it? I felt so claustrophobic marooned in the lighthouse with the pair of them, I began to yearn for lunch-times when I'd be sent out to the shop to buy sandwiches.

I thought of my sisters and Alicia-Rose back in Australia after the holidays and I half-wished I was there with them, maybe living in the outback as a mystic or hermit of some kind. And I remembered when Alicia-Rose was about to go through the Departures gate for the second time and she said I was looking tired and maybe I should give a month's notice to Dream Weddings and set up some little thing of my own. Something smaller and less pressurised, maybe selling wedding hats online? I was touched that she'd noticed how exhausted her old mum was feeling but I didn't think I'd ever be confident enough to go into business for myself. I remembered holding onto her until the last call was announced and then Bill pulled me away and we were both heartbroken all over again. I went home and moped about the house until I felt sick and when I called Australia the following day to make sure Alicia-Rose had arrived safely at her destination, she said I was becoming neurotic and I was to cop on to myself. There's gratitude for you. But I was stunned by my daughter's confidence and proud as hell of her, at the same time.

And then Jay started having an affair with the French model. Broken nose notwithstanding. And I began to think Alicia-Rose might have been onto something, regarding me and Julie going our separate ways. Oh yes, I expect you saw that little dalliance coming but I have to say, I did not. I must have been preoccupied with my own various family dramas but I definitely didn't think Julie's toy boy would ever hook up with her best client of all time.

Poor Julie.

She was well out of Jay's league, wasn't she, that French model? Even though the rock-star was a bit wrinkly and a bit short and his molars were crumbling and he was on heavy withdrawal-medication. And he had breath that smelt like cat food. Sorry, but he did – maybe he ate some weird kind of health food? But he was so incredibly rich! I mean, how on earth did Jay O'Hanlon manage to catch the eye of a top supermodel? Even if the thought had crossed my mind that Jay couldn't be trusted around other women, I'd never have guessed he would have tried it on with someone of her pedigree or that she would've been the least bit interested in a penniless Irish stud. I mean, they're a dime a dozen, good-looking Irish men. A bit of forthright banter, a few moments of intense eye contact, a roguish way of holding a cigarette inside their curled-up hand. Go into any pub in the land and there's ten of them standing idly at the bar. You can take your pick, missus, and good luck to you. But with the money and connections she must have had, you'd think she'd have laughed in Jay O'Hanlon's face. It makes me cringe now looking back at how naïve I really was. I like to see the best in people, that's my problem. But the truth is some people have no conscience whatsoever when it comes to money, power and sex.

What happened was (and I heard this from the woman herself, mind, just a few days ago when she rang me to say she was sorry for causing so much upheaval) our supermodel called unexpectedly to take a look at our goody-bag samples. We weren't expecting her because she was an international model! But anyway, she happened to be in Belfast to take part in a photo-shoot for a prestigious new department store so she took a taxi out to visit Julie and me afterwards. But we weren't in. Because Julie and myself were up a ladder at the castle Julie had finally chosen for the wedding venue, dangling rubber bats off a piece of invisible thread to get a feel for the puppet-show. I know it sounds ridiculous, doesn't it? But actually the bats did look amazingly alive, bouncing up and down with their little wings flapping. And we knew it'd look even better at night, backlit with some yellowish spotlights.

So yes, the model landed out to the lighthouse and who should answer the door but Jay O'Hanlon, topless and wearing his sexiest faded jeans over bare feet. His hair still damp after a quick dip in the miniature sink, and a pot of black coffee and some deep-fried gourmet sausages wafting their aroma up and down the stairwell. It would have been rude of her not to come in and wait, no doubt. And she was powerless to resist our Jay's charms as Julie had been before her. A few pleasant words about the new décor in the lighthouse, a sip of black coffee, a suggestive nibble on a fat pork sausage, and our model ends up on the end of Jay O'Hanlon's legendary doo-da.

Oh, Julie.

The biter, bit.

It started in January, the affair, apparently. I didn't find out about it until March and to this day, I blame myself for not telling Julie when I *did* find out. I caught them at it one afternoon, you see? Doing horizontal gymnastics on my old sofa-bed in the office. The two of them prone on the beautiful cushions I'd chosen with such care and attention to detail. And paid for with my own money. That Jay, naked as a sandboy. Whatever a sandboy is. And her fully dressed, high-heels still on her extremely large feet. The only drawback to being six feet tall, I expect? I mean, she had *massive* feet. Yes, fully dressed except for her pink floral cami-knickers which were hanging from the drawer handle of Julie's desk. The cheek of it! Cheating on Julie Sultana! Doing the wild thing on Dream Weddings' hallowed premises. Her endless, honey-coloured legs wrapped round Jay's neck and him smoking a cigar with his eyes closed. She wasn't saying much but then I saw he had her mouth loosely gagged with one of our stocking samples, 'Winter White' I think it was called. She was giggling and panting and I think she mumbled something about a little Irish house with a huge big chimney on it but then my French isn't the best and she did have a silk stocking lashed across her face.

I don't know what I ought to have done, if there's some sort of handbook available giving guidance on these things. But anyway, I just closed my eyes and stepped back onto the stone staircase. Tiptoed down again all the way to the bottom, went outside and set off along the coastal path for a good long walk. I didn't phone Julie to tell her what I'd seen. And to make sure she didn't discover them too by sending her off on a lengthy errand or something. My mind had gone slightly blank. And so I just sat on an old wooden fence looking out to sea, waiting for them to finish. Had a nice breath of fresh air and felt so pleased with myself that I haven't ever been tempted to cheat on Bill during our twenty-odd years together. Not even one time. This is not my problem, I kept telling myself. This is nothing to do with me. And anyway Julie had stated categorically on several occasions that she didn't genuinely *love* Jay. It was only the hot sex she was keen on and the idea of having a much younger lover. So it wasn't exactly betrayal on a major scale, *not really*.

I thought the French model was only amusing herself with a bit of rough from the Emerald Isle and as soon as the wedding was over, she'd forget Jay and get on with the business of being very rich and famous. And besides, I was still feeling a tiny bit sorry for myself over Alicia-Rose leaving for Australia again. And worrying she might never come back. (She was raving about her new home all over the holidays and I said to Bill, just you wait and see, she'll be emigrating for good next like Ann and Elizabeth.) And okay, maybe I was also being a total cowardly-custard.

But honestly, by then I had lost all faith in my own judgement. Maybe Jay and the model have genuinely fallen in love, I thought to myself. They're both gorgeous and of a similar age. Maybe this is the real thing at last? And we can't go around telling people who they can and can't fall in love with, can we? I mean, that's what western civilisation is based on, isn't it? Personal freedom? And God knows I didn't want to be the one to tell Julie what was going on – she might have punched me in the beak with the shock of it. So yes, I crept back down the stairs and pretended I knew nothing about it. Bubble-integrity and all that. It was getting too much for me, all this kinky-bondage shenanigans. Day and night, there was no getting away from it. It was putting me off sex with Bill to be honest with you. And I didn't want that to happen, no way. The day that Bill's feather-light caresses fail to move me is the day I become an old woman.

So I blocked it out of my mind, and made sure there was plenty of noise when I was coming up the stairs from that day onwards. And I went on washing the dirty dishes in the lighthouse and making hundreds of phone calls and collecting mountains of receipts for our various wedding projects. The rock-star wedding was fixed to take place on May 1st and Julie didn't find out about Jay's affair until halfway through the actual marriage ceremony. And when she did find out, well, there were fireworks a-plenty all right but they weren't all in the sky.

16

Alexander

Alexander and Emma got back together over the Christmas holidays, did I mention that? Not officially back together but things were going that way. The signs were there. Bill told his eldest son not to push things, romantically speaking. To play hard-to-get for once in his life, to treat Emma like he was doing her a massive favour by even speaking to her. And to make a few mysterious calls on his mobile phone and then say it was nobody if she asked him who he was chatting to. So's she'd think he was seeing other girls. And he was to pin a few posters of curvy celebs in skimpy outfits to his bedroom wall, for good measure. Nothing too obvious, no bimbos with their fingers in their mouths, no. But nice arty black-and-white ones, that'd be more convincing, Bill said. Which I declared was grossly and totally unfair behaviour towards a (hopefully) recovering anorexic young girl. But Bill said all was fair in love and war and that Emma needed something else to obsess about besides calories and inches. And it worked. Honestly, my darling husband might be a humble, hard-working plumber but I reckon he could have been a top psychiatrist if he'd had the education. Never mind knowing your inner self! Nothing gets most people fired up like a bit of serious competition.

Emma went raving mad, went absolutely mad as a hatter when she saw the sexy posters in Alexander's room and she tore them off the walls, ripped them to shreds and stamped on them. Quite a feat if you'd seen the state of her at that time. But Alexander just said that was okay, Emma could take the posters down if she wanted to but he was still 'so over' the waif look. And then he nipped into the bathroom to answer a text-message. Emma checked his mobile phone later for missed calls and questioned him endlessly about his social life. But he was giving nothing away. He was magnificent actually. He looked guilty as hell yet he'd done nothing whatsoever except hang about the house for ages contemplating suicide. And driving the rest of us demented with his depressing music played at top volume and his unpredictable mood swings. I was out a fortune on fish and chips around that time, too, trying to pamper my son and keep his appetite healthy.

And then Emma started eating again.

Just little bits and pieces at first. A small orange, a finger of toast with a scrape of butter on it, a solitary carrot grated and sprinkled with finely crushed rock salt and black pepper. But it was a start. Next, she stopped weighing her muesli and even cut the workout sessions down to thirty minutes a day. One time, when we were all having fish and chips in the kitchen (yet again), she said she'd send out for a cheeseburger if that was okay, seeing as the rest of us didn't eat red meat very often. We were stunned. And she did get the cheeseburger, too and she ate every last bit of it. Even the garnish. And no, she didn't pop up to the bathroom afterwards because we were all holding our breath and checking our watches, and she didn't go to the bathroom until the burger would have been safely past the point of no return. Alexander was delighted with himself and so was Bill. I worried that if Emma did transfer her 'free-floating' anxiety onto her relationship with Alexander, we might end up with a stalker on our hands. Or worse, if Alexander changed his mind about loving Emma, *she* might not be able to live without *him*. And the situation would simply flip over. But Bill said Emma was almost dead anyway so the poor girl starting to eat again could only be a good thing, and we'd deal with any resulting problems as and when they arose.

When the time came for her to go back to the clinic in January, Emma said she'd be well again in no time and she asked Alexander to let her have another chance. To give him his due, he didn't agree right away. He said he would think about it. When Emma's taxi set off he didn't cry and he didn't wave goodbye. He just stood on the footpath looking moody while Emma blew kisses to him through the back window. I never thought I'd say this but that was one occasion where the man was a lot smarter than the woman. Bill and Alexander went to the pub to celebrate the success of their little scheme and I took down the Christmas decorations and ate the last of the pretzels and the Brazil nuts. Well, I do hate to throw good food in the bin.

At the end of March, Emma reached her target weight of seven and a half stone and she was released into the community once again. Hooray! Of course, there'd be years of therapy ahead of her and possible relapses and all kinds of setbacks to get over. But Emma was off the danger list and we all cheered down the phone and congratulated her and told her to visit us the minute she got back to Belfast. And she did. She came straight round to our house and formally asked Alexander out on a date. He said he'd check his diary. Casanova Grimsdale! Attaboy!

Well, nearly.

By midnight they were curled up in bed together. Listening to some lightweight pop music on the radio and eating chocolate biscuits. Though he didn't tell her about his crafty scheme to make her jealous. On Bill's advice, Alexander was to maintain his penchant for arty glamour models indefinitely. And the following morning they told us they were getting engaged to be married.

Oh my God! A miracle had happened!

We were so pleased for them both, of course, but we did remind them that Emma's parents had spent a lot of money on the private clinic and they might not be able to pay for a lovely big wedding any time soon. And they shouldn't get their hopes up. But Alexander said not to worry, they had promised themselves a budget of only £1000 to pay for the wedding and the honeymoon (no more and no less) and it was going to be so much fun shopping for bargains and making things on a shoestring. Alexander was earning a regular wage as an apprentice-plumber by then and he said he wanted to spend it on renting a little apartment for himself and Emma. He said they wanted to live on their own as soon as possible and thanks anyway for our offer of a bed-sit. And would you believe, they found a place that very night in the local paper. A lovely brand-new apartment in a converted convent on the Ormeau Road. (Honestly, they're converting anything and everything in Belfast these days. Turning factories and bakeries and convents galore into luxury 'turn-key' flats. It's all down to the halt of emigration and the rise of the white collar sector, apparently.) On the third floor of the development, the flat was. Sorry, the apartment. Two button-flush bathrooms and a sleek modern kitchen, all stainless steel cupboards and green glass bricks. Tiny little place but very nicely designed, with a dainty balcony and a built-in ironing-board. Well, there'd need to be an ironing-board built-in, I thought to myself when I saw it, because there wasn't enough room to erect an old-fashioned one. Five hundred quid per month to rent which I thought was a bit steep. It would amount to almost half of his wages but Alexander said he could afford it and they agreed a date with the owner for moving in.

I told you the rented sector was really taking off here. Time was, you couldn't rent at all in this country unless it was a featureless government unit on some rundown concrete estate. But the fancy building that Alexander and Emma have moved into has ornamental bell-towers, electronic gates and stained-glass windows on the gable walls. It's really fabulous. I wouldn't mind moving in myself, say I wanted to downsize sometime. I hoped they would have nice neighbours but that was only me being fussy again. I'm sure any undesirables will be evicted right away before they do any damage to the hanging baskets.

Emma's massive haul of designer clothes and shoes were safely installed in the built-in wardrobes by the end of the week. Bill and I went round to visit them a few days later and they seemed happy as anything. The metallic fridge was full of yoghurts and fresh fruit and there was a big wooden bowl of mini-chocolate bars on the breakfast counter. They'd bought a nice print of the old shipyard to hang in the sitting room. Alexander was brimming over with pride and enthusiasm and I had to admit I wasn't as gutted as I had been about him dropping out of university. I suppose we're brainwashed into wanting a university education for our children. But these days you can make a better living as a plumber than you can as, say, a science teacher in a grammar school. And as long as our beloved son was happy, we were happy too. We told Alexander and Emma we were delighted with everything. And we gave them a puffy all-white patchwork quilt and a quirky lime-green tea set with gold handles as a house-warming gift.

The funny thing is, next day Emma dropped out of

college too. She said she found being in third level education just too stressful. And she got a part-time job in a fancy gift shop across the street from their apartment building so she could start paying her way in life. And when she saw how long it actually took to earn a hundred pounds she was totally cured of her addiction to high-end clothing and accessories. Which was a brilliant stroke of luck because the private therapy sessions were expensive enough to be getting on with. The engagement was still on, however. Oh yes! Alexander bought Emma a big chunky silver ring with a row of red glass stones on it. It cost £58 from a posh little fashion boutique on the Lisburn Road. The shop assistant wrapped the ring up in a beautiful pink satin box and gave Emma a free sprig of glittery roses for her hair when she heard about their plan to get married on a strict budget. Wasn't that lovely of her? And so, the silver ring was the first thing they bought with their £1000 budget. The second thing was the marriage licence itself from Belfast City Hall. That was £130 (weekday rate). They didn't have an engagement party because Emma was still feeling rather tired after her stay in the clinic, and also from her new job which involved quite a lot of unpacking crates and dusting bronze Buddhas. Instead, Alexander took Emma out to see a comedy play at the Grand Opera House though he did stump up a little extra for a private box that cost £80, including tickets and a bag of chocolates. So, all together they'd spent £268 on a gorgeous quirky engagement ring, a wonderful night out at the theatre and a marriage licence from possibly the prettiest city hall in the UK. I was madly impressed. Mind you, Julie did tell me to shut up and stop 'bloody rabbiting on' about how sensible my son and his wife-to-be were being about the whole thing. Julie found it all a little *too* quirky, to be honest.

"Remember, Mags," she said to me (surprisingly darkly) one day when we were making up black feather corsages for the rock-star's 666 wedding guests, "it's women going crazy with wedding-fever that keeps you and me in a job. So don't go telling *any* of our clients about this shoestring wedding of your Alexander's, do you hear me? We don't want the punters getting any of these poverty-is-cool ideas. There's *nothing* romantic about pinching the pennies, my dear! Nothing romantic in any shape or form."

"Yes, Julie," I said at once. But my heart was singing with joy.

I'd actually forgotten about Jay's affair with the bride-to-be for a few moments (even though I had one of the black corsages *in my hands*) and the knot of guilt that was forever gnawing away at my insides temporarily relaxed. Of course, it came back with a vengeance when I did remember. But no, I kept saying to myself, this is nothing to do with me and maybe it's better if Julie never finds out about Jay's infidelity? And I wouldn't have known about it either if I'd banged the door of the lighthouse shut when I came in that day.

And so on.

Emma and Alexander set the date for their wedding for May 10th. Which was nice, I thought, because by then I'd be well-rested after the 'wedding of the century' and

I'd be really looking forward to the much smaller and more intimate day Alexander and Emma were dreaming of. They weren't going to invite anyone from my side of the family (thank goodness) as we were still smarting from the trauma of our Gothic wake. And not too many from Bill's side either as they would have had to travel from 'across the water', as some people here like to call the Irish Sea. Just close friends and immediate family, really. Emma didn't want to have too much fuss, so close to her remission from the eating disorder. About thirty guests in all, we reckoned. A civil marriage ceremony in the City Hall was duly booked, just like our own wedding day. And then the happy couple were going to serve a modest buffet in their apartment, which they would prepare themselves the day before. They were going to make their own invitations using rice paper from the gift shop and Emma was planning to wear an ivory-coloured evening dress and a pair of shoes she already had. And of course, she had the glittery roses she'd got for nothing – they'd suddenly become one of her most treasured possessions.

"I hope you don't mind," Emma said tearfully as Bill and I took our leave of them after that first visit to their new home. "We did think of asking Dream Weddings to arrange our special day for us but really we don't want anything too grand or complicated. After recent events, you can see why we don't want any fuss and fanfare. The baby and so on? I do hope you understand?"

"Oh, I do understand. I do indeed," I assured them. "It all sounds heavenly if you must know. You have everything under control. And I'd love to just turn up and be a plain old ordinary guest for once in my life. No responsibilities!"

"And thank you for the gorgeous presents," Emma added. "I adore the funny little tea set, really. It reminds me of you."

"You're very welcome," I said to her.

And I meant it from the heart.

17

The Wedding

THE WEDDING.

Ah, the wedding of the century. The Bling-tastic event that should have made Dream Weddings famous throughout the British Isles but instead became a media-byword for disaster. In fact, for a time you couldn't switch on the radio without hearing a lecture on the perils of over-ambition and social-climbing gone mad. Even BBC Radio 4 were having debates about the trend for 'tasteless to the point of nihilism' celebrity marriage ceremonies. So you can see how serious it was, if the likes of R4 were bothering themselves with common folk like us.

Stuck-up old miseries.

And I don't say that lightly. I adore R4 – with those plummy-voiced presenters, it's like Jackanory for grown-ups. Even if they're talking about something completely obscure like Russian food in the seventeenth century or anything to do with classical music, I still lap it up. It's very calming, usually, to listen to. My favourite narrator is Alan Bennett. Do you know what I'd just *love* to hear? Alan Bennett narrating *The Borrowers*, from the original books by Mary Norton. Oh, bliss . . .

But back to the wedding.

You know, over the years, I've seen inside the homes of quite a few so-called intellectuals, and families with old money and honestly, they wouldn't spend Christmas. Thrifty as anything, they are. Everything falling to bits and covered with an inch of dust and dog hairs. Now, don't get me wrong! Dust and decay and a broken Aga is all very well if it floats your boat. But please don't go knocking the rest of us if we like to make a bit of a statement. Just because we like glitter and glitz, or gargoyles for that matter, it doesn't make us bad people or anything.

"Can you actually have too much money," R4 asked the listening public, practically going giddy down the microphone, "literally more money than sense?" And the public seemed to think that, yes, a person could be too rich. And that the pressure to spend it on bigger and better weddings than your peers (and bigger houses and better holidays and so on) could surely trigger bouts of utter silliness. If not bona fide madness.

And yet it had all begun so well.

A Vampires & Rock Chicks theme with millionaire rock-stars and leggy French models galore, £300 goody bags and gallons of pink champagne. I mean, as Julie said herself, what could possibly be described as tasteless about that lot? It was all dead classy. The first day of May and everything was perfect. A bright, balmy afternoon and a clear blue sky above us. A fresh breeze blowing in from across the Irish Sea and not a speck of litter anywhere. Or a cowpat: we'd borrowed a special hoover from the ferry company (the mind boggles). Seven o'clock in the evening, that's when the wedding was due to begin. So's the ceremony could take place just minutes before the celebrations kicked off. All the photographs were to be 'action-shots' in black and white. No hanging around for hours with a light-meter, you see? It was Julie's idea. The castle's imposing ramparts (what was left of them) were festooned with trailing silver and black bannerettes which looked magnificent fluttering in the wind. Very Harry Potter. The butch and solemn-faced security staff were discreetly posted around the site, impeccably dressed in matt-black bomber jackets and loose-fitting slacks worn over formal dress shoes. They each had a two-way radio, a mobile phone and a First-Aid kit as well as the obligatory dark glasses. The couple's official bodyguards had their own little tent placed near the main body of the castle building and they were all ready to deal with any possible assassination-attempts and (or) determined stalkers. So far, so good.

The puppeteers were ready on their platform, belted onto it with safety harnesses actually, the multitude of rubber bats dangling on dozens of invisible wires. The fireworks were rigged to be lit as darkness fell and were under constant scrutiny by a health and safety expert. The magistrate and the Druid were there, dressed up to the nines and looking very important and wise. Each trying to out-do the other in terms of lofty grandness. Busloads of guests began to arrive and file onto the lawn where Julie swiftly directed them towards the pristine marquee for a pre-wedding glass of pink champagne and a selection of vegetarian nibbles. They did look a bit peculiar (the guests not the nibbles) flapping round the site in their vampire garb. In fact the proceedings had all the hallmarks of a downmarket magic convention. But Julie and I had no choice but to keep congratulating the groom on the magnificence of it all.

Privately, I decided that as soon as I got home that night, or by the weekend anyway, I was going to bin my red bedroom curtains and my purple front-room drapes and consign most of the biggest candlesticks to the attic. Goth used to be great, I thought, when it was still an elitist obsession. But now that every Tom, Dick and Harry was in on the game I was beginning to go off it. Yes, I thought to myself, some nice pale and restful curtains that remind me of stone or coffee will do the trick. Well, you never know when Bill or myself might need a doctor in the night. And I definitely didn't want another humiliation like my father's wake on my hands.

But, back to the wedding.

A small orchestra was playing a selection of Indie hits from the 1980's with plenty of haunting cello and violin solos thrown in. 'Eloise' by The Damned was going down well, as was 'Golden Brown' by The Stranglers. The entire scene was lit with soft creamy spotlights, making everyone look younger and more attractive despite the satin cloaks and what have you. And at the centre of it all, on a special podium in the marquee, was the magnificent wedding cake: black icing from top to bottom, complete with overhanging balconies, miniature iron railings and yes, real working lights! The groom and his bride could cut only the top tier after the banquet, we'd warned them. The rest of it was mostly MDF casing and couldn't be touched by anything that might conduct electricity. Such as a long-handled knife. But all in all, it was fabulous, darling! The atmosphere was simmering like a pot-roast in gravy. Snatches of laughter and conversation drifted across the lawn and the photographers were having a field day.

It was Dream Weddings' finest hour.

We didn't worry too much when the bride was an hour late for the ceremony.

"After all, it's practically a woman's duty to keep her future husband waiting at the altar," we joked to some of the guests.

Well, to keep him waiting on the *stage*, really, if we're being honest. So although the groom did seem a bit jumpy as the minutes ticked away, Julie and myself weren't *too* concerned. He was in bits after the first half hour, poor guy. He kept pacing down to the castle gates and looking at his watch. Then he ducked into the bodyguard's tent and came out five minutes later looking a lot more relaxed. But at the time I thought nothing of it. I was too busy helping the last of the guests into their velvet coats and feathered hats and evening gloves, to be overly concerned about the bride's no-show. And it did take quite a while to distribute the black feather corsages and so on. By 8.30 the light had begun to fade slightly in the sky. Not getting dark or anything but just an ominous gathering of clouds that cast a shadow over the marquee and the atmosphere in general. A cold breeze stole into the castle grounds and most of the elderly guests gave up waiting and went back to the marquee to bag a good table. Some of them joking about "not living forever" and those ladies who were wearing low-cut dresses reached for their satin and velvet wraps. Julie instructed the marquee staff to switch on the heaters and start warming the space up a little bit. We hadn't wanted to get the heating going too early, you see. Because when the guests take their seats in a marquee it can get quite stifling, quite early on. So anyway, the faint hum of the blow-heaters duly started up.

And we all went on waiting.

Nine o'clock came and went and the chef (Russian, as it happened) said that some of the food might have to be discarded as it was drying up round the edges. He'd made a lot of ice sculptures on which to display the fruit salads and they were starting to melt. And the vegetarian gravy was drying up and so were the sauces and garnishes. He was very annoyed that his terrific catering was being treated so shabbily and he said he would never work with such amateurs again.

"This entire country is cursed when it comes to food," he said rudely, staring with impatience at Julie and me.

I don't know what *he* was worried about. I mean, he'd got his money and he was safely tucked away in a corner of the marquee with a nice little heater beside him and a stiff drink in his hand. Julie and me were the ones taking all the flak about the bride being so late.

"Oops, watch that passionate temper of yours, my darling!" Julie trilled but I could tell by the tone of her voice she was bricking it. We'd made dozens of calls to the bride's hotel but we were always told by her entourage she'd be setting off shortly.

Liars! The ground underfoot was slightly damp and I noticed my own shoes had a creeping tidemark beginning to show above the sole.

"*Where is she?*" we hissed to one another for the umpteenth time. We feared she'd been kidnapped by terrorists at one point, and was surely about to be ransomed back to us. There seemed no other reason why she could be so late. Well, Julie saw no other reason. I could think of one or two but I said nothing. The truth was too awful to contemplate. Julie was fit to be tied and I was trying not to throw up with nerves.

9.30 came.

9.45.

My stomach was in knots. And I don't mean that as a figure of speech. It was literally in knots. I honestly thought I'd need major surgery to be able to visit the toilet ever again. I decided I was definitely getting too old to be a wedding planner any more. I'd have swapped my PA status for a chippy-girl's pinny in a heartbeat. The hairs on the back of my neck were wet with perspiration and, to make matters worse, Julie was knocking back the vodkas without even the benefit of a mixer. My throat was sore from talking, instructing, laughing, consoling and bitching.

Ten o'clock at night.

Suffering Jesus.

It was pitch black.

It was an out-and-out crisis.

Some of the oldest guests gave up entirely and went home, after collecting their goody bags and telling Julie and me the entire event was disappointing in the extreme. We bundled the loudest complainers into Jeeps and got some of the security staff to drive them back to their various hotels. Then we discovered there was no pink champagne left and that the Russian chef had dumped half the food into a skip behind the marquee, and walked out. The Druid did his best, I have to say, casting a peace and harmony spell over the venue and providing a bit of a sideshow at the same time but the buzz had been completely lost. That impossible-to-define special magic that lifts a wedding out of the ordinary and upwards into something life-changing was gone. And there was nothing we could think of to bring it back.

That's the trouble with weddings: you can spend all the money in the world on the trappings and trimmings. But at the end of the day you do need an actual bride and groom (or a same-sex couple, let's get with the programme) who're willing and able to turn up, preferably on time and actually *get married*. It was off-the-scale of weirdness, watching those OAP witches and warlocks collecting their luxury gift bags and buckling up in the security

Jeeps, shaking their heads and dismissing Julie and me as a pair of total fakes. I felt like shouting at them, had they never made a single mistake in all of *their* lives? I mean, just when did senior citizens become so intolerant in our society? You'd think a lifetime of experience would've made them see the funny side. Wouldn't you?

Julie was looking ashen-faced for the first time in her illustrious career. I thought she was going to faint when I suggested we make an announcement to the crowd that the wedding was cancelled, and simply wrap the whole thing up. But just then, the white bridal limousine came purring up the castle driveway and the guests began to clap and cheer. Well, the ones who weren't already drunk as skunks did. The rest just sat tight in the marquee and tried to warm their feet on the blow-heaters, guarding the plates of food they'd managed to cadge off the furious Russian chef before he departed the event. Some of the guests were having a kip under their car blankets. It felt like there was a war on, that awful atmosphere of doom and gloom and hunger. The groom nipped back into the security tent for what I wrongly assumed was a lemonade shandy (him being off all artificial stimulants except for cigarettes, on his doctor's strictest instructions) and then made to open the car door and lead his beautiful bride to the stage. I mean, to the altar. The beautiful, flower-laden altar where a select group of press photographers and journalists were somehow still assembled and waiting with bated breath. And a battery of cameras, lights, light-reflecting umbrellas and endless loops of electrical cable. And a small generator.

I was physically and emotionally exhausted but Julie was jubilant in a desperate sort of way. She kept smiling and then swallowing hard as if her throat was drying up. And she'd knocked back quite a few vodkas, remember, even though that is totally against Dream Weddings policy. We never, but *never*, drink on a job.

"Selfish bloody tart," Julie whispered to me out of the corner of her mouth. She was actually shaking with relief. "Making us wait for three fucking hours like that, who the hell does she think she is? She's only a gawky model with massive feet. She didn't win a Nobel prize, for fuck's sake. I hate her, Mags. I loathe and despise that woman with every single cell in my body. I hate her a million times over, a million *million* times over. A million trillion times over. I hate her so much I want to rip her head off and spit down her throat."

Well, this is interesting, I thought to myself.

How could Julie ever build on that level of hatred, I wondered, say the truth did come out? Even if she *was* born and bred in Belfast where hatred is taught alongside the ABC (only in certain districts, we're not all crazy). Julie had even started smoking again with the pressure of it all. I mean, cigarettes give Julie a light head usually but she was so upset at the delay she wasn't thinking straight. Here we go, I thought, as the door of the limousine clicked open with a lovely expensive sound. Here we go at last. Happy days and hooray! Quick ceremony, up with the bats, firework display goes off, everybody gets too wasted to notice the food is buggered, the dancing begins and I go home to bed.

Come on.

Except the bride didn't seem that keen to disembark.

Julie and I craned our necks to see into the back of the car. From what we could gather the bride was sobbing gently in the back seat, a glass of brandy balanced dangerously close to the skirt of her billowing black wedding dress. Her make-up was flawless, naturally, and her dark brown hair was piled on top of her head in an elaborate beehive of interlocking braids. The flowers were simply beautiful, a small round posy of blowsy white roses. The most beautiful bride I had ever seen. And also the most depressed and forlorn. Of course, I knew that if she kept on crying, her heavy eye make-up would get smudged and smeared. Oh bugger it! She made Janine Smith look positively skittish.

"What's wrong, my darling?" said the groom.

As Julie tried to jolly along the mood by directing the band to play a more up-tempo tune. 'Never Take Me Alive' by Spear Of Destiny.

We couldn't hear the bride's reply. She just shook her head and drank the brandy and wept some more. The groom swiftly took off his red hat and clambered into the back of the car, closing the door softly behind him. Julie and I exchanged glances. There was an undercurrent of tragedy in the air and not for the first time that day, I had a vision of Jay and the supermodel in a moment of silent ecstasy in the lighthouse office. Her massive feet on the wall above Jay's head. His perfect face relaxed into a satisfied smile. Oh dear God. My heart skipped a beat as Julie looked at her watch and inhaled deeply on a long brown More cigarette and I thought, oh my sweet God, *she has!* That silly supermodel's actually fallen in love with Jay O'Hanlon and she's going to call off the wedding. I staggered a bit and dropped my guest list and handbag but that might have been because the damp ground had made my feet go numb. Julie approached the bridal car to see if she could be of any assistance. Immediately, I slipped my mobile phone out of my pocket and called Bill.

"Please get here immediately if not sooner," I said to him as quietly as I could. "The shit is about to hit the fan. Seriously, I think there's going to be a riot at this blinking thing and I don't want to have to cope with it on my own. I've got a feeling there's going to be violence."

"Isn't Julie there with you?" Bill said at once. "She's surely not skulking off with that Galway-Romeo at a time like this? I'll have serious words with her, if she is, honey."

"Oh, she's here all right," I said, swallowing down my panic. And she was, looking to-die-for in a floaty white Hammer House of Horror-style virginal ballgown and dainty tiara. "Only, I reckon Julie's going to be the one to throw the first punch."

"Has this got something to do with Jay O'Hanlon?"

"It might have. Bill, I know you're going to think I've lost the plot completely but I suspect the bride is about to tell the world she's in love with our Jay. I didn't tell you before but I think they've become rather pally in recent months. And now she's turned up three hours late, in floods of tears. And she won't get out of the car. I think they've been having an affair."

"Ah, for God's sake, it never ends! Look, I'm on my way. You take care, by the way and if it does kick off, just get out of the way. Do you hear me? No heroics, now, I'm telling you," Bill said and he hung up.

I smoothed down my full-length black lace skirt and crisp white blouse and turned around to look for Julie. But I didn't have to look too far because she was standing right behind me.

"What did you say about Jay?" she whispered. "My Jay? Is that silly woman seeing *my* Jay? Tell me the truth, Mags." Fat tears were already running down her face.

"Julie, now look, I'm not trying to say *anything* to you. I really don't know what's going on. I mean, don't cry, please? It might have been a one-off thing? A bit of a laugh, that's all it was. I'm not up-to-date on all this modern rock-and-roll stuff. It probably meant nothing whatsoever. It's how celebrities greet each other these days. Kiss, hand-shake, shag, cup of tea and how are you?"

Oops! Shouldn't have said 'shag'.

Julie's face was a picture.

Not a nice picture, mind. A horrible one.

"What is happening here? This is totally out of order. I don't believe this! You mean, you *saw* them together? When did this happen? Why didn't you tell me, Mags?"

"I'm so sorry, Julie. But what good would it have done? It was only the once, honest. I only saw them together once. It was in March and there's been no hint of anything since. I didn't tell you because . . . because I *couldn't* tell you! You would have thought I was making it up, anyway. Because I didn't like Jay from the start. You know I never thought he was good enough for you. You know I never liked him, Julie."

But Julie's reply was drowned out as the car door opened and the groom stepped onto the lawn and waved to the cheering crowd, before offering a hand to his reluctant bride. She finally emerged to face the music (quite literally) and there were audible gasps at her sheer beauty and fabulousness. Her make-up had survived and there was a huge smile on her face that looked positively painful to Julie and myself but utterly convincing to everyone else. They clapped and cheered even louder and the puppeteers got a bit carried away and they 'released' the bats too early. The yellow spotlights followed the bats' progress as they jerked and flittered their way to the top of the tower and disappeared into a plume of red smoke. The applause reached deafening levels. I tried to think it was all going to be okay. And not just a sad and pathetic group of slightly overwhelmed extras got up in fancy dress and not knowing quite how to conduct themselves. I prayed for the ceremony to be finished and for the fireworks to go off. I just wanted the day to be over. I'd have given my right arm for it to be over.

But it wasn't *nearly* over. It was only just beginning.

"I can't believe it," Julie wept. "He told me he loved me, over and over again. He had my name tattooed on his arm."

"But you don't really love *him*, do you, Julie? You said you didn't love him. So what does it matter if he had a fling with your woman there?" I nodded towards the bride who was now making her way, albeit falteringly, towards the altar.

"It doesn't matter if I *love* Jay or not. That's my business, Mags. But he's gone and let me make an utter fool of myself, not to mention the fact he could have compromised this entire project. We're lucky that spoilt bitch turned up here at all this evening. How did I let this happen? My God! Me, the original control-freak! How did I let this happen?"

"Julie, listen to me. This is going to be all right, trust me. I *am* your best friend, or one of them. And I've told you from the start that Jay was trouble. I told you, you were far too good for him. Maybe it's better that you know the truth? We'll wrap this gig up and put the lot of it behind us."

"I can't *believe* he said all those lovely things to me and he didn't mean any of them," she persisted, looking at me with bewildered eyes.

"Maybe he did mean them at the time, Julie? But then he changed his mind? You know, like you changed your mind about Gary Devine? It's just life, Julie. These things happen. Please don't let this turn of events upset you. This is no reflection on you. It's him! It's Jay that can't be trusted."

But Julie was looking at me with such hurt and sadness on her face it was frightening. I did honestly think she was going to start sobbing uncontrollably. Which for Julie would have been unthinkable. She's not the sobbing type. Her fists were all balled up with frustration and as white as her ballgown.

"Months and months I've been chatting to that woman on the phone about the wedding arrangements, and all the time she was sleeping with my boyfriend! How could she?"

"Look, Julie, I'm so sorry to have to change the subject but I really think we should hurry up this wedding? Yes? The magistrate should be told to begin."

"The sneaky little cow," Julie gasped, and her face was scarily drained of all colour.

"Oh Julie, I'm begging you, will you pull yourself together?" I pleaded. "He's only a toy boy you were amusing yourself with in the afternoons. Talk this through with Jay when the wedding's over but right now we have work to do. They're getting plastered in the marquee and the head chef has gone home. Come on, we still have a wedding to direct!"

"Stuff the wedding!" Julie sobbed and she literally crumpled onto the grass in floods of tears.

At that moment, thank God, the magistrate roused himself and took control of the proceedings for us. He tapped the microphone, warmly welcomed everyone to the wedding and quickly began the brief service while the Druid began to limber up for the Pagan blessing that was to follow. One of the press photographers toppled over the guide ropes in sheer excitement and set off his flash bulb prematurely. And that's not a double entendre. I tried to put my hand on Julie's arm and help her to her feet but she pulled it away and refused to look at me.

"I've been a fool," was all she said. "This is the worst thing that has ever happened to me. An absolute fool!"

"No, you haven't," I told her. "Go easy on yourself."

"An utter fool."

"Get up, Julie. The ground is damp. You'll ruin your dress."

"I don't care, Mags. What's the point of anything, any more? What's the point of Dream Weddings, of the sex war? It's all a waste of time. Men are all the same. And so are women."

"Please, Julie? People are looking."

A small crowd had turned their backs on the bride and groom and were staring at Julie as she lay on the grass, quietly dissolving into sobs that actually overlapped each other. I crouched down beside her and put my arms round her shoulders. Her skin felt cold as ice.

"It's going to be all right, Julie," I said. "He didn't deserve you and you're better off without him. Come on now, where's the old Julie we all love and admire? Eh? What would The Coven say if they saw you like this?"

She didn't reply. She just went on crying. I willed my husband to come gliding into the middle of the crowd and carry me off in his arms. And Julie, too.

"We'll go back to my house when this night is over," I said, "and we'll have a big wedge of quiche and we'll laugh about it. Honestly, we will."

It was then I saw Jay lurking round the back wall of the castle. How he got past security I'll never know but then he *was* reared in the middle of nowhere and I expect he's pretty light on his feet over rough terrain. He was looking rather pale, I have to say. Rather tired and washed-out as if he hadn't slept all night. Come to think of it, he hadn't been hanging around the lighthouse much the day before when we'd been going over the finer details of the wedding. He did look wonderfully in keeping with the surroundings, I have to say, in a pair of amber-coloured jeans and a white shirt open halfway to his waist. A light smattering of chest hair and a perfect torso, his blond hair tousled and hanging in his eyes. His cheekbones catching the evening light in such a way you'd think it was all planned in advance. I thought he looked a bit spectral, like a ghost, to tell you the truth. But that was probably the bruising which still lingered round the sides of his nose. Jay gazed at the bride with tears of longing in his eyes and when she saw him standing there all alone against the moon she began to cry too. A lot of tears at this particular wedding, I noted.

"I'm sorry, but no, no, no," she said to the magistrate. "I just can't do it, okay? I've changed my mind."

"Could you repeat that, please?" the magistrate said, dropping his papers and his spectacles over the edge of the wooden decking and looking totally confused.

"Honestly, baby, you'll thank me some day," the supermodel said to her pint-sized partner, kissing him tenderly on the cheek and dropping her posy of blowsy white roses onto the smooth-swept gravel.

"Jay!" she cried. "Jay, my darling, I'm coming to you! Wait for me!"

The crowd gasped as one.

The bride fled across the low stone walls of the outlying ruins towards her lover while Julie and me stood paralysed with shock. It was so like an overblown 1980's

The Trouble with Weddings

stadium-rock-anthem video. I half-expected Bonnie Tyler to emerge from the dungeon on a fork-lift truck and start rasping and power-ballading about poisonous love affairs and broken hearts in the night. I'm sure Dream Weddings could have arranged it, now I come to think of it, if we'd been given enough notice. I've always had a soft spot for Bonnie Tyler even though she wasn't a Goth. You can't deny she had passion and dignity in abundance, compared to some contemporary pop tarts I could mention.

"I'm so sorry, baby," Jay called out to the French model, wrapping her in his arms and squeezing her very tightly as they finally met up and hugged. Embraced so tightly her cleavage swelled up in the tight black corset and threatened to spill over the edge of it. Her almost-bare breasts were touching Jay's exposed chest in a very erotic way. Their faces were so close together it was a romantic painting come to life. Cheekbones? His and hers. Forget about it. I was almost turned on myself though usually I'm strictly opposed to soft porn in all its various forms. Thin end of the wedge, and all that. We could see everything that was going on, perfectly backlit by the multi-coloured spotlights. I thought they were going to have sex right there and then. They might as well have, mind you: things couldn't have got any worse for Julie and me if they'd stripped off and got it on, on the damp grass.

"I'm so sorry, baby but I just had to see you getting married with my own two eyes," Jay wept into her fabulously braided hair. "I had to see it for myself to believe it was happening."

277

"What the *fuck* is going on here? Is this a joke or what?" The poor old rock-star stumbled a little and his red top hat fell off and rolled away into a patch of specially-planted white roses. "Who the hell's this Jay guy? Is this a set-up? Is this some TV thing? I didn't ask for this. Where the hell is Julie Sultana? I demand this prank be stopped right now!"

Julie was in full agreement there. Her misery at Jay's infidelity somehow transformed itself into a ball of pure anger.

"Stop it!" she cried, pulling off her dainty tiara, leaping to her feet and sprinting across the lawn. Straight into the ruins in her virginal ballgown. "Don't you dare think you can do this to me, Jay O'Hanlon! Don't you dare think this is going to happen! It's not over between us until I *say* it's over. Nobody finishes with Julie Sultana. Do you hear me?"

Well, Gary Devine had but she'd forgotten that, obviously.

And now, so had Jay. It was excruciating to witness.

Oh dear.

The toy boy and the supermodel.

They were kissing and kissing, melting into one another.

I don't think they'd even registered Julie's presence.

The beautiful bride and our Jay were in each other's arms and they were kissing and clinging onto one another as if their lives depended on it. A crack team of surgeons couldn't have parted them at that moment. All tears mingling, and shiny hair braids coming loose, and his arms locked round her impossibly tiny waist. And love, so much love, in the air. The stunned crowd didn't know whether to laugh, cry, clap or shout encouragement to the (new and improved) happy couple. So they did all four. I daresay the sheer extravagance of the day had backfired a little and the guests had grown weary of their capes and cloaks and a five-foot-tall wedding cake with lights blazing in all the 'windows'. The bride (oh, let's call her 'Sophie') finally saw Julie standing there and dashed into the marquee for cover, dragging Jay with her as the cameras went into overdrive.

In a desperate attempt to draw attention away from Julie and Jay and the whole fiasco that was taking place before us, I gave the signal for the fireworks to be ignited. The two technicians were right on it. They couldn't wait to get started, God bless them. Suddenly the air was split with the thunderous cracking and exploding of a thousand white fireworks. The sky was filled with light and white firework 'rain' drizzled down from the ramparts. It was fabulous.

And Julie?

Well, Julie flipped.

Flipped out in a big, big way.

It was a long time coming, I suppose. Forty-one years of being polite and in control can be very draining on the psyche, and now the moment of eruption had finally arrived it was like a dam breaking under the weight of winter floods. Maybe Julie was grieving for her lost childhood (that's the way I like to think of it now) or maybe she simply wasn't ready to say goodbye to Jay

O'Hanlon's mighty love-truncheon. But honestly, I've never seen a woman get so upset. She howled in pain like a wounded elephant, making a noise that wasn't remotely human. I tried to stop her but it was useless. She had the strength of ten men. Julie stormed into the elegant white marquee like a heat-seeking missile, punched Jay to the ground with one swipe, got Sophie's exquisite head in a sweaty arm-lock and plunged the poor woman into the middle of her own wedding cake. Right up to the neck. Held her down in it, I have to say. Like she was attempting to drown the sorry creature in vanilla frosting and apricot jam. Bits of cake and boxes of wiring came tumbling out the sides as Julie gave herself up to a tide of naked rage.

"You rotten slag, you dirty slut, you skinny whore, you two-timing liar, you filthy bitch, you gold-digging tramp, you greedy tart! You grubby tart! You . . . *tart*!"

But no, that was it. She'd run out of insults.

"Stop it, Julie," I cried in panic, trying to pull her off the other woman. "Julie, stop it. They aren't worth it, Julie. It takes two to tango and all that. Julie, stop it! She can't breathe! Stop it for pity's sake! You're going to kill her! Julie! Help me!"

I'm sure Sophie inhaled half a pint of whipped cream and vanilla crumbs before the security staff and Jay managed to pull her out of Julie's clutches. And even then my crazy boss got her hysterically waving hands all caught up in Sophie's elaborate hair-do and pulled out clumps of it by the roots. And as a parting gesture (as two buff young Rambo-look-alike security guards bore her away, struggling and screaming blue murder) she lashed out with her foot and kicked Sophie right in the eye. Oh yes. Julie gave our French supermodel a shiner so big and well, shiny, she'd definitely be off catwalk-duty for a couple of months.

"You silver-tongued bastard, you layabout lounge-lizard, you disgusting liar!" she screamed at Jay, who did (I'll admit) have the good grace to look slightly ashamed of himself. He'd tried to shield his delicate new love from Julie's full force but really she'd have throttled the two of them if it hadn't been for the hired help. She would have strangled them both and still had enough nervous energy left to mow down the confused and giggling guests with a medieval cannon. People were jostling at the marquee entrance, desperately trying to get a glimpse of the unfolding drama. Others were jumping into their cars and trying to flee the scene but they were getting stuck in the narrow carpark entrance.

It was absolutely awful.

"Well, this can't get any worse," I half-laughed, half-wept.

Wrong!

Because suddenly, the marquee was abandoned as the remaining onlookers scattered in every direction and all I saw was a black Volvo S80 coming bumping across the lawn and right into the middle of the banqueting area. It was being driven by the rock-star who had somehow grasped the enormity of what was happening to him. That is, he was getting the big 'E' in front of the world's most glamorous magazine editors. (It was the magazines that were glamorous, by the way, not so much the editors.) I think the car belonged to one of the bodyguards because the rock-star always seemed to travel by stretch-limo, but anyway there he was behind the wheel with the tears blinding him. And it finally dawned on me that he was possibly high on drugs. And shame, naturally. He was crunching the gears and revving the engine in a most alarming way. Chairs and tables and red-velvet tablecloths went bouncing and slithering off the bumper as the rock-star (I really can't name him for legal reasons but let's call him 'John' for the time being) as John tried to run Jay O'Hanlon into the ground. Drove right at him and accelerated wildly, the roar of the car's engine filling the marquee with ugly noise and confusion.

Jay O'Hanlon might have breathed his last among the toppling floral displays and the dried-up vegetarian banquet, had he not had the foresight to leap onto the chandelier and swing to safety via the roof struts. While Sophie rolled under the side of the tarp and rejoined her lover on the lawn outside. Once free, they jumped into one of the security Jeeps and sped away towards the gates as John did a three-point-turn in the black Volvo, ruining what was left of the wedding cake, and followed them. The last of the fireworks spluttered into silence.

My sugar levels bottomed out and I felt weak as a newborn kitten.

I sat down on a chair and gave up.

"Julie, I resign," I said blankly. "I'm too old for this shit. I'm going home."

She looked at me and I saw a smile turn up the corners of her mouth.

Could it possibly be?

Yes?

Yes!

Praise the Lord.

At last, Julie Sultana had come to her senses.

"Well, fuck this for a game of darts," she said calmly. "Let go of me, lads. The show's over. Right! I want you lot to round up whoever's left, give them a goody bag and get them back on the coaches. And you there, you waiters, please start closing up the buffet. Dump the food in the skip and pack away those glasses carefully. They're designer glasses and I want them all counted. Mags Grimsdale, your resignation is not accepted. I don't blame you for any of this. It was my own fault for being such an idiot. As soon as Bill comes, you can go home with him and I'll stay here and sort out this sorry lot. Okay?"

I could have sunk to the ground and kissed her feet, I was that relieved.

"Oh Julie," I said, "I'm so happy you've come back to us!"

Together we walked to the marquee entrance and looked up at the moon.

I was on Cloud Nine.

Whatever that is.

Or I would have been on Cloud Nine.

Had it not been for the sight of my beloved Bill coming driving in the castle gates and immediately colliding with John's out-of-control Volvo. A loud smash and Bill's Chrysler went over on its side and rolled down the hill towards the cliff edge. My beloved husband didn't even have time to register shock, I'm sure of it. One second he was just doing what he does best, trying to locate me in the crowd and bring me home. The next, he was rattling and rolling towards a very low stone wall and a sixty-foot drop into the ocean. John went on out through the castle gates, clipping one of them on his way. It all seemed to be happening in slow motion.

My heart turned inside-out with horror.

"Fucking hell," said Julie, her hands flying up to her mouth.

"Bill!" I screamed, clutching Julie's arm so tightly I probably hurt her. "Bill! Don't be dead. Don't leave me! Bill! Oh my God, somebody make it stop! *Bill*!"

And so on.

It was the worst moment of my entire life. I was frozen to the spot. We all were. The departing guests, the traumatised young waiters, the experienced security staff, even Julie herself. We all stared in paralysed horror as Bill's car slowed down and suddenly came to rest against the wall, battered and broken, all the windows smashed.

You could have heard a pin drop.

"Mags, we have got to be brave now," said Julie in a strangely calm whisper. "Come on. We'll go to Bill together. Hold my hand and take a deep breath."

Julie half-pulled me and I half-ran to Bill on legs that felt like concrete pillars. Every step drained me and there was cold sweat on my face and on my back by the time I reached him. Julie looked into the car first while I stood nearby whimpering and doing a great impression of Charlotte Sultana in the early years. Bill was still moving, just about. Out of the corner of my eye I could see him brushing some broken glass from his face. His hand was covered in blood.

"He's alive, Mags. He's okay. He's still breathing."

Julie beckoned to me to come forward.

I swiftly threw up on the grass, then cautiously pulled Bill's crumpled car door open. He was slumped there, gasping, all twisted and uncomfortable-looking, covered in blood, bits of broken glass, clumps of mud and neatly mown grass.

"Bill, are you all right?" I said hopelessly. "Can you breathe?"

"Just about," he gasped. "I think my leg's broken. And my collarbone. And my hand. And I feel very cold."

"That'll be the shock, love. I'll call an ambulance, Mags," Julie said, brushing a stray piece of cake from her cleavage and slurring her words a bit after so much vodka. "Don't worry, Mags! And don't move him in case he has spinal injuries!" She hitched up her dress and ripped a mobile phone out of the garter on her leg. Julie never goes anywhere without her mobile phone. Thank heaven for Julie Sultana!

"Bill, my darling!" I wept, dropping to my knees beside him, holding his lovely firm hand (the one that wasn't broken) in mine.

He closed his eyes and coughed gently. He tried to say something but all he could do was swallow and moan.

"Talk to me, my love. I think you should try to stay awake and talk to me. Bill, please, please, *please* talk to me!"

And he did say something.

"Never a dull moment with you, Mags Grimsdale," he whispered. "Whatever happens, I love you."

And then he lapsed into unconsciousness. Julie got a waiter to round up some blankets from the First Aid tent and we made Bill as comfortable as we could. Then I knelt there, holding onto his hand, praying for the ambulance to arrive. Thinking to myself, that's the third ambulance that's had to be summoned in this sorry escapade. Because Gary had needed one when he had his car accident on the way down to Galway, and of course Jay had needed one when Gary broke his nose in the Café Vaudeville.

All the while, Julie stayed right beside me with a fire extinguisher (just in case the Chrysler caught fire) and constantly told me everything was going to be all right. She even got some of the men to tie a rope around the car and lash it to a stone outbuilding, just in case the ground underneath us was unsafe. The wedding guests were kept away from the scene and ushered out of the grounds as quickly as possible. She'd also called the police and let them know John was at large in the area, chasing another car while under the influence of (presumably illegal) drugs.

I kept kissing Bill's forehead and thinking I wasn't ready to lose him. Thinking, I wasn't anywhere near ready to cope without him, say the worst did happen. And then feeling weak with shame for even considering my own future at a time like that. But there was no denying I needed Bill as much as I loved him. He was my best friend, really. Despite the wide circle of family and friends that I was blessed with, Bill was the one I get my strength from. He was my soul. I broke down and wept quietly with relief as the ambulance arrived, and again when they told me Bill had a strong pulse and no obvious internal bleeding.

"A lot of pain and some broken bones but he should be okay."

"Thank God," I kept saying, "thank God, thank God, thank God."

And so it was back to hospital waiting rooms and the smell of disinfectant. Julie never left my side. She stayed with me all night and she never mentioned her own heartbreak once. We held hands at one point during Bill's operation (on his leg because the break was messy and jagged) which was kind of weird. But also nice and reassuring. Then at daybreak we sipped hot tea and nibbled on a biscuit or two from the vending-machine to keep our stomachs from grumbling. Well, we hadn't eaten for what seemed like an age.

"I'm really sorry I didn't tell you about Jay earlier, Julie," I said, as the sun rose over the roof of the nurses' apartment block.

"That's okay," she said, patting my arm. "I probably wouldn't have listened anyway, Mags. To tell you the truth, I think I went off the rails a bit there. I must have looked an awful eejit to you and everyone else."

"No, not at all," I said. "He was very handsome and nobody would have blamed you for getting carried away. I'm only sorry it didn't work out. I mean that, now. I'm not just saying it."

"Water under the bridge," she smiled sadly. "Just one of those things."

And so the subject of Jay O'Hanlon was officially downgraded from life-changing watershed to mere office gossip.

Then I was allowed to see my husband.

Bill had one collarbone broken and the other one fractured, a badly broken leg, three fractured fingers, severe bruising on his face and neck, part of the glove-compartment door embedded in his knee, and a spot of short-term memory-loss. He was on the strongest painkillers the hospital staff could legally administer. But his wonderful, loving, caring personality was still intact and we both shed more than a few tears of gratitude.

"Oh, Bill, what are you like?" I wept when I saw him in the bed.

"You should see the other guy," he whispered. "Ah well, at least I'll get a few days off work."

Julie left us there together and went back to my house to check on the boys. We'd phoned them the night before and they were anxious to visit as soon as Bill was up to it. Meanwhile, John had been stopped by the police sometime around midnight as he tore through a neighbouring village. He'd been arrested and charged with dangerous driving. He went quietly in the end, so I'm told, and apologised profusely for causing Bill's many injuries. He hadn't even realised Bill's car had flipped over, he was in such a state. He said he was thoroughly ashamed of himself and offered to go back into rehab.

Sophie and Jay, well, they made a clean getaway and

caught the next flight to Paris. She in her bridal gown and Jay in his white shirt. Lucky sods were on the plane before the police could detain them as witnesses. Who'd have thought, in the middle of all the drama and confusion, that Sophie and Jay O'Hanlon would have had the foresight to bring their passports (and her credit card) with them to the castle? Proving for once and for all that not all supermodels and toy boys are as stupid as they look.

And me? Well, I sat at Bill's bedside chatting to him and saying how it was all my fault and how I'd stop being so needy, and stand on my own two feet for a change, and did he want any more water or lemonade, until I collapsed (again) and was carried out of the ward by my three handsome sons and put in my own bed at home and told to stay in it. They switched on my telly, bought me a lorry-load of magazines and sour worms from the corner-shop, and ordered me to rest. I slept for eighteen hours. First lie-in I'd had in a long, long time. The only thing I did do was call Alicia-Rose to tell her what had happened but also to tell her she wasn't to come rushing back to Belfast. That her dad was going to make a full recovery.

18

See You in Court

I DIDN'T GIVE A LOT OF THOUGHT TO DREAM WEDDINGS IN the days that followed my husband's brush with death. All the more galling because he'd dearly loved the Volvo S80 up until that point, but he didn't want one driven at speed up his crotch, thank you very much. And having the shards of plastic removed from his knee was agony, he said. Sheer bloody agony. Still, on the bright side he was making a good recovery and Alexander was able to take on the smaller jobs for him, for the time being, having just passed his driving test on the first attempt. I was overjoyed that my eldest son hadn't inherited my hopeless driving skills. So even though Julie had given me a few weeks off work, I was still quite busy fielding phone calls from Bill's customers, washing and ironing Andrew and Christopher's rugby kits, calling Alicia-Rose in Australia each day and getting used to living without Bill while he still remained in hospital.

God, I hated the loneliness of being alone in the house on those bright May mornings and afternoons. Yes, just one week on my own and I was getting cabin-fever. Jesus knows how some women manage it for fifty years, pottering about making jam and ironing handkerchiefs. They ought to be canonised! In fact, I don't think I'd have survived without *Diagnosis Murder* and countless cups of hot chocolate. That Barry Van Dyke would do in a pinch, wouldn't he, I thought to myself? Not for me, no. I've found my hero. But for all the other ladies out there who are still looking for theirs, Barry's quite the pin-up.

The Coven rescued Julie in the end, and took her to stay with one of them for a while. Well, they did have no small hand in getting Jay and Julie together in the first place, I suppose. Amanda and Rebecca (the prosecution lawyers, do you remember?) got right on the case. They hired a lawyer friend of theirs to help Bill and he turned up some juicy details from the police report. It turned out John *was* high on cocaine when he knocked poor Bill into the middle of next week, *and* he was currently banned from driving for five years anyway. But even though the stupid guy could well have killed my other half, his team of lawyers told our lawyer he was hoping to get off with a charge of reckless driving. And maybe he'd admit to 'driving under the influence' on the grounds he'd been severely provoked in his actions and was under extreme stress at the time. And also he'd promised to go back into rehab for his drug problems and give lots of interviews telling young people that drugs didn't work. And although they didn't say as much, I knew they were all hoping the shockingly lightweight jail sentences that reckless drivers receive in .this country would be to their advantage. Of course, we were asked if we wanted to settle out of court. But Bill was determined that the case should go ahead because he said celebrities shouldn't be allowed to buy their way out of trouble. He said he wanted John to serve time. Not usually a vindictive man, my husband. But you've got to remember he was on heavy medication. And so both camps withdrew to build their respective cases and we all waited for a court date to be scheduled.

Meanwhile, Julie and Dream Weddings carried on as usual. There was some talk going about the city, naturally, about how the wedding of the century had ended in disaster. But as most of the guests were from out-of-town, there was nowhere for the press to dig their claws in. And the pictures of Julie stuffing Sophie's head into the haunted house wedding cake never saw the light of day because John's people paid them all off. One million dollars for every reel of film. To me, an insane amount of money just to save himself from the embarrassment of being jilted at the altar. But then again, as Amanda and Rebecca pointed out, he had no choice if he wanted to salvage his rock-star reputation.

"Who would buy the silly twat's albums," they said wisely, "if it was known that he was cuckolded for months and then abandoned at the wedding, while he stood up like an eejit in a red-velvet coat with skulls embroidered across his back, and just let it happen?"

Who, indeed? The popular music market is very fickle.

So, as I say, the whole world and his dog knew the wedding had been called off but without a set of juicy pictures to go with it, the story sank into the background after a couple of days. And was overtaken by a scare story about the amount of fat and salt in the average packet of crisps. Litres of oil apparently we're all pouring down our necks each year. Maybe that's why I still get the odd pimple at my age, I thought and immediately decided to go cold turkey on the sour cream pretzels. It was nearly as difficult and stressful as burying my father had been. I woke up in the night yearning both for a handful of crunchy salty pretzels, and for a lovely cosy non-threatening dad in carpet slippers and a zip-up cardigan. Just an ordinary father who grew tomatoes in the greenhouse and read gardening almanacs and maybe kept an allotment or a small quiet dog.

I sincerely hoped Emma hadn't got wind of the oily crisps outrage because it might have set her progress back months. Those shocking pictures of young children drinking big plastic bottles of bright yellow cooking oil even made my stomach heave. And I adored crisps. But Alexander told me Emma had more or less given up watching 'lifestyle' telly and reading glossy gossip magazines as part of her recovery programme. And that she was now reading quality novels in her spare time and they were thinking of rescuing a tiny dog from the animal shelter to take for walks. They'd asked the owner of the flat if they could keep a small pet and he'd said yes, they could, as long as it didn't make a lot of noise. And that if a ground floor apartment with a small garden ever came up for rent, he would let them know.

Anyway, I was having a little lie-down in my bed one evening about eight days after the accident. I was feeling quite worn out from the twice-daily hospital visits by then. God knows how some families manage to care for their relatives for years and years on end. But anyway, I was half-asleep and wondering how Bill would manage the stairs when he came home, and if we should get a stairlift installed, when there was a loud knock at the front door. There was nobody else in the house at the time (Andrew and Christopher were at a pop concert in the Waterfront Hall with a bunch of their mates) so reluctantly I dragged myself out of my cosy bed and went down the stairs to answer it.

"This had better not be some jolly lady collecting for charity or worse some underweight young man who can't speak English selling flipping dusters and making me feel sorry for him," I said crossly to one of Bill's guitars, "because I'm so not in the mood for it today."

Quick tip for you: always keep a dish of pound coins beside the front door for such eventualities. It saves you a lot of time running round the house looking for your purse while some stranger loiters in your front porch, possibly casing the joint for a burglary later on. Then, you can just hand over two quid, grab the dusters or whatever, say thanks and shut the door without getting into a lengthy chat-situation with them. Sorry to sound so cruel and detached but there you are. Ditto carol-singers, cold-callers, et cetera.

But anyway, to my great surprise it was Julie.

"Hello there, Mags Grimsdale," she said sheepishly. "How've you been?"

"Hello yourself, Julie Sultana," I said. "I'm okay. Come in."

"How's Bill?"

"He's much better, He's coming home tomorrow. Just in time for Alexander's wedding. The doctor says he can go if he feels up to it."

"Oh, how lovely for you!"

"Yes, I can't wait to have him home. It's weird going to bed without him."

"I know the feeling," she said in a small voice.

"I'm sorry, Julie."

"Forget it."

Julie was looking fabulous, I have to say. Bob newly styled, gorgeous blue-stone choker round her neck with silver and white flowers dangling from it, knee-length brown leather boots and a swanky new handbag still smelling of leather and luxury. Her perfume was heavy and spicy and I felt my heart aching for the past. The past, when everything was so simple. Before Alicia-Rose went to Australia. Before Julie went off the rails and left me to run the business on my own half the time. Before my Bill was almost killed . . . and I knew it was finally time for me to grow-up.

"These are for you," Julie said sweetly, handing me an enormous bouquet of pink flowers, lots of different kinds including some exotic blooms I'd never seen before. They looked like sleeping tarantulas, to tell you the truth, except they were pink. And there was a dramatic pink grass thing going on around the bottom. Enough cellophane and ribbons to sink a ship. Very Julie,

I decided. I wondered what she wanted from me. Possibly she needed me back early at the lighthouse?

"Well, how lovely!" I said, reaching out for the flowers. "Thanks very much, Julie. You shouldn't have. But they *are* beautiful. What's the occasion?"

"Oh, I think we both know what the occasion is, Mags. To say how very, very silly I've been. And how terrific you've been, taking over for me at the lighthouse when I was busy . . . It won't happen again, I promise. The control-freak is back for good."

"It's forgotten. Really."

"Hopefully everyone else will forget soon, too. People have short memories, Mags. All of this will be ancient history one day. Oh, I thought we might change the name of the business when the court case is over. White Orchid Weddings, did you say once? I think that's lovely."

"Oh, no, Julie. I've changed my mind. I think we should keep Dream Weddings, honestly I do. It feels right. We've been through a lot together and I want to keep it."

"Really? Do you?"

"Yes. I do."

"Okay then. Dream Weddings it is."

"Look, have you time for a cuppa?" I said.

"I thought you'd never ask," Julie purred and she gave me such an intense hug, the lovely pink flowers were almost squashed between us.

"Come through to the kitchen," I told her, setting off down the hall.

Seeing Julie again reminded me of the night of the

accident. Which was unsettling. But also, I was feeling delighted that she was in my house again and obviously missing me loads. "Here, can you pop these into the good room for me?" I asked her. And I passed her back the bouquet. "It's cooler in there. I'll just get the kettle on."

She took the flowers and nudged the door of the good room open with her toe.

"Oh, Mags! It's gorgeous in here," she said, clocking the depleted collection of candlesticks and the new white Roman blind. "Looks twice the size without the Gothic stuff and the purple silk drapes. Where's Goily, though? Have you thrown him out?"

"He's in the garden," I told her, already gathering my best red plates and cups from the dresser shelves and switching on the toasted-sandwich maker. "We thought he would look nicer in the garden."

Well, it's a yard, really. But we call it a garden because it's full to bursting with plants and flowers growing in pots and on a trellis Bill fixed to the wall years ago. There's a little iron seat in the only corner that catches the sun and I like to think it's an artistic sort of spot to relax in. So we'd heaved Goily onto an old skateboard of Alexander's and wheeled him out to his new home and he does look quite settled beside the creeping ivy, I have to say.

"You should have had the room like this for your dad's thingamyjig," Julie said thoughtfully. She's Free Presbyterian so she's not very well up on wake-lingo. Julie's biggest worry at times of bereavement is what hat to wear, but really I can't fault her on that because she wasn't ever close to her relatives on either side when she was growing up. I sometimes wonder how she'd cope if anything happened to The Coven but then I scold myself for being so morbid. Anyway, I have no doubt Julie's friends are immortal. They do give you that impression.

"Oh, I know. I can't believe we didn't think of using the skateboard to move him at the time. The gargoyle, not my father! Oh well, it's done now. Cheese and onion do you?" I said, fetching some Stilton with cranberries from the fridge and a shiny red onion from the vegetable rack.

"Sounds lovely," Julie said, hopping up on a stool at the breakfast counter and playing with her rings and bracelets nervously. "I do miss your sandwiches, Mags. I think I took them rather for granted over the years."

"We've all taken things for granted," I said. "It's human nature."

The kitchen was warm and welcoming and Julie's many bracelets rattled prettily as I chopped the onion and buttered four slices of bread.

"Well," I asked her, "what's up? Come on and tell me all the gossip."

"I went to visit Charlotte yesterday," Julie said suddenly, as the lid of the sandwich toaster hissed down.

Julie always calls her mother Charlotte, never Mummy or Mum.

"How is she?" I asked, pouring tea into cups and hunting through the cupboard for a packet of sugar. Julie takes sugar in her tea, and I don't. I know, it doesn't make sense to me either: her ankles are like straws.

"The same. I told her my new boyfriend had cheated on me with another woman, a client of ours, to be precise. I told her he'd left me for this other woman and I was heartbroken. Well, I wasn't really heartbroken but I wanted to see what she'd say."

"I can guess what she said."

"Yeah? 'Men are all the same,' she said to me. 'When will you ever learn?' That was it! Ten words in all. I counted them. She didn't even ask for details. Wouldn't you think she'd want to know all the gory details, Mags? Any normal woman would."

"No chummy advice on relationships, no anguished cries of motherly outrage? No hugs and kisses, even?"

"Nope. Not a sausage. Same old Charlotte, dry-eyed and cynical to the bitter end. She simply went on folding the jeans and setting out new shoes and handbags on the shelves as if I'd told her I'd broken a fingernail."

"Oh, Julie. I'm so sorry."

"Well, I didn't expect her to be shocked or even mildly upset. But you'd think she could have faked a bit of sympathy for me, couldn't she? Jesus! I mean, she makes chit-chat all day long to her customers, talking about all the events they're going to and coming from. Why doesn't she love me, Mags? Why doesn't she love me the way you love your children? Was it my father's fault, do you think? Did he make her so detached? Or was she born that way? Odd as a fish? Is that why she didn't leave him when it all went pear-shaped?"

"I don't know, Julie. I'd say it's all so long ago now, she'd need therapy to find out. And maybe it would only make her worse? You know, to think she wasted her life because of religion and keeping up appearances? I'm undecided on the therapy debate, to be honest with you. With some people, there's a lot to be said for sticking your head in the sand and just getting on with life. I think Charlotte is one of those people."

"Maybe she is."

"Is that why you went so crazy for Jay O'Hanlon, though? Because he made you feel loved? Because he was so over-the-top you couldn't ignore him?"

"I think so, yes."

"And what about Gary Devine? Didn't he make you feel cherished? He did propose to you, remember?"

"Yes, he did, but I didn't realise in time how nice he was. I think I took him for granted as well. He's moved on, by the way."

"Did you try and make it up with him?" I asked her, astonished. That was very brave, I thought to myself.

"No, I didn't go over there or anything. I just wanted to apologise for all the hurt I caused him. I called him for a chat. But he told me he's met a new girl. A paramedic nurse from when he broke his leg on the way to Galway. They've been out on a few dates. She's only twenty-five."

"Oh. I'm sorry, Julie. Are you bothered?"

"I don't know, Mags. I wanted to be with Jay more than I ever wanted to be with Gary so maybe I didn't love Gary enough anyway? I still don't understand what went wrong between Gary and me. So that's the end of it, I suppose."

SHARON OWENS

"Oh Julie," I said sadly. "Never mind. Think of this as a new chapter in your life. A clean slate and you can start all over again. You have your friends, still."

"Yes," she said then, a familiar smile twitching at the corners of her mouth. "Yes, I suppose I do. That's what I came to tell you, actually. The girls are taking me away for a little holiday. Couple of weeks in the sun somewhere. Bit of shopping, some decent food."

"Well, that's nice. Where are you going, exactly? Italy? Spain?"

"Oh, I'm not sure," she said, and it seemed to me her face was flushing slightly. "I think they said something about Paris."

"Oh my God, Julie Sultana!"

"What?"

"What do you think? Isn't Paris where Jay O'Hanlon hangs out these days? With our old mucker, Bigfoot?"

"I really wouldn't have a clue, Mags. They could be anywhere, for all I care."

"Julie, you are telling me the truth, aren't you? Because I'd hate for you to get into any more trouble over that guy. He's so not worth it."

"Let me see, Mags. What's the toy-boy-related-tally-of-damage so far? My beautiful apartment trashed by Gary. Gary's leg broken and his car written off. Your husband almost killed, you and your kids traumatised, the reputation of Dream Weddings in the balance, me nearly choking that so-called model to death in her own wedding cake. I could have been arrested, never mind that middle-aged pillock in his stupid red coat. And I've

302

been banned from the lovely spa in Galway for life. And it was so nice and warm, too. I hate a cold spa. But anyway I think I've caused enough trouble, Mags, and suffered enough for that particular young man. Don't you?"

"Okay, I get the message."

"Good."

"It was a fling, Mags, nothing more. A fling that got out of hand."

"Yes, but you did seem awfully upset when you saw them together that day. I've never seen you so mad in the entire fourteen years I've known you."

"Mags, one last word about that little drama and then we really will forget about it: I was under a lot of stress, as you may recall. Our biggest commission ever, we could have been in all the magazines. We could have been world-famous and only dealing with millionaires from now on instead of ordinary people."

"Julie!"

"Though of course there's nothing wrong with ordinary people but you know what I mean. I mean, it would have been nice to work without monetary constraints for a change, and we could've put our prices up and taken on fewer gigs. But Jay spoiled our big moment with his wandering eye, and the rest of it. No, I've learned my lesson. No more mixing business with pleasure for me, Mags."

"Okay, okay! So, tell me about this great trip of yours, then," I said. "When do you leave?"

"In a couple of days. We'll see the sights, obviously.

Do some shopping, take in a show and needless to say we'll get blind drunk every night."

"Be careful, Julie," I said. "Don't get too drunk, sure you won't? And don't leave your drinks unattended if you're in a disco or club of any kind. Same rules apply the world over, like I said to Alicia-Rose. Take it in turns to mind the drinks. Tourists are easy pickings for some criminals."

"Mags Grimsdale, you never change. Always playing the mother duck."

"Mother hen."

"Oh yeah. But don't be worrying about me, Mags. The Coven will look after me."

"Em, we'll see about that," I mumbled doubtfully. Thinking of the military jacket they'd bought for Jay. I wondered where the jacket was now but I didn't dare ask Julie.

"I nearly forgot!" Julie said then. "I nearly forgot to give you a little something for your Alexander. For his girlfriend, actually."

"Emma?"

"Yes, Emma. Here it is," she said and she took a small box out of her handbag and set it on the counter between us. Gorgeous little pale blue velvet box, all done up in curly ribbons.

"Crikey, Julie, that looks like a good-quality jewellery box of some kind. I hope you haven't spent too much money on it?"

"Oh, now! Never you mind what it cost. It's a lovely diamond pendant."

"A diamond? Emma will be delighted."

"I got a white diamond so it'd match anything she'll be wearing."

"Gosh, Julie, that's so lovely of you. I'm sure she'll love it. They didn't buy a diamond engagement ring, you see."

"Yes, well, I know they didn't and we can't have that! Now, I'm sorry I can't be there on the day, Mags, but I'll be in Paris by the time the vows are read out."

"Staying out of trouble, I hope?" I said pointing my finger at her like a Mother Superior and giving her my sternest expression.

"Maybe, we'll have to wait and see," said Julie and she laughed her head off.

I couldn't decide, as we polished off the rest of the tea and half an almond cake, if she was really back to normal or not. Back to the same old Julie we all knew and loved. Or if she'd ever been normal to begin with. But she did seem to have got a relative grip on things at any rate. She said she was going to enjoy herself in Paris for a bit and then come home to Belfast all refreshed and ready to begin house-hunting for a place to live. And back to the grindstone at Dream Weddings, of course. We had a lot of ground to gain back.

"It'll be you and me once again, sitting at our desks, Mags. Scoffing M&S sarnies and making funny faces at the customers when they're warbling on, on the telephone."

I took a deep breath and thought of Bill struggling to stand up in the hospital. He was going to need an awful lot of love and support before he was back on his feet.

"Listen, Julie," I said, "I feel it's only fair to tell you, I'm thinking of going part-time until Bill gets better. Just thinking about it at the moment. But I'm quite serious, all the same."

"Oh, now, Mags," Julie said slowly, and suddenly I knew why she'd bought me such a whopper of a bouquet. Not to mention the expensive diamond pendant for Emma. "I'm sure Bill won't want you flapping about and fussing over him like he's some sort of invalid. He'll be fine, my dear – he's a very strong man. And I'm relying on you to keep our little ship afloat while I'm away in Paris."

"Julie Sultana, you never change! I thought you said I could have some time off?"

"Yes, but that was before I knew about this trip. Sorry! Oh, it's not as bad as you think, Mags. Hear me out. Firstly, I'm giving you a pay rise, a big one. And you deserve it, it's not a bribe."

"Keep talking."

"*And* I'm giving you authority to make bigger decisions without asking me first. *And* I'm giving you a travel allowance for any taxis you might have to take in the course of business. *And* I've checked our schedule for the next two weeks while I'm away. You won't have to go to any weddings or clients' houses on your own."

"I'll think about it."

"Terrific! Just you answer the phone and start thinking of new ideas for fantasy weddings. 'Tis an ill wind and all that – all the secrecy surrounding that godforsaken wedding has driven the punters wild. They're all desperate to have an OTT bash in a dramatic location. Maybe the recent bats-in-the-belfry event is going to pay off after all."

"I'll be lonely in the lighthouse without you, though, Julie. I don't know if I fancy two weeks with nothing but the seagulls to keep me company. I'm still feeling pretty shaken, you know."

"Of course you are. Which is why I've patched our phone number through to this house for the time being."

"Julie! You're incorrigible."

"Well, isn't that the best idea? You can answer the phone if you're not busy or you can switch on the answer-machine and get back to them later. Okay? So you can still babysit your gorgeous husband, and everybody's happy?"

She fished the Dream Weddings order book out of her big handbag and laid it gently on the breakfast counter.

"You did say you were bored," she reminded me.

"Did I? Go on, then. I suppose it'll be all right," I sighed.

"Of course it will, Mags. It'll be tip-top. Now, I've got to go shopping for some new clothes to take away on my trip and I'm sure you've got things to do around here for Bill coming home, so I'll be off. And do have a super day at Alexander's wedding. I do hope Bill will be able to make it?"

"Try stopping him!"

"Okay, great stuff! Love to all! Cheerio!"

And she was gone out the front door. Leaving a trail of spicy perfume behind her. I looked at the exotic pink flowers sitting majestically in the good room and I thought of my father and reminded myself that life was very short and we should all make the most of it.

"Have a ball in Paris, Julie Sultana," I said to the pink flowers.

And she did.

That's where she met Henri.

Apparently, Julie was sitting in a dark and shadowy little café on her own, on the last day of her holiday. Just having a private moment to herself (she was crying, to tell you the truth) and she didn't want The Coven to see. So there she was, softly weeping behind a newspaper when she spies this handsome man staring at her from another table. And get this, he was crying too! It was a meeting of minds, Julie said. A meeting of lost souls. So she smiled at him and nodded hello. And this gorgeous guy gets up from his seat and comes over to join her and wouldn't you know it, even though he was French, he spoke perfect English. So they got talking and Julie told him she was getting over a broken heart and that coming to beautiful Par-ee had only reminded her of what she'd lost. And then Henri (he'd introduced himself by then) told Julie he was on his own too. After his girlfriend of five years had left him and gone back to her ex, taking their two children with her. I mean, the two children she'd had with her ex. So Henri hadn't just lost his lady-love, he'd lost the two children as well. So he was completely devastated as you can imagine. And somehow they got chatting and they went for a walk together by the Eiffel Tower. And then for a drink in a bar by the river. By the end of the evening they had swapped phone numbers and agreed to keep in touch. And then Julie was only home in Belfast two hours when Henri turned up at the lighthouse and asked her out on a date. She couldn't believe it. I mean, she was on the only flight to Belfast that morning, but then Henri told her he had rented a private jet. Very romantic, say you choose to forget about wasting aviation fuel and so on. So they went on a date in good old Belfast: out to the Culloden Hotel for a meal and then for a drive to the Giant's Causeway in Julie's white Mercedes convertible, and that's where they had their first kiss. Good old Henri. I don't know if it'll last as they were both on the rebound but he's given Julie her confidence back and that's the main thing.

19

True Love

SHE LOOKED SO BEAUTIFUL ON HER WEDDING DAY, Emma did. Just a few short months after being discharged from a private clinic specialising in eating disorders, and she really did look beautiful. She weighed maybe eight stone which was fair enough considering her height. Although another few pounds would have left us feeling very relieved. But anyway, she did look gorgeous in a simple cream evening dress and wearing Julie's diamond pendant. And it looked amazingly sparkly and bright against Emma's flawlessly smooth skin. Her sleek black bob was trimmed to perfection and two neat slicks of eyeliner were painted perfectly onto her upper lids. Alexander shed a tear or two when she walked into the marriage room and I didn't blame him one bit. So much had changed for both of them in the space of a year.

For all of us, really.

Andrew and Christopher had told us the day before

they were definitely going to Manchester to study
dentistry when they were finished their exams. So I
thought to myself, as Emma and Alexander held hands at
the desk, that fragile little girl up there is the only reason
I might have one of my precious children still living near
me in the years ahead. Still living in this country, in fact.
Who'd have thought it? It'd be a few months before my
youngest two sons would be off on the next phase of their
lives, but still, I knew that once they got settled in
Manchester they would never come back. It happens all
the time. Students make new friends, they get to know a
new town and put down roots. Next thing you know, they
start calling their university town 'home' and only
thinking of Belfast on Saint Patrick's Day, if ever. Bill said
we could move to Manchester if I wanted. Just as soon as
the boys went over, we'd go too, he said. We didn't have
to live in the same house or anything. The lads would
probably want a bit of independence. But we'd buy a
house nearby so they could come round for Sunday lunch
and a chat. Alexander and Emma might consider moving
to England too, Bill suggested, so the family wouldn't be
split up. And I said I would think about it. But in my
heart, I wasn't ready to leave Belfast. I wanted to keep a
family base going in case Alicia-Rose grew tired of the
sweltering heat and the crocodiles, and my youngest two
got tired of asking for 'a brew', and even in case
Alexander and Emma's great love story petered out and
became just another divorce statistic. I mean, I was
almost sure they'd make it but there are no guarantees in
this life. Just look at me and my Bill. All the love in the

world, and he was nearly killed by a rock-star high on drugs.

But that day, I just wanted to be happy and think of nothing except how much wedding cake and chocolate profiteroles and chilled champagne I could get down my neck before I went to bed. And I was planning to break all previous records. In fact, I already had half a bottle of fizz inside me before the marriage ceremony kicked off. I drank it in the kitchen of our house before the taxi came. Bill's leg was still in plaster, don't forget, so he couldn't drive us. And anyway, he was planning to get pretty merry himself at the buffet afterwards. He reckoned he'd be okay in such a small flat because there weren't any big flights of stairs he could fall down. And the management of the building had agreed to let him use the service lift.

When Alexander and Emma were duly declared man and wife, I was first out of my chair, running up the 'aisle' to congratulate them and hug them both before they'd even had time to kiss each other!

Mothers!

You can't take us anywhere.

It was a bit sad that Alicia-Rose couldn't be there but she was listening in on her mobile phone and heard most of the ceremony, interspersed with me sniffling and Bill telling me not to cry. Then it was everybody back to Alexander and Emma's place in a convoy of cars and taxis and we had a fantastic party. All manner of dainty snacks and sauces, decorated and garnished like some cookery show on the television. And some good old Irish stodge for the less adventurous. Big bowls of beef stew and mashed potatoes, mashed carrots and parsnips, caramelised fried onions and neat slices of wheaten bread and rhubarb jam. All laid out on a white cloth and white plates and dishes, strewn here and there with silver glitterballs. They'd kept to their £1K budget but it didn't feel like it, not one bit. Funnily enough, Emma's side of the family were very taken with the beef stew while our lot devoured the much prettier snacks. I suppose we all wanted to be enthusiastic for the bride and groom but the food was delicious and the day was certainly a triumph. We sat around and chatted for hours, just listening to some pop compilation tapes and then we had wedding cake and tea as Alexander and Emma opened the last of their gifts.

They did get some lovely things, mostly household items like a silver-coloured microwave, some fancy cast-iron saucepans, trendy wine glasses and wine racks and a bale of big soft fluffy towels. But there was also quite a tidy sum in cash and they said they would put the money in the bank for a rainy day. Some people sang songs and did a bit of dancing and of course we took lots of photographs. Finally, we threw boxes and boxes of confetti over them and each other (not a problem to sweep up because they had wooden floors) and said our very emotional goodbyes.

They weren't going away on honeymoon just yet, Emma said. They wanted to enjoy being in the apartment for a few days and, when she felt up to it, they would go to Cornwall for a weekend break. They still had the price of the trip to Cornwall in the kitty. Yes, even after all that food, and Alexander's new suit and shoes.

Julie would have been disgusted!

And then, a few weeks later, just after Julie and The Coven came back to Belfast, I read something in a gossip magazine about a mystery prank that had been played on a top model in Paris. Apparently Sophie's very pretty townhouse was filled to the rafters with *tonnes* and *tonnes* of neon-pink disco-foam. The kind of thing they have at those wild open-air parties in Ibiza and those 'happening' types of places. Some person or persons unknown had slipped a nozzle through the kitchen window at the back of the house and flooded the building completely with clouds and clouds of fluffy sticky foam. It went all the way up to the top of the house and was even photographed spilling out of the chimney like a scene from *The Magic Porridge Pot*. No-one was at home at the time of the incident, except for Sophie's cat which thankfully made its escape through the cat-flap.

The commentators said it must have been the work of radical anti-fur protesters: Sophie was known to wear a real fur jacket on her frequent skiing trips. But no-one claimed responsibility and the culprit was never discovered. It was all seen as a massive joke in the media (the Internet nearly collapsed with people logging on to have a gawk and a giggle) until it was revealed that Sophie's collection of designer clothes was completely ruined. Four rooms full of coats, hats, shoes, waistcoats, dresses and handbags. Over half a million pound's worth of Vivienne Westwood, Prada, Gucci, Chanel and so on:

all dyed bright pink and drenched in ugly pink tidemarks. And to top it all, Sophie hadn't insured her collection. Imagine that. Maybe she'd pinched a fair bit of it when no-one was looking backstage or maybe she didn't want to pay the high insurance premiums, but anyway she was out of pocket by half a million quid, and all her lovely cream and gold vintage décor was ruined too.

I did ask Julie once, and only once, if she'd filled Sophie's house with 'doctored' disco-foam just so's she could have the last laugh in the matter. But she said no, she definitely hadn't.

"Honestly, Mags," she said laughing her head off, "you're becoming quite the paranoid princess. Do you really think I'd be that immature? Where would I even get one of those stupid machines? Or a bucket of pink dye? And how would I get them both to Paris without causing a scene at the airport?"

"Didn't we have one years ago?" I said slowly, scanning my memory for a name.

"No, we didn't. Don't be ridiculous!"

"Yes, we did. For that mountain-climber from Enniskillen who wanted us to recreate the Alps in his back garden? You remember, he had a huge garden?"

"Oh, that machine?" Julie said, scratching her head and unwrapping a chicken-and-stuffing bagel. "No, I think I threw that old thing away right after the event. I mean, it got broken, didn't it? It overheated or something."

"I can't recall," I said then, deciding to give Julie the

benefit of the doubt. "Still, I hope there wasn't a hidden security camera anywhere on the premises. I'd say whoever did it could get in serious trouble. The French don't take stalking and sabotage lightly, you know. Especially towards celebrities."

"Oh, I wouldn't imagine there's any evidence kicking about," Julie said lightly. "I'm sure that whoever delivered the foam knew what they were doing and wore a balaclava and what have you. And checked the scene out prior, for surveillance equipment and all. I mean, if they had the balls to do it in the first place, I'm pretty sure they'd have been well organised."

"Well, yes, that's true," I said.

And I do expect it would have helped enormously if the culprit knew someone sympathetic with enough money to be able to rent private jets . . .

∞

There's the phone again.

One minute, please . . .

"Hello, Dream Weddings, can I help you?"

∞

What else is there?

Oh, yes! Saucy moment! I forgot to tell you that when Bill finally saw the tattoo of the angel's wings on my back a few days ago he turned into an absolute sex-fiend. Threw his crutches down on the bedroom floor and ravished me there and then. Gosh, if I'd known the effect it would've had on him, I'd have had it done a lot sooner. He said it was the sexiest thing he'd ever seen in real life and we didn't get out of bed all weekend. Even Andrew and Christopher were giving us funny looks on Monday morning when they went to catch the bus into town.

"What've you two been up to?" Andrew said crossly, hunting everywhere for his wallet. "There's nothing to eat and the house is a mess."

"Oh, nothing in particular," I said innocently. "It's just that with your father and me being so old and decrepit these days, we felt we needed to have a bit of a lie-down."

Yeah, right!

~

Jay and Sophie got married yesterday. It was on GMTV. They got married in the Vatican, which I thought was a lovely touch. Yes, I am being bitchy. She was wearing a simple white dress and he was wearing a neat black suit. It was all very traditional. The reporter said that the mysterious young Irishman had been 'comforting' the famous supermodel since her romance with the King of Rock had ended amicably in May of this year. No mention of the wedding that never was. Well! That's what I call *spin*! Good for them. I hope they're very happy together. I doubt it, but I sincerely hope he doesn't cheat on Sophie the way he did on Julie. Their children will be too good-looking for words, needless to say. I still think

Jay planned this whole thing. That he decided to use Julie to meet wealthy celebrities, when he first found out she was a wedding-planner. But we've got to give him the benefit of the doubt, haven't we? And I read he had a tattoo removed from his arm just before the wedding so that must have hurt. Maybe he does love her?

The 'King of Rock' went on a world-wide, anti-drugs road-show and kept his mouth firmly shut about Jay O'Hanlon and Dream Weddings. Which impressed my Bill so much he decided to settle out of court after all. The money was very swift in coming, along with a letter for Bill to sign, giving up any future claims to compensation. What the heck, we decided. The poor guy had sworn he would never drive again or date again and so we thought we'd give him another chance. After a lot of serious deliberation, Bill bought himself a brand new black Volvo S80 and gave the rest of the money to our children, to help them with their studies. Or in Alexander's case, to save up for a time when property prices weren't quite so ludicrously high.

∞

My father's grandiose headstone of best Irish granite was smashed to pieces this lunch-time. Didn't even last a year. I wasn't surprised but Bill was very upset. Thousands and thousands of pounds it'd cost us in transport costs, engraving fees, special planning permission and so on. But there it was, when we went out to lay some flowers we'd ordered specially. In bits! The cross broken right off the top and the base sprayed with graffiti. Not very neat writing but we think it said: *"The only good Catholic is a dead one."*.

"Why?" said Bill, staring down at the damage. "What is *wrong* with them, Mags? What kind of homes were they reared in? Have they really got nothing better to do with their lives?"

"Oh, Bill," I said, "it doesn't matter. I should have known such a big headstone would attract the wrong sort of attention. I only ordered it to please my sisters."

"It's not your fault, Mags. It's this stupid country of ours. It's whoever decided to allow segregated education."

And so on, he was very annoyed.

But in a strange way (and I know you'll think I'm really barmy now) but in a strange way I think it would have made my father both pleased and proud. Yes, I think he would have been rather chuffed that some teenage tearaways had taken a sledgehammer to his beautiful Celtic cross and sprayed the base with abusive sectarian rubbish. It was on the news, you see? What was left of the gravesite made it onto the local news show this lunch-time, the piece introduced by none other than Tina Campbell. Looking very dapper in a Houndstooth jacket. She interviewed a leading politician from my father's side of the fence, beside the vandalised grave. It was the closest my poor deluded father ever came to getting directly involved in The Troubles.

So anyway I've asked the cemetery bigwigs to leave the damage the way it is for a few months before removing it and preparing the site for a smaller plaque.

Just so Dad can see it and have a good laugh or a good rant, whichever he feels is the most appropriate. If he *is* up there somewhere looking down on us which I sincerely hope he is. Well, my mother did used to say Dad was so completely stupid and gormless, he was bound to get a fool's pardon on Judgement Day. That broken cross looked so bleak and forlorn in the pouring rain in a Belfast cemetery on a cloudy day in November. With a flute band practising somewhere in the background. And an army helicopter droning and hovering overhead, to film any possible outbreaks of civil disturbance during yet another commemorative rally. As I said to Bill at the time, it's what my father would have wanted.

THE END

Published by **poolbeg.com**

The Tavern on Maple Street

SHARON OWENS

Beautiful Lily Beaumont and husband Jack are owners of a
genuine Victorian tavern, situated on one of Belfast's few
remaining narrow cobbled streets. They have been married
for twenty years and have spent that time madly in love
and contented in their own little world with their
regular customers.

But one day, Dublin-based developer Vincent Halloran
comes to Belfast with big plans for Maple Street. The other
traders are keen to sell up and retire, and Jack and Lily
know their ivory-tower days are numbered.

As Christmas approaches, Lily decides to hire four pretty
barmaids and two handsome singers, in a final bid to save
the Tavern. Enter pint-sized man-eater Bridget O'Malley,
lazy art-student Daisy Hardcastle, neurotic Trudy Valentine
and painfully shy Marie Smith. Not to mention the
handsome Devaney brothers with their tight leather
trousers and acoustic guitars.

But is it too little, too late?

Another fairy tale for grown-ups from Sharon Owens
with all the wit and wisdom her readers have come
to expect.

ISBN 978-1-84223-243-9

Published by **poolbeg.com**

The
Tea House on
Mulberry
Street

SHARON OWENS

'*Daniel Stanley came hurrying down the stairs from the first-floor flat and flicked on the lights in the tea house. For a brief moment the old place looked almost cheerful. The dusty curtains, the faded linoleum, the cracked furniture and flaking walls were bathed in a golden light.*'

Penny Stanley's seventeen-year marriage to Daniel is falling apart and so is their shabby tea house on Mulberry Street. But its regular customers love the cosy atmosphere and luscious desserts. Penniless artist Brenda Brown sits in the cafe penning letters to Nicolas Cage. Will they ever be answered? Sadie Smith finds refuge from her diet and her husband's ultra-slim mistress in a slice of the cafe's cherry cheesecake and Clare Fitzgerald returns to the tea house after twenty years in New York.

But the tea house needs more than a coat of paint and as Penny takes action she discovers it is a magical place with secrets of its own.

ISBN 978-1-84223-208-8

Published by **poolbeg**.com

From *The New York Times* bestselling author
of *The Tea House on Mulberry Street*

The BALLROOM on MAGNOLIA STREET

Sharon Owens

It's 1987 and Shirley Winters is a daydreamer who loves
vintage clothes and local pin-up Declan Greenwood. Her
older sister Kate enjoys collecting handbags and lovers with
equal relish, but hates her job in the dole office and her
demon boss Miss Bingham.

When Shirley eventually meets Declan in the ballroom on
Magnolia Street, they fall for each other in a big way. Declan
promptly proposes . . . and sister Kate has a nervous
breakdown. There is no way she is playing bridesmaid to her
younger sister, so the rush is on to find a husband of her
own. Step forward, friendly mechanic and Simon Le Bon
lookalike, Kevin McGovern. He has fancied Kate for years
and can't believe his luck when she finally agrees to go out
with him.

Handsome Johnny 'Hollywood' Hogan owns the ballroom
on Magnolia Street, and every woman in Belfast adores him.
But he loves the one who got away, the beautiful Marion
Greenwood, Declan's mother. Marion's husband, Eddy,
doesn't trust Hogan, even though he and Marion have been
married for twenty years. But to whom does Marion's heart
really belong? And will the truth behind Declan's parentage
be revealed?

ISBN 978-1-84223-205-7